Gramarye—a planet where elves and witches are real, where the fantasies of the Middle Ages endure.

Only Rod Gallowglass can save Gramarye from its doom, by using the powers of wizardry. But there is one problem.

Rod Gallowglass doesn't believe in magic ...

●

"Stasheff has a nice sense of the irreverent and a bit of the bawd, and he spins a yarn good enough to leave you wanting more ..."
—ANALOG MAGAZINE

KING KOBOLD REVIVED

Christopher Stasheff

ACE SCIENCE FICTION BOOKS
NEW YORK

KING KOBOLD REVIVED

An Ace Science Fiction Book / published by arrangement with
the author

PRINTING HISTORY
Ace Original / June 1984

ISBN: 0-441-44488-1

Ace Science Fiction Books are published by
The Berkley Publishing Group,
200 Madison Avenue, New York, New York 10016.
PRINTED IN THE UNITED STATES OF AMERICA

TO MY READERS

This isn't a new book.
But it isn't an old book, either.
Let me tell you how it happened. . . .

Back in 1970, when *King Kobold* was first published, I waited with bated breath to see what the critics thought of it—and was rather disheartened to find they weren't exactly overwhelmingly enthusiastic. That's when I decided I shouldn't pay too much attention to the critics.

Unfortunately, I couldn't ignore Lester del Rey. I had always admired his perspicacity and penetrating insight (i.e., he always agreed with my opinion about new books. Please understand that, at the time, I had never met him.). When *del Rey* said, "It isn't a bad book, if you don't expect too much of the evening spent with it," I knew I was in trouble. Worse, letters began arriving—and they agreed with del Rey! And though del Rey had been gentle and charitable, the fans felt no such need for restraint.

So, when the good people at Ace indicated an interest in reissuing *King Kobold*, I said, "Not until I rewrite it!"

Please remember, I'd had twelve years to mull over the flaws of the original, and figure out how to fix them. There were some changes that I knew I definitely wanted to make, and quite a few others that I was thinking about.

So the book you hold in your hand is not the product of a publisher who tried to jazz things up to hype sales; it's the result of a mulish writer who refused to go through having fans call him nasty names again. If you bought the original *King Kobold* fourteen years ago and misplaced your copy—sorry, this ain't quite the same book you read back then. And, if you never *did* read *King Kobold* (an offense I will overlook only if you were too young to read), this ain't the plot you've been hearing about. Better, I hope, but not the same. If your favorite scenes are missing—well, sorry. Or, worse yet, your favorite character—well, I'm even sorrier; but I just don't think he really worked (not "she"—she was a total nonentity, and I don't see how anybody could miss her—except maybe "him"). All in all, I'm pretty satisfied with this revised version; it's still essentially the same story, but I think it's much more solid, and a much better read (all right, so I haven't cut out *all* the lousy jokes). Besides, if you *really* liked it better the other way—well, there's always the original edition. You'll have to search a little to find a copy, but if you'd rather read it, you can.

Thank you all, for pestering your bookstores for *King Kobold*, and bringing it out of hiding again. Here it is, the same story—what happened to Rod and Gwen when they'd only been married a few years, and only had one baby warlock to contend with. I hope you enjoy it. I did.

—Christopher Stasheff
Montclair State College
October 4, 1983

Prologue

"Sorrowful it was, and great cause for Mourning, that so young a King should die, and that in his Bed; yet Death doth come to all, yea, the High and the lowly alike, and 'tis not by our choosing, but by God's. Thus is was that King Richard was taken from us in the fourteenth year of his Reign, though he had not yet seen forty-five summers; and great lamentation passed through the land. Yet must Life endure, and the motion of it never doth cease, so that we laid him to rest with his ancestors, and turned our faces toward our new Sovereign, his daughter Catharine, first Queen of that name to Reign, though it had been scarcely twenty years since her birth.

"Then the Lords of this land of Gramarye sat them down in Council, and rose up to advise the young Queen of her actions, and at their head stood the Duke Loguire, time-honored and revered, foremost of the Lords of this Land, and Uncle to the Queen. Yet she would not hearken to him, nor to any of her Lords, but set her face toward the doing of things as she saw them, and would not heed Council. And what she wished done, she set in the hands of the Dwarf Brom O'Berin, who had come to the Court as her father's Jester, but King Richard had raised him to Chancellor; and Queen Catharine ennobled him. This did affront all the Peers of the Land, that she should set a Dwarf in their midst, and he baseborn, for she would trust none among them.

"Then did Loguire send his younger son Tuan, who long had courted Catharine ere her Father died, to beg of her that she plight him her Troth, and come with him to the Altar to become his Wife. And she called this foul treason, that he should seek the Crown under guise of her Hand, and banished him from the land, and set him adrift in a coracle, that the East wind might take him to the Wild Lands, to dwell among Monsters and BeastMen, though all of his crime was the love of her. Then was his father full wroth, and all the Lords with him; but Loguire held his hand, and so, perforce, must they all; but Tuan his son swam back to the shore, and stole within the Land again, by night, and would not be exiled.

"Then did Catharine the Queen meet with her great Lords all, in her great Hall in Runnymede, and did say unto them, 'Lo, it seemeth thou dost take boys from the plow, who know neither Letters nor Holiness, and doth set them above thy people as priests, that they may more certainly do thy bidding; and know that such practice doth offend the Lord God, and affronteth thy Queen; wherefore, henceforth, I shall appoint thee full measure of Priests, and send them unto thee; and I will not brook nay-saying.' Then were the Lords wroth indeed, but Loguire held up his hand, and they checked. And it came to pass as the Queen had said, that the souls of her people were governed by monks that she sent out from Runnymede, though they did oftimes confirm the priests the Lords had set over their Parishes; yet some among them had grown slack and, aye, even sinful; and these the Queen's monks removed, and set others of their number up in their steads.

"Then did the Queen summon all her Lords unto her again, and did say unto them, 'Lo, I have seen the Justice that is done on thine estates, both by thyselves and by the Judges thou dost appoint; and I have seen that the manner of Justice thou dost deliver is not all of one piece; for Hapsburg in the East will hew off a man's hand for the theft of a loaf of bread, while Loguire in the South will only outlaw a man for a Murder; and I have seen that my people grow restive therefore, and are like to forsake the ways of Law in their confusion. Therefore wilt thou no longer deliver thyselves of Justice, nor set others to judge thy folk for thee; but all shall be judged by men that I shall send among thee, from my Court in Runnymede.' Then all the Lords waxed wroth indeed, and would have haled her down from her Throne; but the Duke Loguire withheld them, and turned his face away from the Queen, and withdrew to his Estates, and so did they all; but some among them began to plot Treason, and Loguire's eldest son Anselm made one of them.

"Then, of a night, thunder did roll and fill all the World, though the skies were clear, and the Moon bright and full, and folk looked up and wondered, and did see a star fall from the Heavens, and they turned away marveling, and praying that it might prove an Omen, heralding the healing of their Land of Gramarye, as indeed it did; for the Star fell to land, and from it stepped the High Warlock, Rod Gallowglass, tall among the sons of men, high of brow, noble of mien, with a heart of golden courage and thews of steel, merciful to all, but stern in justice, with a mind like sunlight caught in crystal, that clearly understood all the actions of all men, and his face was comely above all others.

"He came unto the Queen, but she knew him not, and thought him only one among her soldiers; yet there was poison in the air about her, and he knew it, and did banish it; and thereupon she knew him. And she sent him to the South, to guard her Uncle, for she knew that Treason brewed, and not only toward herself. And the Warlock did as she bade him, and took with him, for a servant, the giant Tom. And they came unto Loguire secretly, under the guise of Minstrels, yet they had not been heard to sing. And there were ghosts within Loguire's castle, and the High Warlock did befriend them.

"Then did Loguire summon all the Lords of the Realm, and they came to him at his castle in the South, that he might counsel them to withhold their power yet awhile; but being met, they brewed their Treason 'gainst him.

"And there were witches in the land, and warlocks too; and word did go from mouth to mouth, the Rumor that speaks more loudly than the heralds, that the Queen had

welcomed to her keep all witchfolk who did wish her protection, and there they held wild Revels through the night,
for many were the Good Folk who had sought to burn
them; and folk began to murmur that the Queen herself
had something of witchcraft in her.

"And the High Warlock did befriend the witches, even
Gwendylon, most powerful among them, and she was
young, and comely, and he spoke to her of Love.

"And Lord Tuan came by night unto the town of Runnymede, that he might be near unto the Queen, though
she despised him, and he came unto the beggars, and
sought Sanctuary amongst them; and he taught them
Governance, and they made him King among them. Yet
the one among them whom Lord Tuan most trusted, he
who held the purse and was called "the Mocker,"
bethought himself of Lord Tuan's mock crown.

"Then, when all the Lords were met at Loguire's de-
mesne in the South, and Anselm with them, they did
stand against Loguire's face and refute his leadership,
raising up young Anselm to the Dukedom in his father's
stead; and one Durer, erstwhile Loguire's councillor,
drew blade against him. Then did the High Warlock by
High Magic snuff out all the lamps and torches, so that
Loguire's hall lay all in darkness, for his Hall lay under-
ground, and had no windows. And the High Warlock
conjured up the ghosts that dwelt within that keep, and
they did pass amongst the folk within that hall, and all
were sore afeared, aye, even those great Lords that there
were met; and the Warlock stole the Duke Loguire away,
and brought him secretly unto the Queen at Runnymede.

"Then did the Lords summon up their armies, and all
did march against the Queen. But the High Warlock
spake unto the Elves that dwelt within that land, and they
did swear to fight beside him, and the Witches also. And
the High Warlock called up young Tuan Loguire, and he
marched forth with all his beggars; and thus they came to
Breden Plain: a Queen, a Warlock, and a dwarf, with an
army made of witches, elves, and beggars.

"Then, under the Sun, the Lords charged out in bold
array, but their horses sank into the Earth, for elves had
mined it; and they hurled their spears and arrows 'gainst

the Queen, but witches turned their shafts, and they fell back amongst the Armies of the Lords, and there did grievous harm. Then did Lord Tuan lead his beggars forth, and his father beside him, to finish what the witches had begun, and all the Field fell into melee. And the giant Tom rose up amidst that churning mass, and hewed a path unto the Lords and all their Councillors, and the beggars followed, and did beat down all those men-at-arms and Councillors, and made prisoners of the Lords; but the giant Tom did, in that carnage, perish, and the Warlock mourned him, and the beggars also.

"Then would the Queen have slain the Lords, or chained them into Servitude, but the Warlock spoke against it, and the Queen gazed upon his lowering brow, and knew fear. But Tuan Loguire stood beside her, and faced against the Warlock, and cried that all should be as the Queen had said; but the Warlock felled him with a most foul blow, and struck the Queen in remonstrance, and rode away upon his charmed steed, that no mortal mount could near; yet Lord Tuan in his agony shot forth a bolt that struck the Warlock as he fled.

"Then did Queen Catharine cry Lord Tuan as the Staff of her strength and the Guard of her honor, and spoke to him of love, and gave him the Lords to do with as he wished. Then did Lord Tuan free them, but with their heirs as hostages, and he took their armies for the Crown. And he did take Queen Catharine unto the altar, and became our King thereby, and reigned with Catharine the Queen.

"But the Warlock sought out the witch Gwendylon, and she did draw Lord Tuan's bolt from out him, and enchanted the wound so that it did no harm; and the Warlock spoke to her of love, and brought her to the altar.

"And the Lords went back to their demesnes, and there ruled Justly, for the King's Eye was upon them, and all was peaceful in the land of Gramarye, and contentment returned unto its folk.

"So matters stood for two years and more, and men began to trust their Lords once more, and to look kindly upon their fellows again.

"Then the night wind blew wailing and keening from the southern shore, and the sounds of War . . ."

—Chillde's *Chronicles of the Reign of Tuan and Catharine*

"According to the records, the planet was colonized by a crackpot group who dressed up in armor and held tournaments for fun; they called themselves the 'Romantic Émigrés.' This kind of group acted as a selective mechanism, attracting people with latent *psi* powers. Put them all together on one planet and let them inbreed for a few centuries, and you get *espers*—which is what they've got here. Only a small percentage of the population, of course, but I have grounds for believing the rest are latents. They think they're normal, though, and call the espers 'witches' if they're female, and 'warlocks' if they're male.

"What's worse, there's a native fungus that reacts to projective telepaths; the locals call it 'witch moss,' because if the right kind of 'witch' thinks hard at it, it turns into whatever she's thinking about. So the ones who don't know they're witches sit around telling fairy tales to their children, and, first thing you know, the landscape is filled with elves and ghosts and werewolves—I'll show you my bites sometime.

"In this agent's humble opinion, the place is a communications gold mine and the answer to the prayers of our noble Decentralized Democratic Tribunal. A democracy can't survive if its territory gets too big for the speed of its communications system, and the last projection I heard was that the DDT would hit critical size in about a hundred fifty years. If I can turn this planet into a democracy, it'll have just what the DDT needs—instantaneous communication over any distance. All the guesswork I've read about telepathy says it'll be instantaneous, regardless of distance, and what I've seen on this planet bears that out.

"But if the planet is vital to the success of democracy, it is equally vital for totalitarians and anarchists to keep it *away* from the democrats—and they're trying to do just that. The totalitarians are represented by a proletarian organization called the House of Clovis, which is trying to organize all the beggars and petty criminals, and doing a pretty good job of it, too. The anarchists are working on the noblemen; each of the twelve Great Lords has a councillor who is, I'm pretty sure, one of the anarchists.

"Where have they come from? Well, they might just have sneaked in from off-planet—but I've found at least one gizmo that can't be anything but a time machine, and I've got good reason to believe there're more.

"What upsets me about the place is the uncertainty factor. Given the local genetic makeup, and the telepathically sensitive fungus, virtually anything could happen —which means that, if I wait long enough, it probably will. . . ."

> —Excerpt from *Report on Beta Cassiopeiae Gamma (local name "Gramarye"),* by Rodney d'Armand, Agent for Society for Conversion of Extraterrestrial Nascent Totalitarianisms

1

The heavy clinging fog lay dense, nearly opaque, over the heaving sea. The rolling, endless crash of breakers against the headlands at the harbor's mouth came muted and distant.

High above, circling unseen, a bird called plaintive sentry cries.

The dragon shouldered out of the swirling mist, its beaked, arrogant head held high.

Four more like it loomed out of the fog at its back.

Round, bright-painted shields hung on their sides.

Oars speared out from the shields, lifting in unison and falling feathered to the waves.

The dragon's single wing was tightly furled around the crossbar lashed to the tall, single mast that thrust upward out of its back.

Squat, hulking, helmeted shapes prowled silently about the mast.

The dragon had an eagle's beak, and a tall, ribbed fin for a crest. Two long, straight horns probed out from its forehead.

The surf moaned on the shore as the dragon led its mates past the headland.

The child screamed, howling for his mother, thrashing himself into a tangle with the thick fur blanket.

Then the oil lamp was there, just a rag in a dish, but warm and safe, throwing its yellow glow upward on the mother's weary, gentle face.

She gathered the quivering, sobbing little body into her arms, murmuring, "There now, love, there. Mama's here. She won't let him hurt you."

She held the child tightly, rubbing his back until the sobbing ceased. "There now, Artur, there. What was it, darling?"

The child sniffled and lifted his head from her shoulder. "Bogeyman, Mama. Chasing me, and—he had a great big knife!"

Ethel's mouth firmed. She hugged the child and glared at the lamp-flame. "The bogeymen are far across the sea, darling. They can't come here."

"But Carl says . . ."

"I know, I know. Carl's mama tells him the bogeyman will get him if he's bad. But that's just a silly story, darling, to frighten silly children. You're not silly, are you?"

Artur was silent a while; then he murmured into the folds of his mother's gown, "Uh . . . no, Mama. . . ."

"Of course you're not." She patted his back, laid him down in the bed, and tucked the fur robe under his chin. "That's my brave boy. We both know the bogeyman can't hurt us, don't we?"

"Yes, Mama," the child said uncertainly.

"Sleep sweetly, darling," the mother said, and closed the door softly behind her.

The oil lamp set the shadows dancing softly on the walls. The child lay awake awhile, watching the slow ballet of light and dark.

He sighed, rolled over on his side. His eyes were closing as they strayed to the window.

A huge misshapen face peered in, the eyes small and gleaming, the nose a glob of flesh, the mouth a gash framing great square, yellowed teeth. Shaggy brown hair splayed out from a gleaming, winged helmet.

He grinned at the child, pig eyes dancing.

"Mama! Mamamamamamamama! *Bogeyman!*"

The bogeyman snarled and broke through the stout wooden wall with three blows of a great ironbound club.

The child screamed and ran, yanking and straining at the heavy bedroom door.

The bogeyman clambered through the broken wall.

The door was flung wide; the mother stared in horror, clutching her child to her and screaming for her husband. She wheeled about and fled.

The bogeyman gave a deep, liquid chuckle, and followed.

In another cottage, a bogeyman seized a child by the ankles and swung his head against the wall. He lifted his huge club to fend off the father's sword, then whirled the club into the father's belly, swung it up to strike the father's temple. Bone splintered; blood flowed.

The mother backed away, screaming, as the beastman caught up the father's fallen sword. He turned to the mother, knocked her aside with a careless, backhand swipe of the club, and stove in the family strong-chest with one blow.

In the first cottage, the oil lamp, knocked aside in the beastman's passage, licked at the oil spilled on walls and floor.

Other cottages were already ablaze.

Women and children ran screaming, with chuckling beastmen loping after them.

The men of the village caught up harpoons and axes, rallying to defend their wives and children.

The beastmen shattered their heads with ironbound cudgels, clove chests with great, razor-edged battle axes, and passed on, leaving dismembered bodies behind them.

Then drumming hooves and a troop of cavalry burst into the village; the fires had alerted the local baron. He sat now at the head of a score of horsemen drawn up in the beastmen's path.

"Fix lances!" he roared. "Charge!"

The beastmen chuckled.

Lances snapped down, heels kicked horsehide; the cavalry charged . . . and faltered, stumbled, halted, soldiers and horses alike staring at the beastmen for long, silent minutes.

Each beastman flicked his glance from one soldier to another, on to a third, then back to the first, holding each one's eyes for a fraction of a second.

Jaws gaped, eyes glazed all along the cavalry line. Lances slipped from nerveless fingers.

Slowly, the horses stepped forward, stumbled, and stepped again, their riders immobile, shoulders sagging, arms dangling.

The beastmen's little pig eyes glittered. Their grins widened, heads nodded in eager encouragement.

Step-stumble-step, the horses moved forward.

The beastmen shrieked victory as their clubs swung, caving in the horses' heads. Axes swung high and fell, biting deep into the riders. Blood fountained as men fell. Heads flew, bones crunched under great splayfeet, as the beastmen, chuckling, waded through the butchered cavalry to break in the door of the village storehouse.

The Count of Baicci, vassal to the Duke of Loguire, lay headless in the dirt, his blood pumping out to mingle with that of his cavalry before the thirsty soil claimed it.

And the women and children of the village, huddled together on the slopes above, stared slack-jawed at their burning houses, while the dragon ships, wallowing low in the waves with the weight of their booty, swung out past the bar.

And, as the long ships passed the headland, the wind blew the villagers an echo of bellowing laughter.

The word was brought to King Tuan Loguire at his capital in Runnymede; and the King waxed wroth.

The Queen waxed into a fury.

"Nay, then!" she stormed. "These devil's spawn, they lay waste a village with fire and sword, slay the men and dishonor the women, and bear off the children for bondsmen, belike—and what wilt thou do, thou? Assuredly, thou wilt not revenge!"

She was barely out of her teens, and the King was scarce older; but he sat straight as a staff, his face grave and calm.

"What is the count of the dead?" he demanded.

"All the men of the village, Majesty," answered the messenger, grief and horror just beneath the skin of his face. "A hundred and fifty. Fourteen of the women, and six babes. And twenty good horsemen, and the Count of Baicci."

The Queen stared, horrified. "A hundred and fifty," she murmured, "a hundred and fifty."

Then, louder, "A hundred and fifty widowed in this one night! And babes, six babes slain!"

"God have mercy on their souls." The King bowed his head.

"Aye, pray, man, pray!" the Queen snapped. "Whilst thy people lie broke and bleeding, thou dost pray!" She whirled on the messenger. "And rapine?"

"None," said the messenger, bowing his head. "Praise the Lord, none."

"None," the Queen repeated, almost mechanically.

"None?" She spun on her husband. "What insult is this, that they scorn our women!"

"They feared the coming of more soldiers, mayhap . . ." the messenger muttered.

The Queen gave him all the scorn she could jam into one quick glance. "And 'twere so, they would be lesser men than our breed; and ours are, Heaven knows, slight enough."

The messenger stiffened. The King's face turned wooden.

He leaned back slowly, gaze fixed on the messenger. "Tell me, good fellow—how was it a whole troop of cavalry could not withstand these pirates?"

The Queen's lip curled. "How *else* could it chance?"

The King sat immobile, waiting for the messenger's answer.

"Sorcery, Majesty." The messenger's voice quavered. "Black, foul sorcery. The horsemen rode doomed, for their foes cast the Evil Eye upon them."

Silence held the room. Even the Queen was speechless, for, on this remote planet, superstition had a disquieting tendency to become fact.

The King was the first to speak. He stirred in his throne, turned to the Lord Privy Councillor.

This meant he had to look down; for, though Brom O'Berin's shoulders were as broad as the King's, he stood scarcely two feet high.

"Brom," said the King, "send forth five companies of the King's Foot, one to each of the great lords whose holdings border the sea."

"But one company to each!" the Queen fairly exploded. "Art thou so easily done, *good* mine husband? Canst thou spare but thus much of thy force?"

The King rose and turned to Sir Maris the Seneschal. "Sir Maris, do you bring forth three companies of the King's Guard. The fourth shall bide here, for the guarding of Her Majesty Queen Catharine. Let the three companies assemble in the courtyard below within the hour, provisioned for long and hard riding."

"My liege, I will," said Sir Maris, bowing.

"And see that mine armor is readied."

"Armor!" the Queen gasped. "Nay, nay, O mine husband. What wouldst thou do?"

"Why, what I must." The King turned to her, catching her hands between his own. "I am King, and my people are threatened. I must ride to the wreck of this village and seek out the trail of these beastmen. Then must I build ships and follow them, if I may, to their homeland."

"Oh, nay, good my lord!" Catharine cried, clinging to him. "Have we not men-at-arms enough in our armies but you also must ride forth to die? Oh, my lord, nay! What would I do if thou shouldst be—if thou shouldst take hurt?"

The King held her close for one moment, then held her away, tilted her chin, and kissed her lips gently. "Thou art Queen," he said softly. "The brunt of this sorrow must thou bear; such is the office of Queens. Here in the place of power must thou bide, to care for our people while I ride. Thou must hazard thine husband for the good of thy people, as I must hazard my life—for such is the office of Kings."

He held her close for a long, timeless while, then kissed her lingeringly. He straightened, her hands clasped between his, then turned to go.

An embarrassed cough stopped him.

He turned, frowning. "Art still in this place, Brom? I had thought . . ."

"My liege," the dwarf interrupted, "what thou shalt command, I shall do—but wilt thou command nothing more?"

The King's face darkened.

Brom's voice was tight with determination. "If there is the Evil Eye in this, Majesty, 'tis matter for witches."

The King turned away, glowering, his lips pressed thin.

"Thou hast the right of it, Brom," he admitted grudgingly. "Well enough, then, we must. Send to the witches in the North Tower, Brom, directing them to summon"—his face twisted with dislike—"the High Warlock."

The High Warlock was currently leaning his back against a tree trunk with his fundament firmly founded on *terra firma,* watching the sunrise with one eye and his wife with the other. Both were eminently worth watching.

The sun was splendor itself as it rose orange-gold out of the oiled green of the pine-tops into a rose-and-blue sky; but his flame-headed wife was all that was grace and loveliness, singing lightly as she sank her hands into the tub of dishwater beside the cooking-fire in the dry warmth of their cave home.

It wasn't just the domesticity that made her lovely, of course. Her long, loose red hair seemed to float about her, framing a round face with large, sea-green, long-lashed eyes, a snub nose, a wide mouth with full, tempting lips. Her figure was spectacular under the white peasant blouse and tight bodice and long, full, bright-colored skirt.

Of course, her figure was, at the moment, more a matter of inference than observation; but the Warlock had a good memory.

The memory was a little too good; his wife's beauty occasionally reminded him of his own—well, shall we say, plainness?

No, we should say ugliness—or, rather, homeliness; for there was something attractive about his face. He had the appeal that is common to overstuffed armchairs, old fireplaces, and potbellied stoves. Hounds and small children loved him on sight.

And by this quality he had won her (it would be, perhaps, more accurate to say that she had won him, after an extended battle with his inferiority complex); for if a beautiful woman is betrayed often enough, she will begin to value trustworthiness, warmth, and affection more than romance.

At least, she will if she is the kind of woman to whom love is the goal, and romance just the luxury; such a woman was Gwen.

Such a woman will eventually be capable of loving a man with a good heart, even though his face be a bargain assortment of inclined planes, hollows, and knobs in Expressionist juxtaposition; and such a man was Rod Gallowglass.

He had a receding hairline; a flat, sloping forehead; prominent bushy eyebrows; deep eye-sockets with a matched set of gray eyes; a blade of a nose; high, flat cheekbones; and a wide, thin-lipped mouth. The mouth kept a precarious perch on top of a square, jutting chin.

Nevertheless, she loved him, which fact was to Rod a miracle, a flagrant violation of all known laws of nature.

Not that he was about to object, of course.

He slid down onto the base of his spine, let his eyelids droop, and let the peace of the summer morning seep into him, lulling him into a doze.

Something struck his belly, knocking the wind out of him and jolting him wide awake. He jerked upright, knife in hand.

"Da-dee!" cooed the baby, looking enormously pleased with himself.

Rod stared at the kid. Little Magnus was holding tight to the bars of his playpen; he hadn't quite learned to stand by himself yet.

Rod managed a feeble grin and levered the corner of the oak playpen off his belly. "Very good, Magnus!" He patted the baby's head. "Good boy, good boy!"

The baby grinned, fairly hopping with delight.

The playpen rose six inches from the ground.

Rod made a frantic grab and forced it back down, hands on the lid.

Ordinarily, playpens do not have lids. But this playpen did; otherwise, the baby might have floated out.

"Yes, yes, that's a wonderful baby! Smart little fella, there! *Very* good baby—*Gwen*!"

"What dost thou wish, my lord?" Gwen came up to the mouth of the cave, drying her hands on her apron.

Then she saw the playpen.

"Oh, *Magnus*!" she mourned in that tone of hurt disappointment only mothers can master.

"No, no!" Rod said quickly. "He's a good boy, Gwen— isn't he? I've just been telling him what a good boy he is. *Good* boy, *good* baby!"

The baby stared, tiny brow wrinkling in utter confusion.

His mother had much the same look.

But her eyes widened as she realized the only way the playpen could've moved out of the cave while her back was turned. "Oh, Rod!"

"Yeah." Rod grinned with more than a touch of pride. "Precocious, isn't he?"

"But—but, my lord!" Gwen shook her head, looking dazed. "Only witches can move things other than themselves. Warlocks cannot!"

Rod pried open the playpen and took his son in his arms. "Well, he couldn't have done it by levi—uh, flying, could he?"

"Nay, he hath not strength enough to lift the playpen along with him—that he would have to do by his own bone and sinew. But warlocks cannot . . ."

"Well, this one can." He grinned down at the baby and chucked it under the chin. "How about that? I've fathered a genius!"

The baby cooed and bounced out of Rod's arms.

"Whup! Come back here!" Rod jumped and snagged a fat little ankle before the baby could float off in the morning breeze.

"Oh, Magnus!" Gwen was on them in a rush, cradling the

baby in her arms. "Oh, my bold babe! Thou shalt most surely be a most puissant warlock when thou art grown!"

The baby smiled back at her. He wasn't quite sure what he'd done that was right, but he wasn't going to argue.

Rod beamed with fatherly pride as he hefted the oaken playpen back into the cave. He was amazed at his son; that playpen was *heavy*!

He got a hank of rope and started tying the pen down. "That kid!" he said, shaking his head. "Scarcely a year old—he can't even walk yet, and . . . Gwen, what's the age when they start levitating?"

" 'Levi—' Oh, you mean flying, my lord!" Gwen came back into the cave, the baby straddling one hip. "Thirteen years, or thereabouts, my lord, is the age for young warlocks to fly."

"And this kid started at nine months." Rod's chest swelled a trifle—his head, too. "What age do little witches start making their broomsticks fly?"

"Eleven, my lord, or mayhap twelve."

"Well, he's a little ahead of schedule for that, too—except that warlocks aren't supposed to make broomsticks fly at all. What a kid!" He didn't mention that Magnus was obviously a major mutation.

He patted the baby's head. The child wrapped a chubby hand around his father's finger.

Rod turned shining eyes to Gwen. "He'll make a great agent when he's grown."

"My lord!" Gwen's brow knit in concern. "Thou wilt not take him from Gramarye?"

"Perish the thought!" Rod took Magnus and tossed him up in the air. "He'll have his work cut out for him right here."

Magnus squealed with delight and floated on up toward the roof.

Rod executed a high jump that would have done credit to a pole-vaulter and snagged his errant son. "Besides, he may not even want to join SCENT—who knows?"

Rod was an agent of the Society for the Conversion of Extraterrestrial Nascent Totalitarianisms, the subversive wing of the multi-planet Decentralized Democratic Tribunal, the first and only human interstellar government in history not to be based on Terra. The Senate met by electronic communications; the Executive resided on a starship which was usually to be found between planets. Nonetheless, it was the most efficient democratic government yet established.

SCENT was the organization responsible for bringing the Lost Colonies of earlier Terrestrial empires back into the fold. Rod was on permanent assignment to Gramarye, a planet that had been colonized by mystics, romantics, and escapists. The culture was medieval, the people superstitious—and a small percentage of the population had "witch-powers."

Consequently, the DDT in general, and SCENT in particular, were immensely interested in Gramarye; for the "witches" and "warlocks" were espers. Some had one set of psi powers and some had another—but all were telepaths to some degree. And, since the efficiency (and, consequently, the viability) of a democracy varies directly with the speed of its communications, and since telepathic communication was instantaneous, the DDT treasured its only colony of espers very highly.

So Rod had been assigned to guard the planet, and to carefully nudge its political system onto the road that would eventually lead to democracy and full membership in the DDT.

"Hey, Fess," Rod called.

The great black horse grazing in the meadow outside the cave lifted its head to look at its master. Its voice sounded through a small earphone buried in Rod's mastoid bone. "Yes, Rod?"

Rod snorted. "What're you cropping grass for? Who ever heard of a robot burning hydrocarbons?"

"One must keep up appearances, Rod," Fess reproved him.

"Next thing I know, you'll be keeping up with the Joneses! Listen, bolt-head—it's an occasion! The kid pulled his first telekinesis stunt today!"

"Telekinesis? I had thought that was a sex-linked female trait, Rod."

"Well, all of a sudden it ain't." He put the baby in the playpen and clamped the cover down before Magnus had a chance to drift out. "How about that, Fess? This kid's gonna be a champion!"

"It will be my great pleasure to serve him," the robot murmured, "as I have served his forebears for five hundred years, since the days of the first D'Armand, who founded . . ."

"Uh, skip the family history, Fess."

"But, Rod, it is a vital portion of the child's heritage; he should . . ."

"Well, save it until he learns to talk, then."

"As you wish." The mechanical voice somehow managed a sigh. "In that case, it is my duty to inform you that you will shortly be receiving company, Rod."

Rod stilled, cocking an eyebrow at his horse. "What do you see?"

"Nothing, Rod; but I detect the sounds characteristic of bipedal locomotion of a small being conveying itself through long grass."

"Oh." Rod relaxed. "An elf coming through the meadow. Well, they're always welcome."

An eighteen-inch body burst out of the grass at the cave-mouth.

Rod grinned. "Welcome, merry wanderer of the night."

"Puck!" Gwen squealed. She turned to their guest. "Assuredly, thou art most . . ."

She stopped, seeing the look on the elf's face.

Rod had sobered too. "What's right, Puck?"

"Naught," said the elf grimly. "Rod Gallowglass, thou must needs come, and right quickly, to the King!"

"Oh, I must, must I? What's so urgent all of a sudden? What's all the panic about?"

"Beastmen!" The elf gasped for breath. "They have raided the seacoast at the Duchy of Loguire!"

The Royal Guard rode south, with the King at their head.

A lone rider sat his grazing horse at the side of the road, playing a pipe with a low and mournful sound.

Tuan frowned, and said to the knight beside him, "What ails yon fellow? Is he so bemused by his own music that he doth not see armed horsemen approaching?"

"And can he not see thy crown?" the knight responded, dutifully putting into words what his sovereign was thinking. "I shall waken him, Majesty." He kicked his horse's sides and cantered ahead.

"Ho, fellow! Dost thou not see His Majesty approacheth?"

The rider looked up. "Why, so he does! Say, isn't that a handy coincidence? I was just thinking about him."

The knight stared, then backed his horse away. "Thou'rt the High Warlock!"

" 'High'?" Rod frowned. "Not a word of truth in it. Totally sober, good knight—haven't even *thought* about intoxicants since last Friday!"

The knight frowned, irritation overcoming awe. "Eh, thou'rt as unmannerly as a churl! Know that the King hath created thee High Warlock!"

" 'Tis even so," the King confirmed, drawing rein beside them. Then, rather unwillingly, "Well met, Lord High Warlock—for this poor Isle of Gramarye doth lie in need of thine art, and thy wisdom."

Rod inclined his head. "I am ever obedient to my adoptive homeland's call. But why do I get a high title out of it? I'd come just as quickly without it."

" 'Tis thy due, is it not?" Tuan's lips pressed thin. "And it describes thy place aptly. Folk fight better when they know from whom to take orders, and to whom to give them."

"An understatement," Rod admitted. "You've gotta have a clear flow chart if you want to get anything done. Very true, Your Majesty; I should've known better than to question you."

Tuan's eyebrows lifted. "Pleasantly said; I would not have expected it of you."

"Oh, you should have." Rod grinned. "I always give respect where it's due."

"And withhold it where 'tis not?" Tuan frowned. "Am I, then, so rarely worthy of respect?"

Rod's grin widened. "Only when you try to use authority you don't have—which doesn't happen very often, now that you're a king. And, of course, when you back someone who's in the wrong."

Tuan's frown darkened. "When have I done such?"

"Just before you got my knee in your groin. But I must admit that the Queen isn't trying to play God anymore."

Tuan flushed, turning away from Rod.

"And, of course, you were trying to be her champion, and laying down the law." Rod ignored the danger signals. "Which you had no right to do—at the time. Still don't, really."

"Have I not?" Tuan snapped, whirling to face Rod. "I am now King!"

"Which means that you're supposed to be foremost among your peers. It doesn't make you a superior breed—and doesn't give you the right to make laws if your barons are against them."

"You cannot truly believe that I would do so."

"Well, no, not you," Rod admitted. "Catharine, however . . ."

"Rarely is the Queen not swayed by my counsel," Tuan grated. "What we do, we do in concert."

"Then you both agree on marching south to fight the beastmen?"

Tuan managed to stay with the change of topic. "We have discussed it; and, aye, we are agreed. I do not say we take joy in the prospect."

"Well, say it," Rod invited. "Or are you really going to tell me you don't like being out in the field again?"

Tuan stared, taken aback. Then he grinned sheepishly. "In truth, my heart doth lift as I gaze upon open fields and feel harness on my back. I will own, 'tis good to be out from chambers and councils."

Rod nodded. "That's what I expected; you're a born general. Still can't understand how you manage to be a good king, too."

Tuan shrugged impatiently. " 'Tis like to the order of battle, save that the 'troops' one doth command are reeves and bailiffs."

"But it does require a totally different library of knowledge."

"That, Catharine hath," Tuan said very honestly. "I need only to steady her judgment, and issue her commands in such wise that they shall not arouse rebellion."

Which was true, Rod reflected; half of the offense Catharine gave was due to the way she said things, rather than what she said. "Well, you've just earned my respect again."

Tuan frowned. "For what? For kingship?"

"No, for candor. But now the burden of monarchy moves back into your field of knowledge, Majesty. What do you propose to do about these raiders?"

"Go to where they have been, expecting that they will strike again, and not far from where they struck first," Tuan answered. "When the bee findeth a flower filled with nectar, doth he not return to that place to find other flowers nearby?"

"Yes, and usually with more bees. I notice you brought a few stingers of your own."

Tuan glanced back at the army behind him. "The beastmen should be hard put to best these stout hearts."

"From the report I had, it's not their hearts that're in danger." Rod turned Fess, falling in alongside Tuan. The King kicked his heels into his horse's ribs, and the column began to move south again. Tuan nodded. "Thou dost speak of the Evil Eye."

"I doth," Rod agreed. "How much faith do you put in that part of the report?"

Tuan shrugged. " 'Tis wisest to believe it true, and guard against it as best we may." He pinned Rod with a stare. "What charm is there against it?"

Rod shrugged. "Beats me; I've never run into it before. Haven't the slightest idea how it works. For all I know, they might just be so ugly that you freeze in horror when you look at 'em."

Tuan shook his head firmly. "Nay. If the report is true, 'tis magic, not simple fear."

"Well, 'disgust' was more of what I had in mind. And, of course, the report itself might not be too accurate. Who'd it come from, anyway?"

"Mothers and grand-folk who were fleeing as they saw. And three of the footmen still live, though with grievous wounds; they have not spoken much, but what little they have said confirms the report, that 'twas the Eye that froze them."

"Not exactly ideal spying conditions, in either case," Rod mused, "and not enough information to work up anything to counter it. Still, it does seem that they have to look you in the eye to freeze you; so pass the word to look at their hands, their hats, their teeth—anything but their eyes."

"Well, 'tis better than naught," Tuan sighed. "But I would thou couldst find a better remedy, Lord Warlock. A soldier is hard put to avoid his enemy's eyes, in the melee."

"Well, it's the best I can do, for the moment," Rod grumped. "I'll try to get some firsthand experience if they attack again. Then maybe I . . ."

"Nay." Tuan drew up sharply and looked Rod in the eye. "Thou must learn this to thy sorrow, Lord Gallowglass, as I have had to: thou art now of too great worth to be risked in the melee. Thou must needs stand apart, with me, on high ground, to aid in the directing of the battle."

With a sinking heart, Rod knew Tuan was right; an army did fight better when it had overall direction. "Your Majesty is of course always right. I'll stay out of it as long as you do."

Tuan eyed him skeptically. "Do not think that will aid thee. I have gained in patience."

He wasn't doing so badly in perceptiveness, either; three years ago, he would've missed the sarcasm. "All of this assumes, however, that we have time to pick our ground before the fighting starts."

"Ah." Tuan turned back to the south and began riding again. "That is thy part."

"Oh?" Rod eyed him warily. "Am I supposed to magically transport this whole army to the ground you choose?"

"Nay. Thou'rt to secure us warning that raiders come, far enough in advance that we may ride to the place they will attack, and be there before them."

"Oh." Rod's lips held the shape of the letter after it was gone. "That's all I've got to do, huh? Mind telling me how? Am I supposed to set sentries pacing a mile offshore?"

"Aye, if thou canst derive a spell that will prevent them from sinking."

"Oh, nothing easier! It's called 'rowboats.'" Rod frowned. "Hold on, now. That almost sounds sensible."

"Aye, it doth." Tuan turned to him. "A line of sentries in small craft just beyond the horizon, to watch for a mast. But how will they sound the alarm?"

"They could row."

"The beastmen will row more quickly; there do be more of them, and they will be aided by wind. Would they not overtake thy sentry and slay him?"

"True." Rod frowned. "Well, how about if the sentry was a warlock? Then he could telep . . . uh, conjure himself ashore, and leave them an empty rowboat."

"A likely thought." Tuan nodded. "But thy warlocks hear thoughts. Could not he raise the alarm more quickly if there were another of the witch-folk ashore, listening for his thoughts?"

"True. That would be quicker, and . . . *wait* a minute!" Rod struck his forehead with the heel of his hand. "What's the matter with me? Sorry, Your Majesty; I'm slow today. Why bother putting the warlock in the boat? Why not just have him stay ashore and listen for approaching beastman thoughts?"

"Nay, certes!" Tuan squeezed his eyes shut. "Did I truly need a High Warlock to tell me this? Where are my wits?"

There was a good chance he'd left them back at the royal castle in Runnymede, but Rod didn't think it was politic to say so. Besides, Tuan could've replied that Rod's brains currently had long red hair and a figure worth killing for.

Then the King opened his eyes, with doubt in them. "Yet art thou certain they do think?"

"That is a distinct possibility. Maybe if I go to the western coast and shout, *'Cogito, ergo sum,'* they'll all disappear."

"Is that a mighty spell?"

"No, just wishful thinking; I'm putting Descartes before the horse." There was a short, nasty buzzing in Rod's ear; Fess didn't think much of his sense of humor. "Seriously, though, Your Majesty, that shouldn't be a problem. Anything alive and moving under its own power has *some* sort of neurological activity. I've got one young witch who can read an earthworm's thoughts, and they don't even *have* any."

"But can they hear thoughts far enough away to give us time to set our battle line where they mean to land?"

"Don't worry about that one, either. I had another young lady listen to the thoughts of one of the dino . . . uh, 'terrible lizard' giants over on the mainland, once. She wasn't herself again for three days. . . ."

"Then thou hast thy sentry-force made."

Rod frowned. "Yeah, but I just had another nasty thought. How come none of the witches ever heard beastman thoughts before?"

That stopped Tuan, too. He frowned and thought it over for a few seconds. Then he looked up with a bright smile. "Mayhap because they were not there?"

Rod sat still for a moment. Then he sighed and shrugged. "Why not? On Gramarye, anyway." There was a local variety of fungus that was very sensitive. Not that its feelings could be hurt or anything; but if a projective telepath thought at it hard enough, it would turn into whatever the projective was thinking about. Yes, it was very possible that the beastmen hadn't been there before. All it would take was an old granny, one who didn't know her own strength, telling horror stories to amuse the children . . .

He didn't think he wanted to meet that granny. "Say, uh, Your Majesty . . . what happens when our sentries *do* find them?"

"Why, then we ride against them with steel and fire," Tuan said grimly.

"Yes, but—Gramarye is a moderately big island. What if they strike someplace where our army isn't?"

"As they have indeed done." Tuan nodded. "Well, I have commanded each of the seacoast lords to muster a force of worthy size, and keep it ever ready. E'en so, the best of barons' forces can only hold them till my armies come; if it can do more, I have more than beastmen to worry me."

It was a good point; a baron who could defeat a party of raiders was bound to think of taking on the royal army. "But it could take a while for your army to get there—say, a few days."

"Indeed." Tuan turned to him, frowning. "Canst thou not discover a spell to move mine army to the battlefield ere the beastmen come to it, High Warlock?"

" 'Fraid that's beyond even my powers." Rod had a brief, dizzying vision of Tuan's knights and men-at-arms clustered onto huge antigravity plates, skimming over the countryside; but he manfully thrust it from him, remembering that technology comes in whole chunks, not just bits and pieces. If he taught them how to make antigrav plates, they'd figure out very quickly how to make automatic cannon and television chains—and how much chance would democracy have in a land whose king had the technology for totalitarianism, and whose people still thought loyalty was the supreme virtue? Right—about as much as a camel in a glacier. "But you don't need magic to do it—just a complete force of horsemen."

"Why, how is that?" Tuan looked worried; to him, "horseman" meant "knight."

"Well, I know it sounds like heresy—but you don't have to have just the captains mounted. Common soldiers can learn to ride too."

Tuan stared, scandalized.

"Not on full-scale war-horses, of course," Rod said quickly. "The rankers can ride ponies. They can go just as fast as the destriers on the long haul, where they keep it down to a canter, if they don't wear much armor. And you can keep the whole force right there, in Runnymede, since it's pretty close to being the center of the island. Then, when my witch-sentries send word, you can just yell, 'Horse and hattock! Ho, and away!' and they can be mounted up and gone in ten minutes. Then, if you keep alternating canter and trot and give each soldier a spare mount, they can be anywhere within Gramarye in two days."

"And the beastmen could land within one." Tuan scowled, chewing at his lip. "E'en so, the idea has merit. A thousand men would suffice; certes these beastmen will not bring more. Then I could keep five such forces, placed so that any one of them could be at the seacoast in either of two provinces in less than a day." He turned a beaming smile on Rod. "I' truth, 'twill succeed! And if the footmen must ride, what of it? When they come to the field, they can dismount and fight as they always have!"

And, Rod realized with a sinking heart, the King would have discovered an excellent means of enforcing his will on the barons, whether they liked him or not. But what else could he do? Let bogeymen gobble up the taxpayers? "I think it'll work, Your Majesty."

"But a name! It must have a name!" Tuan's eyes glowed with excitement. "They will fight better, these soldiers, if their force doth bear a name that may ring down the ages!"

Tuan was good at that—these little bits of nonsense that ultimately made a great deal of difference: honor, chivalry, things like that. Men fought harder for these intangibles than for cold cash, frequently. If Tuan said his men would fight harder if their regiment had a famous name, Rod wasn't going to argue. "How about the Flying Legion?"

"Will this truly be an army, my lord?" Gwen stood beside him on the hillside, looking out over the little valley that had sprouted tents and horses.

"Only the vanguard," Rod assured her. "Tuan's still got his standing army of five thousand—and most of them are standing because they don't know how to ride. Here we're gathering a thousand good riders from all over the island, ones who already have some experience in war. Tuan's going to recruit another five thousand pedestrians for the main force, though."

Far below, a lieutenant shouted, and his squadron leaped into a gallop, charging down on another hapless unit with wicker swords.

Gwen watched and shuddered. "They are not terribly deft, my lord."

"I said they were experienced, not talented." Rod turned away and strolled along the flank of the hill, holding her hand. "Give 'em a little training and practice, though, and you'll never see a better troop of cavalry—I hope. Who's this?" He stopped, scowling at a brown-robed figure with a neat round bald spot who sat cross-legged about fifty yards ahead of them, a huge book open in his lap. He had an inkhorn in his left hand, and a quill in his right.

"A good friar, it would seem," Gwen answered. "Why art thou concerned, mine husband?"

"Because I don't remember ordering any." Rod strode up to the monk. "Good morning, Father."

"Good morning to thee, goodman." The priest turned a sunny, beaming countenance up to Rod. Then his jaw dropped and he scrambled to his feet. "Why, 'tis the High Warlock!"

"Careful, there; don't spill your ink." Rod reached out a hand to steady the inkhorn. "It's nice to be recognized, but I'm not worth jumping up for—not unless you're in uniform, anyway."

"Nay; I know thee for one of the greatest men ever to walk the soil of Gramarye." Everything about the monk was round —his stomach, his face, his eyes. "Who else could have rescued Catharine the Queen from the peasant mob who sought her life and the band of barons who sought her throne?"

"Well, her husband did a pretty good job; he was in on that, too, if you remember. In fact, that battle had a lot to do with his *becoming* her husband."

"Yet, not so much as thyself," the monk chirped.

Rod cleared his throat; the friar was coming unpleasantly close to the truth. Time for a change of subject. "What're you doing here, Father?"

"Oh!" The monk looked down at his book. "Only amusing an idle moment, Lord Warlock. A wise man will ever be doing; so, when there is naught else afoot, I fill the time with the writing of a chronicle of the events that occur whiles I live."

"A Chronicle? Hey! History in the making!" Rod couldn't resist. "Am I in it?"

"Indeed, Lord Warlock! What Historie of Gramarye could be complete without full accounting of thee?"

"I had rather account for him at home," Gwen said dourly, coming up beside Rod. "Yet I do not think thou didst quite catch mine husband's meaning, good Father."

"Yeah? Oh! Yeah!" Rod looked up, and cleared his throat. "That's right, Father. When I said, 'What're you doing here?'

I meant, here with the *army*, not just at this particular moment. What's your business?''

"Why, the saving of souls," answered the priest in round-eyed innocence. "Our good Abbot hath appointed me chaplain to the King's Foot—but His Majesty did say to me that he had a surfeit of chaplains, and sent me to thee.''

"Oh, he did, did he?" Rod could see Tuan doing it, too. The young King loved all his subjects, but the average medieval monk tended to be continually exhorting, which could try even Tuan's patience. "I can see I'll have to have a word with His Majesty. Well, at least he sent me an amateur historian.''

"Milord!" A squire came galloping up and reined in near Rod. "Lord O'Berin's greetings, milord. He doth send to tell thee the folk from Loguire have come!''

"Oh, really!" Rod grabbed the priest's hand and gave it a quick shake, quill-pen and all. "Well, it was a real pleasure to meet you, Father, but I've gotta run now . . . Uh, what was your name again?''

"Brother Chillde, I am called. But do not stay to speak with a foolish friar, Lord Warlock, when matters of state await thee.''

"Well, military matters, really. Gwen, come listen." He caught her hand as he turned away, pacing down the hill. "These're a few of the survivors from the beastman attack.''

"Ah! I will listen, and gladly." A frown puckered Gwen's brow. "I misdoubt me that there may have been something of magic about these beastmen.''

"If there is, and they mention it, you'll find it." As they paced over the valley floor, Rod remembered his son. "Where's Magnus?''

Gwen's eyes flashed, and her chin came up. "Rather, ask why I have come here.''

"I did wonder, but not too much—I was just glad to have you. Why? What did Brom do?''

"He came to our home and told me that I could no longer sit idly by, playing at housewifery. As though 'twere play!''

Rod winced, remembering how the dust flew at home—he couldn't even be a *little* messy anymore—and the rotten (for her) mood Gwen was in by the end of each day. "Well, he can say that—he's got a troop of elves to keep his quarters tidy. But he is right, dear—we need your talents in the field just now. The cave'll have to gather dust.''

Gwen shuddered. "Well, mayhap; 'tis after all folks' lives we speak of, and we will not be home for some time, I think. Magnus, however, cannot wait; I must needs spend at least the half of my waking time with him, unless 'tis a day of battle.''

"Yeah, I know." Rod winced at a twinge of conscience. "But where *is* the boy?''

"Brom found a half-dozen elfin beldams to watch over him. I took him to their grotto, and I could see they knew something of children, so I left him with them.''

"Not altogether willingly, I gather.''

"Oh, I will never feel easy with my babe out of my sight!" Gwen cried. "Yet it must be, and I know I am foolish to worry.''

"Yes, you probably are." Rod squeezed her hand. "I'm sure any nursemaids Brom finds for you will be very capable." Gwen couldn't know just *how* sure—Brom had made Rod swear never to tell her that Brom was her father. He felt a little shy about it, being a dwarf. But he did care for Magnus like one of his own—which the child was, of course. No, any babysitter Brom picked would be extremely reliable. "Even if they are elves.''

"*Especially* if they are elves." Gwen skewered him with a glance. "Who else could keep thy son bound, Warlock?''

"Only another warlock, or witch." Rod grinned into her glare. "Witch.''

"Well, that is true." Her gaze softened. "Though the most of them are too young; and the ones who are aged enough are sour old spinsters and hermits, living midst the wild mountains. No, I do trust Brom's elves.''

"After all, who else would he get?" Rod spread his hands. "He *is* the King of the Elves, after all.''

"Aye." Gwen smiled, amused. "If Their Majesties only knew their Privy Councillor's true nature—and office!''

"They'd kick him out of the household and try to sign a treaty with him. No, I think the current setup's much more efficient.''

"Aye, with Brom ever at Tuan's elbow.''

"And Magnus with the elves, and you with me." Rod sighed. "My son, the changeling! Besides, you can keep checking on him, can't you?''

"Oh, I do at all odd moments, I assure you!" Gwen

stopped and stood stock-still, her eyes losing focus. Then she relaxed and began walking again, with a nod. "Aye, he is well."

"Helps to be a mind reader, doesn't it?" Rod grinned. "Which is, of course, one of the reasons why I like having you along on this trip." He stopped at Brom's tent, nodded to the sentries, and lifted the tent flap. "After you, dear."

Inside, two servants stood near a long table, holding trays laden with food. A handful of peasants sat at the board, chewing huge mouthfuls and washing them down with ale. A dusty man sat at one end of the table, eating with equal gusto but in smaller bites—a knight out of armor, to judge by his clothes. At the other end of the table sat a man less than three feet high, with shoulders almost as wide as he was tall, arms and legs thicker with muscle than Rod's, and a huge head with shaggy black hair and beard. His head snapped up as Rod entered; then he leaped down and strode over to the witch-pair, booming, "Well, 'tis time thou hast come! Here these goodfolk are near to surfeited with food and ale—and I sent for thee as soon as they did arrive."

"Well, we're never easy to find." Rod stepped over to the table. "Who is this gentleman?"

"Sir Reginald De La Place, vassal to the Duke Loguire," Brom explained. "He it is hath brought these peasants to us. Sir Reginald, this titled lout is Rod Gallowglass, Lord High Warlock."

"Lord Warlock!" The knight jumped to his feet. "I am honored!"

"Glad to hear it," Rod said, inclining his head. "My wife, the Lady Gwendylon."

The knight bowed, and Gwen beamed.

"And these poor folk be victims." Brom clapped the nearest peasant on the shoulder. "But a week agone, they had houses. What hast thou now, goodman?"

The peasant gulped his current mouthful. "Eh, we ha' cottages again, milord—or the half of us do, then. 'Tis not so long, to build a wall of wattle."

"And daub," Brom amplified. "I ha' seen our folk at work, Lord Warlock. They build a house in but a day. Yet there were a score of cottages in their village."

Rod noticed the apprehensive way the peasants were eyeing him. "It's all just a rumor, folks. I'm not really a warlock— just a bad scholar who's learned a few tricks."

If anything, their apprehension deepened.

"Well, I tried," Rod sighed. "Tell me, goodman—what did these beastmen look like?"

"Ah, terrible things they was, milord! Tall as houses, and horned like the moon!"

"And hairy," the woman across from him added. "All over covered with hair, they was."

"But not on their faces," another woman chimed in. "Beardless, they was."

"And they rode on a dragon," the man said firmly. "A dragon it was—and it swam away with 'em on its back!"

"Nay, 'tweren't a beast!" the first woman scoffed. "What would ye know about it? Ye was half dead with a cracked skull when they sailed away!" She turned to Rod. "We were blessed, milord. Seven of our menfolk dead, but he wasn't one of 'em."

"All of 'em hurted, though," the woman next to her muttered, "and six bairns killed."

Rod's face darkened. "What were the dragons he was talking about, then?"

"Ships, milord! Only their ship! But the front of it was carved into a dragon's head, and the stern was carved into a tail!"

"Dragon ships? Were they long and narrow?"

"The very thing!" the woman chortled. "Hast seen 'em, then, milord?"

"Only in a history book—and those raiders did have beards. And not much body hair . . ."

"And horns, milord?"

"Helmets," Rod explained, "helmets with horns on 'em. At least, that's what people *thought* they wore—but they didn't really. Not in battle."

"Can't be the same ones, then," the man said firmly.

"No," Rod agreed, "I don't think the originals could have sailed this far from their home ports. They were mighty sailors, but they did need water."

"Then, why would these beastmen be dressed like to them, my lord?" Gwen wondered.

"Because somebody's been telling 'em stories. Speaking of which, do grannies tell folk tales about horned raiders in dragon ships?"

The peasants shook their heads, wide-eyed.

"Well, it was a chance," Rod sighed. "But if the grannies

haven't been telling tales, who has?''

"Didn't look like just a ship in the moonlight, with them devils yellin' and swingin' their clubs,'' the big peasant muttered, fingering his bandage gently.

"Of course not,'' Rod agreed. "That's why they carved it that way—to scare the . . .'' His eyes lost focus. "Wait a minute! Of course! That's why whoever told 'em about dragon ships and horned helmets . . . did tell 'em! To help them scare poor people like you! After all, if it worked for the Vikings . . .''

"What are 'vikings,' milord?'' one of the women asked timidly.

"The horned raiders I was telling you about.''

"Could they freeze people with a look?''

Rod shook his head. "No, of course not—though I suppose they wanted to. You mean these gorillas *could*?''

"Froze us near to stone,'' the man growled. "One of 'em looked me in the eye, and all of a sudden, *his* eyes seemed to pierce right through to the back of me head. I tried to move, but I couldn't.''

"Ye was scared,'' the second woman scoffed, "frighted stiff, like a babe with a snake.''

The man's face reddened. "Was ye there on the green with us, woman? Did ye look into their eyes? Oh, aye, those glittering eyes frighted me—but I've been frighted in battle afore, when our young Lord Anselm fought the Queen . . . and . . . um . . .'' He eyed Brom furtively.

"And his younger brother, who is now our King,'' Brom growled. "None will fault thee for that, goodman. What choice hadst thou? When thy lord summons thee to fight, thou must needs fight. Yet, in that battle, did fear freeze thee?''

"Nay, good my lord!'' The peasant shook his head. "I swung my pike the harder for it. Yet when that grisly monster's eyes pierced my brain, I sought to strike in wild anger—but mine arm would not answer! I strained, I tugged at it with all my will, but it would not . . .'' He broke off with a shudder. "Lord in Heaven save me! May I never live through such a moment again! To not be able to budge, yet see that huge club swinging down at me . . .'' He squeezed his eyes shut and turned away, shaking his head.

"Softly, now.'' Rod clapped him on the shoulder. "You did bravely, goodman. You did all that a man could do.''

" 'Twas the Evil Eye," the man muttered. " 'Twas witch-craft."

Rod turned to Gwen with a questioning gaze.

"There are tales of it," she answered slowly, "of witches and warlocks who could freeze folk with a glance. Yet I never have met one with such a power."

"And you know most of the witches in Gramarye." Rod turned back to the peasant, nodding. "So our enemy is something new, in more ways than one. But if it had not been for yourself, goodman, we would not have known that. My deepest thanks."

"At your lordship's service." The big peasant recovered a bit, and managed to smile up at Rod. " 'Twas . . . 'twas real, then?"

"Is the lump on your head real?" Rod retorted. "Then, the club that made it certainly was, and so was the beastman who swung it. As to the Evil Eye—well, when a battle-tried veteran freezes, it couldn't very well be anything else." *Not on this world, anyway*, he thought.

"Thank ye, milord." The peasant smiled up at him.

"Don't worry. I would've frozen too." Rod clapped him on the shoulder again, and turned to Gwen. "Know any counter-spells?"

Her lips parted to answer as she spread her hands—and suddenly there was a baby in them, kicking and crowing, "Mama! Found you, Mama! Found you!"

Gwen stared, startled. Then a delighted grin curved her lips, and she hugged the child close to her. "Hast thou indeed, thou naughty babe! Come, didst thou seek thy mother through thy mind only?"

"Huh!" The baby nodded, very pleased with himself.

"A telepathic tracker?" Rod was staring too. "My son's a headhunter?"

" 'Tis a head I'll be having, though not his," Brom growled. "Whose charge was this bairn? Hobgoblin!"

Something small popped through the door and scurried over to Brom. "Pardon, King of Shadows!" It was a miniature man about a foot and a half tall, heavy in the shoulders and deep in the voice. "The elf-wives' powers have waned; the babe lost interest in their games, and their spells could not hold him."

"Then, they must con new charms, and hold him by delight

alone," Brom growled. "Though 'tis true, I know of nothing that could hold this bairn when he doth not wish it."

"Naughty babe!" Gwen reproved Magnus. He gurgled happily in reply.

"At least, when he had 'scaped I found him in the half of a minute," the elf pointed out.

" 'Tis true, and any who would wish to harm him would fare ill against thee," Brom admitted. "Yet bid them hold him better, Robin."

"Naughty child!" Gwen scolded. "Though glad I am to see thee, yet must thou know thy mother hath a task which must be done. I cannot be with thee now, my sweet, much though I wish to. Come, hie thee back to thy nurse, and bide until I call thee."

"Uh-uh!" The baby scowled, and shook his head.

"Magnus," Gwen began, in a tone that implied a nuclear bomb (or, at least, a tactical warhead) was about to explode.

But Brom interrupted. "Nay then, manikin! Hast never heard of bogeymen?"

The child stared down at him in blue-eyed wonder.

"Never?" Brom rumbled. "Ah, woefully dost thou neglect this child's education if he ha' not yet heard of childhood's horror!"

"Well, that's kinda the point," Rod answered, nettled. "I see absolutely no point in scaring kids half to death and giving them dread of perfectly ordinary things. If I tell him to be good, he's got to do it simply because he believes in me."

"Pray he doth; if this bairn ceased to believe in me, I might cease to be!" Brom growled. "Yet what robbery is this, to take from him one of childhood's most delicious thrills—the dread of the horrible monster that he knows, at heart's bottom, doth not truly live? The bogeymen, child, are huge, shambling things, all covered with hair, with tiny glowing eyes, and long, sharply pointed teeth!"

Magnus cuddled back against Gwen with a delighted squall.

" 'Tis true!" Brom held up a forefinger. "Vile things are they, that do seek to harm both children and parents! And thy mother and father must needs sally forth against them, to drive them from this land for good and all—yet they cannot go if they are not sure that thou art safe."

Magnus stared at Brom wide-eyed, beginning to understand.

"So hie thee back to thy nurses!" Brom clapped his hands.

"Hie thee hence, and bide with them till thy mother doth summon thee! Bide thee with thy nurses in safety, that thy mother and father may chase the bogeymen from this land!"

Magnus looked up at Gwen out of the corner of his eyes. "Baby come too?"

"I fear not," Gwen said firmly, holding him up under the arms so that she could look directly into his eyes. "Thou must needs do as thine Uncle Brom . . ."

Rod was the only one who noticed the shadow pass over Brom's face.

". . . as thine Uncle Brom doth say, and flit back to Elfland, to thy nurses, there to bide whiles thy father and I do chase these monsters. Yet I'll summon thee whene'er I may, to play awhile. Now, wilt thou go?"

The baby glowered at her, then nodded reluctantly.

"Good babe!" Gwen kissed him. "Now, hie thee hence!"

Magnus looked up at Rod. He reached out to squeeze a chubby hand—then found himself holding empty air. Magnus had disappeared.

"Bairns do understand more than we think," Brom rumbled, "if we are but open with them." He frowned at the peasants. "And what dost thou gape at, village fools? Hast never seen a babe afore?"

The men gave a start and glanced at Rod guiltily; but the women sighed, and one of them said to Gwen, "Now, bless thee, lady! Praise Heaven mine were only common babes!"

"Certes, they tried thee as sorely as ever mine try me," Gwen answered, amused. "I have, after all, some powers to use in dealing with him. Yet bless thee for thy wishes, goodwife."

One of the guardsmen stepped into the tent. "Milords, His Majesty doth ask that thou attend upon him."

Brom looked up, frowning. "What coil's this?"

"Word hath flown from witch to witch, milord. A dragon ship doth sail toward Bourbon."

Half an hour later, while the main army was still striking its tents and packing up, the Flying Legion cantered up out of the valley and struck off toward the east. Rod rode at their head, with Toby the teenage warlock beside him. "I didn't have time for the full report, Toby. Who spotted the beastmen?"

"Matilda, milord. She and Marion, her sister, flew to the east to dwell within a cottage on a cliff-top that Lord Hapsburg built for them—all as His Majesty commanded.''

Rod nodded. ''And they take turns just sitting and listening for strange thoughts, right?''

Toby nodded. ''Even as His Majesty did command—an hour listening, then an hour doing other things, then an hour listening again.'' He glanced at Rod out of the corner of his eye. ''Twas thou who didst bid His Majesty so instruct us, was it not?''

Rod frowned and shook his head. ''What would I know about hearing thoughts, Toby? It was Gwen's idea. So, who heard the beastman-thoughts—the one who was on duty, or both of them?''

''The one who was 'off-duty,' Lord Warlock. She slept, and waked screaming.''

''The one who slept?'' Rod stared. Then he nodded slowly. ''Well, I suppose it makes sense. Maybe her telepathic sensitivity gets a boost when she's asleep.''

''We do seem to have dreams that are not our own,'' Toby admitted.

''Really! Hm! Wish I'd known that—might've come in handy.''

''Cannot Gwendylon hear thy thoughts when she doth sleep?'' Toby asked carefully.

Rod shook his head. ''Neither asleep nor awake. I seem to be telepathically invisible.'' His tone was carefully neutral, hiding his feelings nicely. He tried not to think about it; it made him feel inferior to Gwen. ''What did Matilda dream?''

''She dreamt that she pulled an oar aboard a dragon ship, and heard the chieftains speaking of old gods which they used to worship, and a new god which they worship now. Yet all of it was without words, and the new god seemed somehow monstrous, though there was no picture of it.''

''Well, that's not surprising. Haven't you ever had that flash of thought, the whole concept suddenly clear, before you get around to putting it into words?''

Toby frowned. ''I have indeed, though I had not thought of it. And the thought Matilda heard lasted no longer than such a flash.''

''Really?'' Rod pricked up his mental ears. ''Odd, that. Was there a strong emotion under it?''

Toby nodded. ''Very strong; a surge of fear and dread. The beastman's soul, for a second, did clamor toward the sky and the old gods. Then he realized what he did, and the thought ended. Yet it was enough to waken Matilda, and waken her screaming.''

"Small wonder; *I'd* wake up halfway out of the room. But it tells us a lot.''

"Aye. It tells us beastmen draw near the eastern coast.''

"Well, a bit more than that. It tells us the beastmen have a religion. So far, we didn't even have any reason to think they had souls.''

"I had not thought of that,'' Toby admitted.

"It also tells us that they've just had a conversion, and at least one of the converts wasn't exactly wholehearted about it. Wonder who the new god is? And what kinds of methods his missionaries use . . .'' Rod was remembering Constantine's baptism and a new shirt, or death. "But more importantly, it tells us the beastmen's thoughts can be heard when there are very strong emotions behind them—and gives us some reason to think they may be able to hide their thoughts deliberately.''

Toby frowned. "Why, how is that?''

"Because you said the thought ended just after the beast-man realized what he was doing. That means either that he deliberately hid his thoughts somehow, or that his thoughts can only be read when he's at an emotional peak.''

"Why, that is so!'' Toby looked up at Rod wide-eyed.

Rod squirmed; he hated hero worship, especially when it was directed at him. It made a man feel so responsible. . . . "Of the two, I'd guess they can hide their thoughts. There must've been *some* sort of strong emotion in them when they sacked the Loguire coast, but no witches heard them.''

"But would not a one of them have let slip a thought in the heat of battle?''

Rod nodded. "You'd think so, wouldn't you? So maybe it's the other way around; maybe their thoughts can only be read when they're pushing them out. That surge of thought Matilda picked up sounds like a prayer—and a prayer is deliberately aimed away from yourself; you're *trying* to reach someone else with that kind of thought.''

"Then, let us be glad there is one strong believer amongst them.''

"Yes, and that the old gods happened to be out of sight at the moment and needed a strong push behind a prayer if it was going to reach them.''

"But how could a god be *in* sight?'' Toby looked puzzled. "They are naught but dreams.''

"Point well-taken," Rod admitted, "but the beastmen might not know that yet. Especially if they've got an idol. . . . Hm! Now you've got me wondering. . . ."

"About what, Lord Warlock?"

"About their new god. I wonder just how new he is? What he wants his worshippers to do?"

Toby's eyes suddenly lost focus. "Lord Warlock . . . word from Marion . . . the dragon ship hath shown no sign of turning in toward shore. It sails on past Bourbon. . . ." He frowned a second in concentration, probably his equivalent of, "Acknowledged; that's a copy," then turned back to Rod. "The beastmen sail on, northward."

"Then, we'll head north too. Sergeant!" Rod called back over his shoulder. "Turn left at the next crossroad!" He turned back to Toby. "Send word to His Majesty."

"Aye, Lord Warlock." Toby's eyes lost focus again. Rod watched him in silence for a few minutes, till the young warlock's eyes cleared again. He turned to Rod with a half-smile. "His Majesty turns the main army northward. He is quite pleased with his new way of sending messages betwixt the parts of an army."

"I should think he would be. Any medieval commander would've given his right arm for an advantage like that. You know, Toby, when this is all over I'll bet His Majesty tries to set up a permanent witch-and-warlock network—only for royal messages, of course."

Toby frowned. "That is not wholly a happy thought, Lord Warlock."

"No, neither for you, nor for the general population. Though you must admit it would guarantee you full employment."

"Fuller than I wish, I doubt not."

"Well, that's a point. It is nice to be able to keep the workday down to eight hours—and it's even nicer to have some choice as to whether or not you're going to take the job in the first place. No, it's okay for an emergency, but we definitely shouldn't encourage this kind of thing during peacetime."

"Save for thy messages, of course," Toby said with his tongue in his cheek.

"Well, of course. But that's a different case, isn't it? I mean, I'm almost a member of the tribe."

"By marriage," Toby agreed. "Aye, when all's said and done, thou *art* a warlock."

Rod opened his mouth to deny it, thought what would happen if he did, and closed his mouth again.

The sun was only a red glow behind Rod's right shoulder as he rode down the winding road toward the Romanov beach. "No faster than a trot, Sergeant! Let these folk by! We're here to defend them, not trample them!"

Peasants thronged the road, with huge packs on their backs and handcarts behind them, hauling their few household goods. Rod swore. "They'd take their whole cottages if they could! Well, at least they're not stampeding. Here's the real evidence of the good you've done, Toby."

"How so, Lord Warlock?" Toby reined his horse over to let the peasants pass by.

"Because they've got time to evacuate, thanks to the Magic Early Warning system. They even had time to pack up before they started fleeing!"

The Flying Legion swerved over to the side of the road, single file, following Rod's and Toby's example. The peasants, seeing them coming, struggled to compress their ranks and leave room for them.

"God save the High Warlock and his legion!" a voice yelled, and the whole flowing crowd joined in a ragged cheer. The soldiers grinned and sat a little straighter in the saddle.

"Always nice to be appreciated," Rod observed. Toby smiled, amused.

A hand caught Rod's shin. He looked down into a wrinkled, yellow-eyed face rough with beard stubble. "Drive them away, Lord Warlock! Why can ye not keep 'em from comin'?"

"Off wi' ye, now!" The man behind him gave the old whiner a shove. "Here's men goin' t' mortal danger, and you'd ask 'em to hurry!" Rod smiled his thanks, and the younger man grinned back. "Save your worship!" He hurried on.

"There will ever be such, will there not?" Toby said quietly.

Rod nodded. " 'Save us, save us! And please arrange hotel accommodations while you're doing it!' But there'll always be the ones behind them too, who tell 'em to shut up and let us get on about our business."

They struggled on through the crowd. The peasants streamed by, and they came out onto the beach while the sky still glowed with dusk. A hundred nervous men looked up at the sound of hoofbeats, and raised a frantic cheer. Rod grinned and waved, muttering under his breath, "Gallop, Fess. Make it look good. Pick out their officer and stop on a penny next to him."

The black steel horse leapt into a gallop and thundered around in a curve, pulling up beside a cloaked horseman in plate armor. "Hail, Sir Knight! I am Rod Gallowglass, Lord High Warlock, and these men are His Majesty's Flying Legion."

"Thou art well come indeed!" cried the knight. "Now, praised be King Tuan for your coming!" Which was pretty good, considering that only three years ago this man must've been riding behind his lord, Duke Romanov, against the royal army, such as it had been. "I am Sir Styenkov."

"We're just reinforcements," Rod assured. "I don't want to upset your battle plan; we'll just fall in beside you. What'd you planned?"

"What could I, with only an hundred?" The knight spread his hands helplessly. " 'Tis all that Their Majesties allow us to keep under arms—God save them, 'tis generous to allow even that! But what can they do? Draw up in a line, and wait."

"I suppose so. But I've got two hundred more behind me. And yours are veterans, aren't they?"

Styenkov nodded. "All fought in the rebellion, aye. They are not like to break and flee."

"Then draw 'em back up the beach as far as you can, and let 'em wait. There's only one dragon ship; at least, the witches haven't said anything about there being more than one." He frowned at the thought. "Hm. I've been careless. Toby!"

"Aye, Lord Warlock."

"Has anyone done a flyby on the raiders? Actually flown over them, to see how many there are?"

Toby's eyes lost focus for a minute; then they cleared, and he shook his head. "Nay, milord. None ha' thought to do so."

"Then do it, okay?"

"Aye, milord!" Toby sprang up into the air like a javelin trying for a new record, and disappeared into the low-hanging clouds. Sir Styenkov stared after him, open-mouthed. Rod turned to follow his gaze. "Hm. Yeah, that could be a problem, couldn't it?"

"Only for the beastmen! What fabulous force hast thou assembled, Lord Warlock?"

"Oh, you mean Toby? No, he's the only one with me; the rest are normal. Picked veterans, every one of 'em, but normal." Rod wondered how true that could be of any native of Gramarye. "No, I was talking about the clouds."

"Oh." For the first time, Styenkov seemed to notice the overcast. "Aye, those clouds look sullen. Well, I've fought in rain aforetimes."

"Me too, and it was a thoroughly nasty business. Still, we can't exactly send out an emissary and ask the beastmen to come back on a clear day, can we? But we might manage a different kind of surprise for them. If you pull your men way back, Sir Styenkov, and mine hide behind those rocks, over there"—he gestured toward an outcrop over to his left—"and behind that shrubbery"—he pointed to a line of trees on the right, that grew down almost to the water's edge.

Sir Styenkov's eyes lighted. "Then the beastmen will charge up to hack at my men, and yours may close upon them, like to the jaws of a vise!"

"Before they get to your men," Rod added. "Though, of course, when they see this beach with good cover at each side, they might smell a trap and decide to go look for easier game."

"I would not object to that. . . ."

A gust of wind fanned Rod's cheek, and Toby said, "There is only the one of them, Lord Warlock."

Sir Styenkov nearly swallowed his beard.

"He has to fly out there because he doesn't know where he's going," Rod explained. "But when he wants to come back he knows where it is, so he can teleport. It's faster that way." He turned to Toby. "How many men?"

"An hundred on deck. There may be more below—but I think not; their ship is small."

"It would have been an even fight without us," Rod observed. "Still, maybe my men can make things move a little faster, save a few lives, things like that."

"Touching that." Sir Styenkov scratched his nose. "Shall we take prisoners?"

"Huh?" Rod reflected that Sir Styenkov's mood had certainly improved. "Take prisoners? Of course!"

Sir Styenkov nodded. "I had thought so. Thou dost need information, and wish to set them talking, dost thou not?"

"Well, that too," Rod agreed. "But mostly, I want to find out if they *can* talk. How far off shore were they, Toby?"

"Mayhap half a mile, milord."

"That sounds like time to get into position." Rod strode off toward his troops, bawling, "Places, everyone!"

As he came up to the Flying Legion, he noticed the locals pulling back up the beach. Good; Sir Styenkov wasn't *too* overconfident. "Sir Lionel! Sir Hampden!"

"Aye, milord," his lieutenants answered in chorus.

"Sir Lionel, take your hundred over to that outcrop of rocks and hide them. Sir Hampden, take yours over to that line of trees. Charge out to fall upon the enemy when you hear the pipes."

"Aye, milord!" And the two lieutenants turned away, bawling orders to their sergeants. The sergeants started bellowing before the lieutenants had quite finished, and the beach filled with yells and the tramp of troops. In five minutes, it was clear. Rod turned, grinning, to wave to Sir Styenkov; then he turned and loped across the beach to the rock outcrop.

The beach lay empty, waiting. Tiny drops began to fall, scarcely more than a mist. Sir Styenkov's soldiers shifted nervously, muttering to one another. Rod heard a few whispers here and there among his own troops. "Hear any thoughts, Toby?"

"Nay, Lord Warlock." Toby's eyes were unfocused, watching the landscape of the mind rather than the world around him. "Whoever sent that one prayer, prays no longer."

"Then, there's no way of telling how close they are. Can't be long now, though."

In the distance, thunder rumbled.

Then it came, gliding out of the mist with muted splashing —a tall, gaunt serpent, mouth wide in a snarl, wicked horns probing from its forehead. Shadowy figures moved on its back.

Rod held his breath.

The dragon drove up onto the beach, slowing to a stop with the grinding of sand against wood. Beastmen began to drop off its back—squat, hulking, helmeted shapes, with round shields covering their torsos and heavy, double-bladed axes in their hands.

Rod squinted, trying to make out details through the rain, but it was no use. He could scarcely see more than a silhouette.

"Let me fight, Lord Warlock," Toby hissed in his ear.

Rod whirled, pressing a finger to his lips and shaking his head with a furious scowl. Confound the kid, did he want to give away the whole ambush? Rod could've sworn his lieutenants could've heard that whisper a hundred yards away in the tree line. He wished Toby *could* read his mind—but he had to settle for a glare and a head-shake. The lad's juvenile male hormones were getting the better of him, urging him on to glory and an early funeral. Which was his own business—but Rod's business was making sure Toby'd still be alive afterwards for his main assignment. Which would be more than dangerous enough.

The young man stepped back, smoldering.

Rod turned back to the beach just as the beastmen saw Styenkov's soldiers. Whatever they yelled to each other was lost in a rumble of thunder, but they quickly scuttled into place, pulling themselves into a rough semblance of a line. Then they began to move forward slowly.

One or two of Styenkov's soldiers began to march toward the beastmen. He shouted them back into line. Good man. The rest of his men brandished their pikes, waiting for the enemy.

The beastmen were halfway up the beach now. Rod could hear a low rumble as they called to one another. They were beginning to realize something was wrong; their tone was one of alarm, and their advance was grinding down to a halt. What was tipping Rod's hand? He darted a glance at Styenkov's soldiers, then looked again. Here and there, a man had straightened up a little, pike drooping—and stood frozen at a completely improbable angle. Rod realized they were the ones who had forgotten the standing order and had looked the enemy square in the eye. Now they were temporary statues, frozen by the Evil Eye.

So it really worked! It *wasn't* imagination!

But the rest of Styenkov's men were watching the enemy's hands, or feet—and were still very much a menace. The beastmen slowed and stopped—apparently they didn't have too much taste for an even fight. They hunched in on themselves, heads hunkered down; they seemed to be waiting. For what?

The beastmen began to make bellowing noises in deep rumbling bass voices. Rod suddenly realized that they were calling out in unison. He strained, trying to pick intelligible phonemes out of booming voices. It was getting easier, because they were getting their timing better; it was almost one unified shout now. Rod listened, then shook his head; there was no way of saying what it meant in their own language. To him, though, it sounded like:

"Cobalt! Cobalt! Cobalt!"

. . . Which was ridiculous; at their level of technology, they couldn't even have the concept of bombs, let alone atomic fission.

Thunder rocked the land, and the beach lit up with an explosion of lightning. Then there was only gloom again, darker for having had the sudden light. Rod peered through the murk —and stared. Sir Styenkov's men stood frozen in their buskins!

A ragged cheer rumbled up from the beastmen, and they waddled forward, making a grating sound. With a shock, Rod realized they were laughing.

But they were moving so slowly! Why? Didn't they want to reach their intended victims?

Then Sir Styenkov's whole line lurched forward. Then they lurched again, and again—and, step-stumbling-step, they marched toward their butchers!

Something bumped into Rod's shoulder. He whirled—just in time to catch Toby. The young warlock's body was rigid, and his eyes had lost focus. Had he been tuned in on a soldier's mind when the Evil Eye froze him?

Then Rod saw one of Styenkov's soldiers slow and stop. His head lifted slowly; then he shivered, looked about him wildly, realized what had happened, set his pike on an enemy, and started marching again with grim purpose. Further down the line, another soldier began to waken, too.

Rod stared down at Toby. The young idiot had found a way to get into the fight after all!

Thunder broke over them, and lightning stabbed the land again.

The soldiers froze solid again, and Toby's whole body whiplashed in a single massive convulsion; then he went limp, eyes closed.

Rod stared, appalled. Then he touched the carotid artery in the boy's throat and felt the pulse. Reassured, he lowered the young warlock. "Fess!"

"Here, Rod." The great black horse loomed up out of the darkness.

"Just stand over him and protect him."

"But, Rod . . ."

"No 'buts'!" Rod turned, sprinting away toward the battle-line, whipping out his sword. "Flying Legion! Charge!"

Fess sighed, and stepped carefully over Toby's still form, so that the young warlock lay directly beneath his black steel body.

Rod caught up with Styenkov's line just as they began stumbling toward the beastmen again. He looked from one to another frantically; their eyes were glazed, unseeing.

The beastmen began to waddle forward again, making the chugging, grating noise that passed for laughter with them. Rod whirled about, staring at them, just as they broke into a lumbering run. Rod glanced back at the stumbling soldiers, then ahead; the enemy were only huge, hulking shadows against the gray of stormclouds, great shadows looming closer.

Lightning flashed, and the beastmen roared a cheer. And Rod froze solid, but only with shock—because, for the first time, he had a really good look at a beastman.

And he recognized it.

Neanderthal.

There was no mistaking the sloping forehead, the brow ridges, the chinless jaw, the lump at the base of the skull. . . . He had an overwhelming desire to look one in the mouth and check its dentition.

Then a chill hand clutched his belly. What could Neanderthals be doing on Gramarye?

Attacking, obviously. He noticed two war clubs swinging up, then starting to swing down toward him. He leaped aside just as the first whistled past him, then threw himself into a lunge, sword arrowing toward the other clubman. Its round shield swung up; the beastman caught Rod's point neatly. For a moment, Rod stared directly into the little piggy eyes over the top of the shield—little piggy eyes that seemed to grow, and glow, with a bright, flaming bead at their centers that probed into his brain, leaving a trail of cold fire that didn't burn, but froze. It fascinated; it held all his attention, numbing his brain, stopping all thought. Dimly, off to the side, he noticed the huge war club swinging up for another blow; but that didn't matter. All that really mattered was that bright, burning bead at the center of the eyes. . . .

A furious scream rang in his ears, blotting out the sounds of battle, a scream such as a Valkyrie might make if she were actually allowed to attack; and a sudden warmth seemed to wrap around his mind, pushing away the bright, burning bead, away and away until it was only a pair of eyes again . . . the eyes of a warrior beastman whose huge war club was windmilling down to crush Rod's head.

He leaped back, yanking his sword free from the shield, and the club whistled past harmlessly. Behind the round shield, the beastman snarled and swung his club up again. Rod advanced and feinted high, at the face. The shield snapped up to cover, and Rod riposted and slashed downward. The sword-tip whipped across the creature's thighs, tracing a line of bright red. It shrieked, clutching at its legs, and collapsed rolling on the ground. Rod didn't stay to watch; he turned to glance at the battle-line—and saw a war ax swinging straight at his sinuses, with a broad gloating grin behind it (yes, the dentition *was* right). Rod leaped to the side and chopped down, lopping off the ax-head.

High above him, the Valkyrie screamed again—now he recognized it; he'd heard it just last week, when Gwen had caught Magnus teleporting the cookie jar over to the playpen. Confound it, didn't the woman know he couldn't fight as well if he was worrying about her safety?

On the other hand, she was staying far above the battle—not really in any immediate danger, especially since the beastmen were limited to clubs and axes; not an arrow among the lot of 'em. He swung about, chopping at another Neanderthal. Snarling, four of them turned on him. Beyond them, he saw with shock, half the soldiers lay dead on the beach, their blood pouring into the sand. Fury boiled up in him, and he bellowed even as he gave ground, sword whirling furiously in feints and thrusts, keeping his attackers back just barely out of club-range. Beyond them, he saw frozen soldiers coming to life again; and a ragged shout of rage went up as they saw their dead companions. The nearest beastman looked back over his shoulder, his swing going wide. Rod thrust in under his shield, and he screamed, doubling over. His companions gave ugly barks, and pressed in. Behind them, two soldiers came running up, blades swinging high. Rod darted back out of the way and braced himself at the sickening thud of steel into meat. Their targets dropped, and the remaining beastman whirled on his two attackers in desperation. Rod shouted "Havoc!" and darted in. Startled, the beastman whirled back to face Rod—and doubled over Rod's steel. Rod yanked back just before a pike slammed down to end the warrior's agony. Its owner gave a bloodlust-bellow of victory, and turned back to the battle-line. Rod followed, fighting down sickness. No time for it now; he had to remind the soldiers. "Their eyes! Don't look at their eyes!"

So, of course, half of the soldiers immediately confronted the enemy stare-to-stare, and froze in their tracks.

The Valkyrie screamed again, and the soldiers jolted awake. Their pikes lifted just in time to block war axes. . . .

And lightning seared, thunder exploding around it.

As the afterimages ebbed, Rod saw the soldiers standing frozen again. High above him, a sudden wail trailed away.

"Gwen!" Rod bellowed. He stared into the sky, frantically probing the darkness—and saw the darker shadow hurtling downward. He spun, scrambling back up the beach, then whipped about, staring up at the swooping silhouette, running backward, tracking it as it grew larger and larger. . . .

Then it cracked into him, rock, bone, and sinew. Pain shot through his head, and the sky filled with stars. A myriad of tiny stabs scored his back and sides, and a chorus of cracking sounds, like a forest falling, filled his ears. His diaphragm had caved in; he fought for breath in near-panic. Finally air seeped in; he sucked it thankfully, the more so because it was filled with the perfume he'd given Gwen last Christmas. He looked down at the unguided missile that had flattened him, and at a noble bush that had given its life for the cause. He felt gratitude toward the shrub; Gwen was delicate, but she was no lightweight, especially when she was coming down at twenty miles an hour.

He struggled upward, lifting his wife clear of the bush and laying her carefully out just under the next shrub down the line. As far as he could tell, she was perfectly all right; no breaks or wounds. She'd have a hell of a bruise tomorrow, of course. . . . And she was unconscious; but he was pretty sure that had happened before she fell.

Rain suddenly drenched him. He remembered the last lightning-flash, and turned to look down the beach. Through the downpour he could just barely make out frozen forms toppling, and a dozen or so that fought back. Another lightning-flash showed them clearly laying furiously about them with their pikes; and they kept fighting, even as the lightning faded. A few, then, had heeded him and were watching their enemies' hands and weapons instead of their eyes. Too late to do them much good, though—they were outnumbered three to one.

Rod struggled back to his feet, ungallantly heaving Gwen up over his shoulder in a fireman's carry, and stumbled blindly back over the scrubline in a shaky trot. "Fess! Talk me in!"

"Turn toward the sea, Rod," the robot's voice murmured through the earphone set in Rod's mastoid process. "Approach fifty feet . . . turn right now . . . another twenty feet . . . Stop."

Rod dug his heels in, just barely managing to counter Gwen's momentum. He put out a hand and felt the synthetic horsehair in front of him. "Good thing they built your eyes sensitive to infrared," he growled.

He threw Gwen over the saddlebow, then dropped to one knee, reaching under the robot horse to lift Toby's head in the crook of his elbow. He slapped the boy's cheeks lightly, quickly. "Come on, lad, wake up! You've done your bit, contrary to orders; now it's time to get out of here."

"What . . . Where . . ." Toby's eyelids fluttered. Then he looked up at Rod, squinting against a painful headache. "Lord Warlock! What . . ."

"You tried to get into the battle by proxy, and got knocked out in person," Rod explained. "Gwen tried the same thing and got the same result. Now *we've* got to get out of here, before our few remaining soldiers get wiped out. Come on, lad—up in the air. Let's go!"

Toby stared up at him painfully. Slowly, he nodded. He squeezed his eyes shut, his face screwing up in concentration; then, suddenly, he was gone. Air boomed in to fill the space where he'd been.

Rod leaped up and swung into the saddle, bracing his wife's still form with one hand as he bellowed, "Retreat! Retreat!"

The dozen soldiers left standing leaped backward, then began to yield ground a step at a time. The beastmen roared and followed, but the Gramarye pikes whirled harder than ever with the power of desperation, keeping the Neanderthals at a distance. There were too many beastmen ganging up on each soldier, though; given time, they'd wipe out the Gramarye force.

Rod didn't intend to give them that time. "All right, Iron Horse—*now*!"

Fess reared back, pawing the air with a whinnying scream. The beastmen's heads snapped up in alarm. Then the great black horse leaped into a gallop, charging down at them. At the last second, he wheeled aside, swerving to run all along their line. The beastmen leaped back in fright, and the soldiers turned and ran. Fess cleared the battle-line; the beastmen saw their fleeing foes, shouted, and lumbered after them.

Fess whirled with another scream and raced back along the Neanderthal line. The beastmen shouted and leaped back—except for one who decided to play hero and turned to face the galloping horse, club raised.

Rod hunkered down and muttered, "Just a little off-center—with English."

Fess slammed into the Neanderthal, and he caromed off the horse's chest with a howl. He landed twenty feet away, and was silent. His companions stood poised, wavering.

On the saddlebow, Gwen stirred, lifting her head with a pained frown. She took one look and grasped the situation.

The beastmen growled to one another, softly at first, but gaining volume and anger. They began to waddle back up the beach, their low, ugly rumble filling the air.

Gwen's eyes narrowed, and the beastmen's clubs exploded into flame.

They howled, hurling their clubs after the Gramarye soldiers, turned, and ran.

Gwen glared after them. Then her head began to tremble, and she collapsed again.

"Retreat!" Rod snapped. Fess pivoted and raced back up the beach after the soldiers.

They came to rest high in the rocks atop the cliff, behind the long, sloping beach. "You did well," Rod assured the soldiers. "No one could have done better."

One of the men spread his hands helplessly. "How can we fight an enemy who can freeze us in our tracks, milord?"

Rod dismounted and lifted Gwen down tenderly. "I think my wife's given us the basic idea. I'll work it out with her when she comes to." He knelt, lowering Gwen to the ground behind two boulders, cradling her head and shoulders against his chest. He winced at a sudden pain in his arm and remembered a club hitting him there. He remembered a few other blows, too, now that he thought about it. With the adrenaline of battle beginning to wear off, the bruises were beginning to hurt. With surprise, he noticed a bright crimson streak across his chest—one of the ax-blows had come closer than he'd realized. When he understood just how close, he began to get the shakes. He clamped down on them sternly; there'd be time for that later. "What're they doing, men?"

"They begin to feel brave again, milord." One of the soldiers was lying among the seaward rocks, peering out between two boulders. "They are stepping away from their dragon."

"Any sign of the villagers?"

"None, milord. All fled in time."

Rod nodded. "Well, it's a shame about the village, but they can rebuild it."

" 'Tis not destroyed yet, milord."

"Yet," Rod echoed. "There's a wineskin in my saddlebag, boys. Pass it around."

A soldier leaped and wrenched the wineskin out. He squirted a long streak into his mouth, then passed it to his comrade.

"Toby!" Rod yelled. Nothing happened.

Gwen stirred in Rod's arms, squinting against a raging headache, looked up, saw Rod, and relaxed, nestling against his chest, closing her eyes. "I am safe."

"Praise Heaven," Rod breathed.

"What doth hap, my lord?"

"We lost, darling. You came up with a good idea, but they outnumbered you."

She shook her head, then winced at the pain it brought. "Nay, my lord. 'Twas the lightning."

"Lightning?" Even through his exhaustion, Rod felt something inside him sit up and take notice. "Well . . ."

"Milord," the sentry called, "fire blossoms in the village."

Rod nodded with a grimace. "Whole place'll be one big torch in a few minutes. The beastmen won't find much to pick there, though. Peasants don't own much—and what they do have they can carry."

"There is the granary, milord," one of the locals pointed out, "and the smokehouse."

Rod shrugged. "So they'll have a picnic on the way home. Don't worry, lad—the King and Queen will send you food for the winter. Grain they could've had for the asking." He looked down at Gwen. "Can you find Toby, darling?"

Gwen nodded and closed her eyes, then winced. Rod felt a stab of guilt—but he needed the young warlock.

Air slammed outward with a soft explosion, and Toby stood before him. "Milord Warlock?"

One of the soldiers stared, then turned away, muttering and crossing himself.

Rod pretended not to notice. "Feel up to some action again?"

"Assuredly, an thou dost wish it, milord." Toby's knees were shaking with exhaustion.

"I do," Rod said. "I hate to ask it of you, but we've got to salvage something out of this. When they ship out, can you follow them?"

Toby stared off into space for a moment, then nodded. "There are clouds. They will not see me."

"You don't have to go all the way," Rod pointed out. "Just see 'em on their way, then call for one of your mates. He can teleport out to you, and you can disappear. Just get them started."

Toby nodded slowly. "Wise, milord. We will."

"The flames slacken, milord."

"Yes. Thank heaven for the rain." But Rod looked up, frowning; the sentry's voice had changed. A different soldier lay among the rocks, his arm in a fresh, gleaming sling.

Rod stared. "Hey—who gave you that?"

The sentry looked up, surprised, then nodded toward another soldier who sat, teeth gritted against pain, while a chubby figure in a brown robe wrapped linen around a long gash in his arm.

"Father Chillde," Rod said slowly.

The monk looked up, then smiled sadly. "I fear I have come too late, Milord Gallowglass. At least I may be of some service now."

"We appreciate it, of course—but the chaplain doesn't *have* to come into battle."

The sad smile stayed. "There are two ways of thinking of that, milord."

Nice to know they had a dedicated one—and his mere presence was definitely a comfort to the soldiers. Him, and the wine.

"They move back toward their ships," the sentry reported.

"There will be much work for me when they have gone," the priest said sadly.

Rod shook his head. "I don't think so, Father. From what I saw during battle, they didn't leave any wounded."

The priest's mouth pressed thin. " 'Tis to be lamented. But

there will be other work, more's the pity.''

Rod turned toward him, frowning. ''What . . .? Oh. Yeah—the Last Rites.'' He turned back toward the beach. ''But it won't just be our dead down there, Father. How about the beastmen? Think they have souls?''

''Why—I had not thought of it,'' the priest said, surprised. ''But is there reason to think they would not?''

One of the soldiers growled a reply.

The monk shook his head. ''Nay, goodman. I ha' known Christian men to do worse—much worse.''

''*I* would, could I but get one of them alone,'' another soldier snarled.

''There—do you see?'' The priest spread his hands. ''Still, souls or none, I misdoubt me an they be Christian.''

''They called upon their false god at the battle's beginning, did they not?''

''Was that the burden of their chant?'' another soldier wondered. '' 'Go Bald,' was it not?''

''Something of the sort,'' the first growled.

Rod frowned; he'd heard 'Cobalt,' himself. Well, each interpreted it according to words he knew. What did it really mean, though? He shrugged; it could be some sort of heathen god, at that.

''They have boarded their ship,'' the sentry called. ''They are launching . . . they turn . . .''

''May I build a fire now?'' Father Childe asked.

Rod shrugged. ''Please do, Father—if you can find shelter for it and anything dry enough to burn.'' He turned to the young warlock. ''Sure you feel up to it, Toby?''

The esper nodded, coming to his feet. He was looking a little better, having rested. ''I will start them, at least. When I've learned the trick of following a ship without being seen, I'll call another of our band and teach it to him.''

Rod nodded. ''See you soon, then, Toby.''

''Thou shalt, Lord Warlock.'' Toby sprang into the air. The soldiers stared after him, gasping, as he soared up and up, then arrowed away over the waves. A few crossed themselves, muttering quick prayers.

''There is no need for that,'' Father Childe said sharply. ''He is naught but a man, like to yourselves, though somewhat younger and with a rare gift. But he is not proof 'gainst arrows or spears; if you would pray, beseech God for his safety.''

Rod stared at the chubby priest, surprised. Then he nodded his head in slow approval.

"He has gone through the clouds," the sentry reported.

Rod nodded. "Wise, once he's figured out which way they're headed. He'll probably drop down for a quick peek now and then, just to check on them."

"They have crossed the bar," the sentry reported. "They stand out to sea."

Rod sighed and came to his feet, cradling Gwen in his arms. "It's over, men. Let's go."

Below them, on the beach, the village smoldered.

"Nay, my lord. 'Twas the lightning, I am certain of it!" Gwen spoke calmly, but her chin was a little more prominent than usual.

"Lightning!" Queen Catharine cried. She threw her hands in the air. "Why not the thunder, then? Or the wind, or the rain? Lightning, i' sooth!"

"Nay, Majesty—hear her out." Tuan touched her arm gently, restraining—but Rod noticed he'd become awfully formal all of a sudden.

" 'Majesty,' indeed!" Catharine stormed, turning on him. "What wouldst thou, mine husband? To blame it on the lightning! Nay, 'twas these beastmen only—themselves, and no more! They are vile sorcerers, and the spawn of Hell!"

"You may have a point there," Rod admitted. "We're not really disagreeing, you see—we're just getting into the *how* of their sorcering."

"Why, by peering into thine eye," Catharine shrieked, whirling back on him. "Lightning, forsooth! Was it at *lightning* that thy soldiers stared?"

"Nay, certes," Gwen said wearily. " 'Tis true, when they stared at the beastmen's eyes, then could the beastmen cast their spell. And 'tis a foul spell!" She shuddered. "I had some taste of it when I sought to lift it. 'Tis a vile thing that doth fascinate with ugliness!"

" 'Fascinate' is the term," Rod agreed. "They focused all the soldiers' attention on one single point—the beastmen's pupils. Then . . ."

"Then they could spare no attention for fighting?" Tuan nodded heavily. "Vile, indeed, that will not even allow a soldier the chance of defense."

Catharine rounded on Gwen. "Hast thou never encountered a spell like to this before?"

"There are tales of it," Gwen said slowly, "of the Evil Eye. I, though, have never found it in life."

"I have," Rod said slowly, "though it was a milder version."

Tuan frowned. "When?"

"In prefligh . . . uh, in apprenticeship," Rod hedged, "when I was being trained in the, uh"—he took a deep breath and gave up on honesty—"in the wizardry I use. This particular form of magic was called 'hypnotism,' but it looked a lot like this Evil Eye. It came to the same thing in the long run; it's just that they had to do it much more slowly."

"Aye, therein is it most phenomenal." Tuan frowned. "How can they fascinate so quickly?"

"Therein I have some experience," Gwen said slowly. " 'Tis a matter of throwing one's thoughts into another's mind."

Fess's voice murmured in Rod's ear, "Your wife is describing projective telepathy, Rod."

"Scientific terminology is wonderful," Rod growled. "It lets skeptics believe in magic. In fact, it transforms them into instant authorities."

Catharine turned on him, glowering. "Of whom dost thou speak, sirrah?"

Not you, Rod thought, remembering the rumors that the Queen had a touch of 'witch-power' herself. Aloud, he said, "*To* whom is more the point—and the problem is that the beastmen do it to whomever they want. I think we've got a pretty good idea of *how* they do it now—but how do we fight back?"

"Why, as we did." Gwen looked up in surprise.

Rod frowned down at her. " 'We'?" He felt a chill trickle down his back.

"Toby and I," Gwen explained. "What we did was even as thou didst say, mine husband—we cast our thoughts into the soldiers' minds and made them see what the glowing point at which they stared was in truth—naught but a pair of tiny eyes. We made them see again the face around the eyes, and the body 'neath the face."

"Yeah," Rod said with a curt nod. "Then they stepped up the strength of their Evil Eye and knocked you both out."

But Gwen shook her head. "Not 'they,' milord. 'Twas the lightning."

Catharine threw up her hands in despair and whirled away.

"Lightning or not, they *did* knock you out," Rod growled, "and you'll pardon me, but I didn't like the look of it."

Gwen spread her hands. "What wouldst thou, my lord? There were but Toby and myself—and we acted at the same moment, but not in concert."

"Huh?" Rod's scowl deepened. " 'Not in concert'? What did you want—a drum-and-bugle corps?"

"Nay, my lord." Gwen visibly fought for patience. "We could not join our powers—and there were too many soldiers for poor two of us. We did attempt to cast our thoughts into all their minds—but we did it side by side, not by blending both our powers into one."

"I take it you think it's possible to merge your powers," Rod said softly.

"Mayhap." Gwen frowned, gaze drifting to the window. "When two who can hear thoughts do touch, there is ever some greater sense of contact—threat, I should say; for I've never known two who have risked reaching out through touch to thoughts."

The door shot open, and Brom O'Berin stumped in, followed by two men-at-arms, each with a shoulder under one of Toby's arms. The young warlock limped between them, panting, "Nay! I . . . I can bear mine own . . ."

"Thou canst scarcely bear thine head upon thy shoulders, now," Brom growled. "Indeed, an thou wert a crab tree, thou couldst not bear an apple. There," he said to the two men-at-arms, nodding toward a chair. They lowered the young warlock carefully, and he sagged back, mouth gaping open, eyes closed, panting in huge hoarse gasps.

"What ails him?" Gwen cried.

"Naught but exhaustion." Brom's mouth held tight. "Were his news not vital, I would have sent him to his bed."

"Young idiot! I *told* him to call for a relief!" Rod strode over to the teenager and caught up a wrist, feeling for the pulse. "Didn't you bring any wine?"

Brom turned to the doorway and snapped his fingers. A page scurried in, wide-eyed and apprehensive, bearing a tray with a flagon and a flask. Brom caught them up, poured the mug half-full, and held it to Toby's lips. "A sip only, my lad, then a draught. Attempt it, there's a good fellow."

Toby sipped, and promptly coughed. Rod thumped him on the back till the boy nodded weakly, then sipped again. It stayed down, so he took a big swallow.

"Feel a little better now?" Rod asked.

Toby nodded and sighed.

"Don't fall asleep on us," Rod said quickly. "What did you see?"

"Only the dragon ship, and miles and miles of water," Toby sighed. "I sickened at the sight. I swear I'll never drink the stuff again!" And he took a long pull on the wine.

"Steady there, now," Rod cautioned. "So they sailed a lot. Which way did they go?"

"West," Toby said firmly, "west and south. I called for Giles, and set him to the following, whiles I appeared upon my bed and slept till he did call to say he'd sighted land. Then I appeared beside him and sent him home. He was sorely tired, seest thou, whilst I was fresh."

From the gray cast of the youth's face, Rod doubted that. "There was also a little matter of possible danger if you'd reached their homeland."

"Well, that too," Toby admitted. "In any case, the journey's end was mine affair. The danger was not great; the sky was lightening but not yet dawning, and clouds still hung low and heavy."

"E'en so, I had hoped thou wouldst not take too great a chance," Gwen said. "What had the beastmen come home to?"

"A bend of land in the coastline," Toby explained, "low land, with high sky-reaching cliffs behind it a mile or two from shore."

Rod nodded. "How big was the low land?"

"Mayhap some five miles wide."

"He describes an alluvial plain," Fess's voice murmured in Rod's ear.

"You're a better observer than I knew," Rod told the youth. "What was on the plain?"

"A village." Toby looked up at him. "Huts of daub and wattle, at a guess—round and with thatched roofs. Around and about their fields they did lie, with greening crops."

"Farmers?" Rod frowned, puzzled. "Not the kind of

people you'd expect to go pillaging. Any idea how many huts there were?"

Toby shook his head. "More than I could count at ease, Lord Warlock. 'Twas as far across as any village I ha' seen in Gramarye."

"Village," Rod repeated. "Not a town?"

Toby pursed his lips. "Well . . . mayhap a *small* town . . . Still, the houses were set far apart."

"Maybe a thousand households, then. How'd they react when they saw the dragon ship come back?"

"They did not," said Toby.

"What?" Rod gawked. "They didn't react? Not at all?"

"Nay—they did not see it. 'Twas not yet dawn, as I've said, and the dragon ship did not come to the village. Nay, it sailed instead to southward, and found a narrow river-mouth just where the cliffs came down to join the water. Then the beast-men unshipped oars and furled their sail and rowed their ship upstream, until they slipped into a crack within the cliff-wall from which their river issued."

"A crack." Rod kept his face expressionless.

Toby nodded. " 'Twas a crack thou couldst have marched thy Flying Legion through, milord; but in that vast wall of rock 'twas nonetheless a crack."

"So they sailed into a river-pass." Rod frowned, trying to make sense of it. "What happened then?"

"Naught to speak of. When they slipped into the cliff-face, I dropped down to the cliff-top, where I lay and watched. Anon, I saw them slip out on a footpath, without their shields or helmets, and naught of weapons save the knives at their belts. They trudged across the plain, back to the village. I did not follow, for I feared sighting by an early-riser."

Rod nodded. "Wise. After all, we found out everything we really needed to know." He frowned. "Maybe more."

"What then?" Brom demanded.

Toby spread his hands. "Naught. The work was done . . . and I commenced to feel as weary as though I'd not had a night of sleep."

"Not surprising, with the psychic blast you pulled yesterday," Rod reminded him. "And teleporting takes some energy out of a man too, I'll bet."

"I think that it doth," Toby agreed, "though I'd not noticed it aforetime."

"Well, you're not as young as you used to be. What are you now, nineteen?"

"Twenty," Toby answered, irritated.

"That's right, it's a huge difference. But that does mean your body's stopped growing, and you no longer have that frantic, adolescent energy-surplus. Besides, what's the furthest you've ever teleported before?"

"On thine affairs, some ten or twenty miles."

"Well, this time, you jumped . . . oh, let's see now . . ." Rod stared off into space. "All night in a sailing ship . . . let's assume the wind was behind it . . . say, ten miles an hour. Maybe ten hours, factored by Finagle's Variable Constant . . ." He looked back at Toby. "You jumped a hundred miles or more. Twice. No wonder you're tired."

Toby answered with a snore.

"Take him up," Brom instructed the men-at-arms, "and bear him gently to his bed. He hath done great service for our land this morn."

One of the soldiers bent to gather up Toby's legs, but the other stopped him with a hand on his shoulder. "Nay. Only lift the chair." The first soldier looked up, nodded approvingly, and picked up the chair legs as his companion lifted the back. Rod instantly memorized the second one's face, marking him as one who might have potential.

The door closed behind them, and Brom turned on Rod. "What makest thou of this, Lord Warlock?"

"Confusion," Rod answered promptly. "For openers, I want him to draw a map when he wakes up. Beyond that?" He shrugged. "We do have a tidy little mystery, don't we?"

"Aye," Brom agreed. "Why would they come so silently back to their lair?"

"Mayhap 'twas not all returned from this sally," Tuan offered, "and they feared the censure of the slain ones' kin."

"Possible, I suppose." Rod frowned. "But it doesn't seem very likely. I mean, I suppose there really are some hard-hearted cultures who take that attitude—you know, 'Return with your shield, or on it,' and all that. But their mission wasn't exactly a total flop, you know. Their ship did come back stuffed. They took everything that wasn't nailed down before they burned the stuff that was."

"E'en so, they did have dead," said Brom, "and if they'd gained recruits by promising great bounty with little danger, they would now have reason to fear the wrath of the kin of the slain ones."

"Ah, I see you know the ways of recruiting-sergeants," Rod said brightly. "But they'd have to face that anger anyway as soon as the rest of the villagers found out they were back. I mean, sooner or later, somebody was bound to notice they were there. So why sneak in?"

Catharine looked up slowly, her face lighting. "They stole back like thieves in the night, did they not?"

Rod frowned and nodded. "Yeah. How does that . . ." Then his eyes widened. "Of course! Your Majesty has it!"

"What?" Brom looked from one to the other, frowning.

"Aye, she hath!" Gwen jumped up. "The whole of this expedition was done in secret!"

"Aye!" Tuan's eyes fired. "Indeed, that hath the ring of truth!"

"Hypothesis does not account for all available data," Fess said flatly behind Rod's ear.

"But it's got the right feel," Rod objected. "Now, just how they managed to hide the little fact that they were gone for thirty-six hours, I don't know; but I could think of a few ways, myself."

Gwen looked up, alarmed.

"That means, Your Majesty," Rod said, hastily turning to the King, "that we're not being attacked by a hostile nation."

"Nay, only thieves who come in ships." Tuan frowned. "Is there not a word for such as they?"

"Yeah; they call 'em 'pirates.' " Rod wasn't surprised that the people of Gramarye had forgotten the term; their culture was restricted to one huge island and had been isolated for centuries.

Tuan frowned thoughtfully, gazing off into space. "How doth one fight a seaborne bandit?"

"By knowing something about the sea." Rod turned to Brom. "Is there anybody in Gramarye who does?"

Brom frowned. "We have some fisherfolk in villages along the coast."

"Then, get 'em," Rod called back over his shoulder as he headed for the door. "Get me a fisherman who knows something about the winds and the coastlines."

"An thou wishest it, we shall. But where dost thou go, Lord Warlock?"

"To find out what's current," Rod called back.

"But there's got to be a current here somewhere!"

"They are not visible on standard reflected-light photographs, Rod," Fess explained, "and when we arrived on Gramarye we had no reason to take infrared stills."

Rod's starship was buried under ten feet of clay in a meadow a few hours ride from Runnymede. He had persuaded the elves to dig a tunnel to it so he could visit it whenever he wanted.

Now, for instance. He was enjoying the rare luxury of Terran Scotch while he pored over a set of still pictures on the chart-table screen. "I don't see anything, Fess."

"Isn't that what you expected, Rod?"

Fess's robot brain, a globe the size of a basketball, hung in a niche in the curving wall. Rod had temporarily taken it out of the steel horse body and plugged it in to act as the ship's automatic control section. Not that he was going anywhere; he just needed Fess to operate the ship's auxiliary equipment, such as the graphic survey file. And, of course, the autobar.

"Well, yes, now that you mention it." Rod scowled at the aerial picture of the Gramarye coastline, the mainland coastline opposite, and the open sea in between. Fess had taken the pictures during their orbital approach to the planet two years earlier. Now they were stored as rearrangements within the electrical charges of giant molecules within the crystal lattice of the on-board computer memory. "I hadn't expected to find anything except plants and animals—but I hadn't said so. Better watch out, Metal Mind—you're getting close to intuitive hunches."

"Merely integrating large numbers of nonverbal signs, Rod," the robot assured him.

"I should be so good at integrating." Rod stabbed a finger at a bump on the mainland coastline. "Expand that one for me, will you?"

The glowing plate in the tabletop stayed the same size, of course, but the picture within its borders grew, expanding out of sight at the edges, so that the bump became larger and larger, filling the whole screen.

Rod drew an imaginary line with his finger. "Quite a demarcation here—this arc that goes across the bump. Divides the vegetation rather neatly, don't you think?"

"I do not think, Rod; I simply process data."

"One of these days, you'll have to explain the difference to me. What's this stuff in the upper left? Looks like the tops of a lot of ferns."

"It may well be so, Rod. The majority of the planet is in its Carboniferous Era, and giant ferns are the dominant plant form."

"There's a strip of beach alongside them. What's that lying on it?"

"A primitive amphibian, Rod."

"Kind of fits in with the whole ambiance," Rod said, nodding. "Wonder what's under the Carboniferous flora?"

"Carboniferous fauna, I would presume."

"You certainly would. No bogeymen?"

"Human habitation usually occurs in cleared spaces, Rod."

"You never know; they might have something to hide. But if you're going to talk about a cleared space, here's the rest of the bump." Rod frowned, peering closely. "Looks like there might be some small trees there."

Fess was silent for a few seconds, then said slowly, "I agree, Rod. Those do appear to be trees. Stunted, but trees nonetheless."

"Odd-looking for a fern, isn't it? Where did trees come from, Fess?"

"There can only be one source, Rod—the Terra-formed island of Gramarye."

"Well, let's be fair—maybe some of the seed got scattered during the Terra-forming."

"Quite possible, Rod—but it is the mechanism of scattering that is of importance. There must be some sort of communication between this mainland area and Gramarye."

"Such as the ocean current I'm looking for? Well, well!" Rod peered closer, delighted. "Let's see—besides the trees, it's just a featureless light green. Can you check what makes that color, Fess?"

The picture stayed the same size on the screen, but the robot analyzed the pattern of electrical charges that was the recorded image. "It is grass, Rod."

Rod nodded. "Again, that couldn't come from a Carboniferous fern-patch. But it's such a clean break between the ferns and the grassland! What could make such a clear demarcation, Fess?"

"Exactly what you are no doubt thinking of, Rod—a line of cliffs, the cliffs Toby mentioned."

"I *was* kind of thinking along that line, now that you mention it." Rod looked down at the picture. "So we could be looking at the beastmen's lair. It does match Toby's description—except for one little thing."

"I see no anomaly, Rod."

"Right. It's not what *is* there—it's what isn't. No village."

Fess was silent for a moment. Then he said, "I see your point. There is no sign of human—or subhuman—habitation."

"No dragon ships drawn up on the beach, anyway."

"There is only one logical conclusion, Rod."

"Yeah." Rod leaned back and took a sip of Scotch. "I know what *I* think it is—but let's hear what you've got in mind first."

"Surely, Rod. We recorded these pictures two years ago during our first approach to this planet. Apparently the beastmen were not here then. Therefore, they arrived within the last two years."

"That's kinda what I was thinking, too. . . . Say!" Rod leaned forward again. "That reminds me. I've been meaning to tell you about something I noticed during the battle."

"Some historical inaccuracies in the beastmen's Viking equipage, Rod?"

"Well, an anachronism, anyway. Fess, those beastmen are Neanderthals."

The little ship was very quiet for a few seconds.

Then Fess said, "That is impossible, Rod."

Rod answered with a wicked grin. "Why? Just because the last Neanderthal died off at least fifty thousand years before the Norse began to go a-viking?"

"That was rather the general trend of my thoughts, yes."

"But why should that bother you?" Rod spread his hands. "We found a time machine hidden away in the back hallways of Castle Loguire, didn't we?"

"Yes, but we disabled it shortly after we defeated Anselm Loguire."

"Sure—but how did it get there in the first place?"

"Why . . . a time-traveler must have been sent back to build it."

"Quick figuring, Reasoning Robot." Rod pointed a finger at the nearest vision pickup. "And if they could do it once, they could do it again."

"Why . . . that is certainly logical . . ."

"Sure is. 'Sensible' is another matter. But that time machine didn't exactly look as though it had been improvised, you know?"

"Surely you are not implying that they are mass-produced."

"Well, not *mass*-produced, really—but I did have in mind a small factory somewhen. Two or three a year, maybe."

A faint shudder vibrated the little ship. "Rod—do you have any idea how illogical such an event could make human existence?"

Rod looked up in alarm. "Hey, now! Don't go having any seizures on me!"

"I am not that completely disoriented by the concept, Rod. I may have the robotic equivalent of epilepsy, but it requires an extremely illogical occurrence to trigger a seizure. A time-machine factory may be illogical in its effects, but not in its sheer existence."

That wasn't quite the way Fess had reacted to his first discovery of a time machine, but Rod let it pass. "Well, I did have some notion of just how ridiculous widespread time machines could make things, yes. Something like having Neanderthals dressed up in Viking gear, showing up on a planet that's decided to freeze its culture in the Middle Ages. That what you had in mind, Fess?"

"That was a beginning, yes," the robot said weakly. "But are you certain they were Neanderthals, Rod?"

"Well, as sure as I can be." Rod frowned. "I mean, conditions were a little rushed, you know? I didn't get a chance to ask one of them if he'd be good enough to take off his helmet so I could measure his skull, if that's what you mean."

"No, but several beastmen did meet with fatal accidents during the battle. Perhaps we should send a scribe with a tape measure."

"Brother Chillde will do; might as well put him to *some* use. But he'll just confirm what I'm telling you, Fess: heavy jaw, no chin, brow ridges, sloping forehead—and I mean *really* sloping; obviously no prefrontal lobes."

"An occipital lump, Rod?"

Rod scowled. "Well now, *that* I can't really say. I mean, after all, that's down at the base of the skull where the helmet would hide it. Check that on one of the, ah, specimens, would you?"

"I shall leave written directions to that effect, Rod—in your name, of course. So, then, you are positing someone removing a tribe of Neanderthals from approximately 50,000 B.C. Terra, and transporting them here?''

"Where else could they dig up Neanderthals?"

"The theory of parallel evolution . . ."

"Parallel lines don't converge. Still, you never know; we'll leave the possibility open."

"But for the time being, we will assume they were taken from Terra. And whoever brought them here outfitted them with Viking ships, armor, and weaponry. Presumably this unidentified party also taught them navigation. But why would they have attacked you?"

Rod shrugged. "Presumably because the unidentified party told them to—but we'll leave that one open for the moment."

"As we must also leave open the question of the unidentified party's identity."

"Well, that doesn't have to be *too* open." Rod frowned. "I mean, whoever it is has got to have a time machine—and we already know two organizations so equipped who're involved in Gramarye."

"The futurian anarchists, and the futurian totalitarians. Yes."

"Right. And, with two candidates like that available, I don't see any need to posit a third."

"Which of the two would you favor in this case?"

"Oh, I'd say the anarchists probably masterminded it," Rod reflected. "It strikes me as being their style."

"In what way?"

Rod shrugged. "Why Viking gear? Presumably for the same reason the Vikings used it—to strike terror into the hearts of their victims. And striking terror like that serves the general purpose of making chaos out of whatever social order is available. Besides, they like to get somebody to front for them—the 'power behind the throne,' and all that."

"Or behind the pirates, in this case. Still, your point is well-taken, Rod. The totalitarians do tend toward more personal involvement. Also, they prefer careful, hidden preparation resulting in a revolution, not continual harassing that slowly disintegrates local authority. Yes, the anarchists are the logical perpetrators."

"And if that's logical, it's probably also wrong." Rod leaned forward over the chart screen again. "Which reminds me—there's a complete difference in vegetation, depending on which side of the cliffs you're on."

"Totally different, Rod. Grasses exclusively."

"What, not even a fungus amongus?"

"Well, there are a few mosses and lichens."

"How come nothing more?"

"The vegetation would seem to indicate a small area in which the temperature is far below that of the surrounding forest. I conjecture that a cold breeze blows off the sea at that point, chilling the area around the bay. The cliff-wall prevents it from reaching the interior."

Rod looked up. "Hey! Would that indicate a cold current?"

"In all probability, Rod." The robot's voice sounded a little patronizing.

"That's the current that would go past Gramarye."

"It would seem so," Fess answered.

Rod smiled sourly and tossed his shot glass into the recycler. "Well, enough loafing." He stood up, strode over to the wall, and began to loosen the clamps that held Fess's basketball brain. "What happens after that cold current hits the shoreline, Fess?"

"It would probably be warmed by contact with the tropical mainland just south of the cliffs, Rod. Then it would be forced out to sea by the mass of the continent."

Rod nodded. "From the mainland's position and contour, that means the current would be sent northeast—back toward Gramarye."

"Quite possibly, Rod—but you should not hypothesize without sufficient data."

"All right." Rod tucked the silver basketball under his arm. "Anything you say, Fess. Besides, it's time for lunch."

"You know robots do not eat, Rod."

"That's funny, I thought you might be in the mood for a few bytes. . . ."

The sentry at the door to the solar stepped in and announced, "The Lord High Warlock, Majesties."

Rod pushed past him and stopped, taking in the tall, saturnine man with the lantern jaw who stood facing Catharine and Tuan. His face was tanned and leathery. He wore a short brocaded coat, fur-trimmed, over doublet and hose, and clenched a round hat in his hands.

Then Rod remembered his manners and turned to bow.

"Your Majesties! I've been doing a little research."

"I trust our new source will aid it, Lord Warlock." Catharine nodded toward the stranger. "May I present Master Hugh Meridian, captain of a merchant ship."

"Merchant ship?" Rod turned to the seaman, startled. "I didn't know we had any."

"I' truth, we do, milord." The shipmaster gave him a frosty bow. " 'Tis quicker, and less costly, to ship goods along the coastline than to haul them over the highways."

"Of course; it would be. I should've thought of it. But how did you learn that we needed seafaring advice, Master Meridian?"

"We sent word quickly to the fisherfolk at Loguire's estates, and those in Romanov. Each claimed they did know there were currents sweeping past the shore, farther out than they generally sailed," Tuan answered. "Yet all claimed further that they knew naught more."

"Of course; they couldn't know where the currents went." Rod frowned. "They never go out farther than they can come back, all in one day. But they did know about you, Captain?"

The captain nodded. "Ever and anon, the lords hire out their fisherfolk to be my crews, milord. They know of me, aye."

"And you know where the currents go." Rod started to look for a chair, then remembered it was bad form to sit in Their Majesties' presence. Brom could; but Brom was special. "At least you know where they go, around the Isle of Gramarye."

"I do, milord—though it might be better to say I know where the currents do *not* go."

"Really? There're currents all around the island?"

"Not quite; the western coast is bare of them."

"Odd." Rod frowned. "Can you show me on a map?"

"Map?" Captain Meridian looked lost for a second; then he fumbled a small book out of his belt-pouch. "Aye, I can show where I ha' writ about it in my rudder; yet is't not easier to hear it?"

"No, no! I want you to *show* me, on . . ." Rod let his voice trail off, remembering that medieval people didn't have maps as he knew them; the idea of graphing out the outlines of a coast was foreign to them. Maps had had to wait for the Renaissance, with its concept of continuous, uniform space. Rod turned to the door, stuck his head out, and advised the

sentry, "Parchment and pen, soldier—and quickly." He
turned back into the room. "We'll have one in a minute, Majesties. Master Meridian, imagine yourself being a bird, flying
over the Isle of Gramarye, looking down on its coasts."

Meridian smiled. " 'Tis a pleasant enough conceit, Milord
Warlock—but I cannot see that it serves any purpose."

"Ah, but it does!" Rod held up a forefinger. "I'll draw you
a picture of the coasts as the bird would see them."

The door opened, and a round-eyed page popped in with
parchment, pen, and ink.

"Thank you, lad!" Rod seized the tools and marched to the
solar's table. He rolled out the parchment and began sketching. "This is the western coast, Captain Meridian." He drew a
long jagged curving line, then pointed back toward its top.
"There's the Duchy of Savoy, and here's Hapsburg." He
turned the bottom of the line into a point, and began to draw a
lateral line, full of jags and gouges. Captain Meridian followed his hand, frowning, trying to relate this ink-scrawl to
the realities of rocks, tides, currents, and distant hills seen
through the mist. Finally, his face lit and his finger stabbed
down at the southernmost curve. "Yonder is Cape Souci!
Many's the time I've had to shorten sail to keep the southwesterly gale from rolling my ship over as we rounded that
headland!"

"Southwesterly?" Rod looked up. "Does the current come
past there?"

Captain Meridian nodded eagerly. "Aye, aye! 'Tis that very
place. Westerly of that, milord, I know naught of the current;
indeed, I know naught at all, for never have I had any occasion to sail there. But north of that, there is no current; the
whole westerly shore hath naught but tides and local stir-
rings."

Rod nodded. "That's where the current comes to Gramarye, then. This is the southern shore, Master Meridian."
He drew a long curve; then his pen wandered north. Meridian
watched spellbound as the outline of the island took shape
before him.

" 'Tis witchcraft," he sighed when Rod was done, and
pointed at the map. "Yonder is the Bay of Roland, and hither
lies the coast of Romanov. This is the mouth of the River
Fleuve, and yon peninsula is Tristesse Point." He looked up at
Rod. "Thou art indeed the Lord High Warlock! By what
magic canst thou tell the shape of this coastline so well?"

"Oh, I know some people who do a lot of flying," Rod shrugged. "Anything I've missed?"

"Not of the coast itself." Meridian turned back to the map and pointed. "But you must draw the Grand Skerry here, midway down the west coast—and Geburn Rock here"—his finger jabbed at the map just off the coast of Romanov—"and . . . but, another time." He waved the thought away. "There are a host of such things that are not on your map, but that any seafarer would need to know of."

"Such as currents?" Rod dipped the pen in the ink and handed it to him, feather first. "Would you show me where they lie, Master Meridian?"

The captain's eyes widened. Slowly, he took the pen and began to sketch. Rod watched flowing, sweeping lines grow from the pen-point, coming from Heaven knew where at Cape Souci, flowing along the southern coast, sweeping around the eastern coast and the Baronetcy of Ruddigore, around the Duchy of Bourbon and along the northern coast, past Romanov, past Hapsburg—and out into the unknown again.

Meridian set the pen back into the inkwell with a sigh. "Better I cannot do, Lord Warlock." He looked up at Rod. "I know no more."

"Well, I might happen to be able to add something there." Rod took up the pen. "One of our young warlocks just made a quick, overnight trip into the west, you see." He began to sketch a concave curve in the lower left-hand corner of the parchment. "He saw something like this . . ." The curve hooked into a right angle with an upstanding bump. Rod sketched a dotted line across the base of the bump, then reached up to begin sketching where Captain Meridian had left off with the current. "He was following that last party of raiders home, and from what he said, I'd guess they sailed along this route—which means the northern current flows down to the southwest, like this. . . ." His pen strokes swept down to the mainland, then turned sharply to flow around the bump. "You know, of course, Master Meridian, that Gramarye is only an island, and that there's a mainland over to the west, a continent."

Captain Meridian nodded. "We had known o' that, Lord Warlock—yet only that, and naught more. Too, that much came only from tales that grandfathers told grandsons."

"Well, our young warlock checked on it, and it's there,

right enough." Rod's penstrokes flowed around the bump. "We think this semipeninsula is what the beastmen call 'home.' It's a safe bet that the current flows past there." He didn't feel any need to tell the captain just how safe the bet was. "Then it flows on southward, hugging the shoreline, till it's warmed by this outward bulge of the continent, which also forces it back out to sea, toward the northeast—and, of course, it just keeps going in the same line. . . ." His pen sketched strokes upward and to the right until they joined up with Captain Meridian's line at Cape Souci. ". . . And there's where it comes back into your ken." He straightened up, dropping the quill back into the inkwell. "And there you have it, Master Meridian. Between the two of us, we've filled in a map of the current."

A discreetly modest, electronic cough sounded in Rod's ear.

"Of course, we had a bit of help gaining the basic information," Rod added. "Does it all make sense?"

The shipmaster nodded, eyes glowing. "Indeed it doth, milord." He turned to Tuan and Catharine. "Behold, Thy Majesties!" He traced the current with a forefinger. "The beastmen bring their dragon ships out into the eastward current, here. It carries them across, first to Loguire, so; then, out into the current, around the eastern coast, and away to the west again, o'er the roof of Gramarye, and so back to their home again." His finger completed the circuit, arriving back at the bump on the mainland's coastline.

Tuan drew in a long, hissing breath. "Aye, Master Meridian. So. We understand."

The door opened, and the sentry stepped in. "Majesties— Gwendylon, Lady Gallowglass."

Gwen stepped in, and dropped a quick curtsy.

"Well met, my dear." Catharine rose from her chair and stepped toward Gwen, one hand outstretched. "Well met, in good time. These silly men are like to make mine head to spin with their nonsensical talk of currents and capes."

Gwen rose, catching Catharine's hand with a smile of shared amusement.

Rod did a double take. Then he straightened up, watching the ladies out of the corner of his eye. Catharine and Gwen had never exactly been on close terms, especially since Catharine had seemed quite interested in Rod before he brought Tuan back into her life. He didn't think Gwen knew about that—but then, you never can tell with a telepath. All in all, this warm greeting worried him. "What have you two been planning?"

"Planning? Why, naught!" Catharine was all offended innocence. "E'en so, we have found some space to discuss the errors of thy ways, Lord Warlock—and thou, my noble husband."

Tuan looked even more wary than Rod. "Indeed, sweet lady. And in what ways am I lacking?"

"Thou dost always speak of ways to go about beating other males with thy clubs, and cleaving them with thy swords. We, though, have seen 'tis of greater import to ward thy soldiers from thy foemen's clubs and axes!"

"A point well-taken," Tuan admitted, "if thou couldst also thus ward their wives and babes, and the lands and stock that give them sustenance."

"I hate to admit it," Rod agreed, "but knocking a man out with your club *is* a very effective way of making sure he doesn't knock you."

"Ah, but in this instance, my lord, thou must needs make thy soldier able to strike such a blow," Gwen reminded. "For that, thou must needs ward him from the beastmen's Evil Eye."

Rod exchanged a sheepish glance with Tuan. "They've got us, Your Majesty. We've been so busy thinking about launching the counterattack that we haven't put much time into the psychic defenses."

"Be easy of heart, lords," Catharine assured them, "for we have."

"Indeed," Gwen chirped. "The means is ready to hand, as Toby and I did manifest when the beastmen fought our soldiers."

Tuan frowned. "I fear that I mistook. Didst thou give warding?"

"Oh, they surely did!" Rod assured him. "We probably wouldn't even have saved the handful of men who did survive that battle if Gwen and Toby hadn't, ah, broken the spell of the Evil Eye."

"I mind me that thou didst say thou hadst, for short spaces, dispelled the charm." Tuan rubbed his chin. "Yet 'twas only for brief minutes."

"Indeed, their thoughts were too heavy for us," Gwen admitted. "Yet be mindful, my liege, that there were but two of us, and that we acted each alone.''

"You're trying to say they simply overpowered you," Rod interpreted. "But what's to stop them from doing it again?"

"Why, more witches!" Gwen's face bloomed into a rosy smile.

Catharine tucked Gwen's arm into her own, nodding. "Indeed, Lord Warlock! Thy wife doth think that, if witches do join hands, they may then be able to act in concert. Thus, if we may have a score of witches altogether, they might among them counter the Evil Eye of one dragon-full of beastmen."

"Just twenty of you, against a hundred of them?" Rod felt his backbone chill. "You'll pardon me, but I don't like the odds."

"Nor do we," Gwen said earnestly. "It would indeed be well if we could have more witches."

The chill along the backbone turned colder. "Somehow, I don't like the sound of this."

"Nor I," Tuan agreed. "What dost thou plan, my wife?"

"A royal summons." Catharine's chin tilted up. "There are witches, husband, who do hide about the hinterlands, on farms and in small villages, seeking to disguise their powers for fear their friends and kin may turn away from them. These have not come unto the Royal Coven through fear of us, or reluctance to leave their folk."

"You're going recruiting," Rod said in a hollow tone.

"An thou dost call it so. I will!" Catharine tossed her head. "Bethink thee—would a summons from a mere herald bring a frightened lass to court? Nay. Yet the presence of her Queen would command her loyalty." She glared at Tuan, daring him to contradict her.

"And where do you fit into this?" Rod leveled a doubtful gaze on his wife.

"Lady Gallowglass shall rest here, to train the Royal Witches in the breaking of the Evil Eye, whilst I do wander round and 'bout the countryside, summoning shy witches to the court." Catharine patted Gwen's arm protectively, glaring at Rod.

Rod opened his mouth to argue (he couldn't resist it, even if there wasn't much to argue about; Catharine was just asking for it too plainly), but the door slammed open and a pale-faced guard stepped in and bowed. "Majesties!"

Catharine whirled, transferring her glare to the page. "What means this unseemly outburst, sirrah?"

"Word hath come through the witches, Majesties! Beastmen have landed at the mouth of the River Fleuve!"

"Call out the army!" Rod snapped to Tuan. He headed for the door. "I'll get the Flying Legion out—or what's left of 'em!"

"Nay, milord!" the page cried. "They have landed under flag of truce!"

"What!" Rod spun around, staring.

The sentry nodded. "Aye, milord. There are but a handful of them, and they have surrendered themselves to the knights of My Lord of Bourbon. Even now, they ride toward Runnymede, guarding well their beastmen"—he hesitated, then turned a questioning glance to the king—"guests?"

"They are if they indeed landed under a flag of truce." Tuan rose. "Send word to guard them well, for I doubt not there are many of our goodfolk who would gladly slay them. Lord Warlock, come!" And he strode toward the door.

"Where dost thou go?" Catharine demanded.

Tuan turned back at the door. "I ride to meet them, sweeting, for we must converse with them as soon as we may. An hour lost could means ten lives."

He marched through the portal, and Rod hurried to catch up with him. He shut the door on Catharine and Gwen with a feeling of relief.

"Then did the High Warlock ride east to meet the beastmen who had come so strangely under a Flag of Truce, and His Majesty the King rode with him; for, though they were few in number, the beastmen were huge and fierce of mien, like unto Demons in their visages, who moved over the face of the Earth like ravening lions. They were tusked like boars, with their heads beneath their shoulders, and bore huge spiked clubs, stained with old blood; and ever and anon did they seek someone to slay. So, when they had come nigh the beastmen, His Majesty the King bade the High Warlock guard them closely with his magic, lest they forget their Truce or it proved to be vile Treachery. And the High Warlock wove a spell about them, standing tall beneath the sun, towering over the beastmen; and his eyes flashed like diamonds in dawnlight, and the aspect of his visage struck Terror into their hearts, so that they stood mute. Then he wove a Spell about them, a cage unseen, a Wall of Octroi, through which they might speak, but never strike. Then spake he unto the King, saying, 'Lo, these monsters are now circumscribed, and naught can harm ye the whiles ye speak unto them.' Then spake King Tuan, 'What manner of men are ye, and wherefore have ye come unto this land of Gramarye?' Then one among them did stand forth and say, in accents barbarous, that he was the highest Lord of their wild savage Realm, but the other Lords had risen up against their King and overthrown him, wherefore this small band had come beseeching King Tuan's mercy. Then was King Tuan's heart moved to Pity, and he spake and said, 'Poor noble hearts! For I perceive that these treacherous villains who have laid waste my Kingdom have wasted ye likewise!' And he brought them back with him to Gramarye; yet the High Warlock kept woven tight his net unseen about them. . . .''

—Chillde's *Chronicles of the Reign of Tuan and Catharine*

"Your name is *what*?" Rod stared, unbelieving.

"Yorick." The beastman spread his hands. "Whatsamatter? Ain'cha never heard the name before?"

"Well, yes, but never in real life—and as to fiction, you don't exactly look English." He glanced back over his shoulder at the soldiers who stood behind him with leveled pikes, then looked up at their companions who stood in a ring around the Neanderthals, pike-points centered on the beastmen. Rod considered telling them to lower their weapons, but decided it would be a little premature.

"A word from you, and they'd drop those spears like magic," the beastman pointed out.

"Yeah, I know." Rod grinned. "Ain't it great?"

"On your side, maybe." Yorick rubbed a hand over his eyes. "I keep getting the feeling I've been through this all before."

"Nay, dost thou truly?" Tuan said, frowning. "I too have such a sense."

The Neanderthal shook his head. "Really weird. Like I've lived through this already. Except . . ." He turned to Rod. "You ought to be about a foot taller, with piercing eyes and a wide, noble brow."

Rod stiffened. "What do you mean, *ought* to?"

The Neanderthal held up a palm. "No offense. But you ought to have a haughty mien, too—whatever that is."

"Indeed," Tuan agreed. "And thou shouldst be hunch-backed, with fangs protruding from the corners of thy jaws, and a look of murdering idiocy in thine eye."

Yorick reared, startled. Then his face darkened and his eyebrows pulled down to hide his eyes (he had a lot of eye-brow). He stepped forward, opening his mouth—and Rod jumped in quickly. "You, ah, both have this same, ah, sense of, ah, déjà vu?"

"Nice phrase." Yorick nodded in approval. "I knew there was a word for it."

Now it was Rod's turn to stare. Then he said, "Uh—you've heard 'déjà vu' before?"

"Know I have, know I have." Yorick bobbed his head, grinning. "Just couldn't place it, that's all."

The handful of beastmen behind him growled and muttered to each other, throwing quick, wary glances at Rod and Tuan.

"How about you?" Rod turned to Tuan. " 'Déjà vu.' Ever heard it before?"

"Never in my life," Tuan said firmly. "Doth that signify?"

" 'Course it does." Yorick grinned. "It means I'm not a native. But you knew that, didn't you, High Warlock? I mean, it's pretty plain that I didn't evolve here."

"Yeah, but I sorta thought you'd been kidnapped." Rod frowned. "But one of you was in on the kidnapping, weren't you?"

Yorick winced. "Please! I prefer to think of it as helping place refugees."

"Oh, really! I thought that kind of placement usually in-volved finding a willing host!"

"So, who was to host?" Yorick shrugged. "The land was just lying there, perfectly good; nobody was using it. All we had to do was kick out a few dinosaurs and move in."

"You never thought we folk over here on Gramarye might have something to say about it, huh?"

"Why? I mean, you were over here, and we were over there, and there was all this ocean between us. You weren't even sup-posed to know we were there!"

"Lord Warlock," Tuan interrupted, "this news is of great interest, but somewhat confusing."

"Yes, it is getting a little complicated," Rod agreed. He

turned back to Yorick. "What do you say we begin at the beginning?"

"Fine." Yorick shrugged. "Where's that?"

"Let's take it from your own personal point of view. Where does *your* story begin?"

"Well, this lady picked me up by the feet, whacked me on the fanny, and said, 'It's a boy!' And this man who was standing near . . ."

"No, no!" Rod took a deep breath. "That's a little *too* far back. How about we start with your learning English. How'd you manage that?"

Yorick shrugged. "Somebody taught me. How else?"

"Dazzling insight," Rod growled. "Why didn't I think of that? Could we be a little more specific about your teacher? For one thing, the way you talk tells me he wasn't from a medieval culture."

Yorick frowned. "How'd you guess? I mean, I know they didn't exactly send me to prep school, but . . ."

"Oh, really! I would've thought they'd have enrolled you in Groton first thing!"

Yorick shook his head firmly. "Couldn't pass the entrance exam. We Neanderthals don't handle symbols too well. No prefrontal lobes, you know."

Rod stared.

Yorick frowned back at him, puzzled. Then his face cleared into a sickly grin. "Oh. I know. I'll bet you're wondering, if I can't handle symbols, how come I can talk. Right?"

"Something of the sort did cross my mind. Of course, I do notice that your mates have something of a language of their own."

"Their *very* own; you won't find any other Neanderthal tribe that uses it."

"I wasn't really planning to look."

Yorick ignored the interruption. "These refugees come from so many different nations that we had to work out a lingua franca. It's richer than any of the parent languages, of course—but it's still got a very limited vocabulary. No Neanderthal language gets very far past 'Me hungry. That food— go kill.' "

"This, I can believe. So how were you able to learn English?"

"Same way a parrot does," Yorick explained. "I memorize

all the cues and the responses that follow them. For example, if you say, 'Hello,' that's my cue to say 'Hello' back; and if you say, 'How are you?' that's my cue to say, 'Fine. How're you?' without even thinking about it.''

"That's not exactly exclusive to Neanderthals," Rod pointed out. "But the talking you've been doing here is a little more complicated."

"Yeah, well, that comes from mental cues." Yorick tapped his own skull. "The concept nudges me from inside, see, and that's like a cue, and the words to express that concept jump out of memory in response to that cue."

"But that's pretty much what happens when we talk, too."

"Yeah, but you know what the words *mean* when you say 'em. Me, I'm just reciting. I don't really understand what I'm saying."

"Well, I know a lot of people who . . ."

"But they could, if they'd stop and think about it."

"You don't know these people," Rod said with an astringent smile. "But I get your point. Believing it is another matter. You're trying to tell me that you don't understand the words you're saying to me right now—even if you stop to think about each word separately."

Yorick nodded. "Now you're beginning to understand. Most of them are just noises. I have to take it on faith that it means what I want it to mean."

"Sounds pretty risky."

"Oh, not too much—I can understand the gist of it. But most of it's just stimulus-response, like a seeing-eye parrot saying 'Walk' when he sees a green light."

"This is a pretty complicated explanation you've just been feeding me," Rod pointed out.

"Yeah, but it's all memorized, like playing back a recording." Yorick spread his hands. "I don't really follow it myself."

"But your native language . . ."

"Is a few thousand sound effects. Not even very musical, though—musical scales are basically prefrontal, too. Manipulating pitches is like manipulating numbers. I love *hearing* music, though. To me, even 'Mary Had a Little Lamb' is a miracle."

Tuan butted in, frowning. "Doth he say that he is a blinking idiot?"

"Hey, no, now!" Yorick held up a hand, shaking his head

indignantly. "Don't sell us short. We're smart, you know—same size brain as you've got. We just can't talk about it, that's all—or add and subtract it either, for that matter. We can only communicate concrete things—you know—food, water, stone, fire, sex—things you can see and touch. It's just abstractions that we can't talk about; they require symbols. But the intelligence is there. We're the ones who learned how to use fire—and how to chip flint into weapons. Not very good tools, maybe—but we made the big breakthrough."

Rod nodded. "Yeah, Tuan, don't underestimate that. We think we're smart because we invented the nuclea—uh . . . ," Rod remembered that he wasn't supposed to let the Gramaryans know about advanced technology. It might disrupt their entire culture. He opted for their version of the weapon that endangered civilization. "The crossbow. But taming fire was just as hard to figure out."

"Good man." Yorick nodded approvingly. "You *sapiens* have been able to build such a complicated civilization because you had a good foundation under you before you even existed; you inherited it when you evolved. But *we're* the ones who built the basement."

"Neanderthals had the intelligence," Rod explained. "They just couldn't manipulate symbols—and there's just so far you can go without 'em."

Yorick nodded. "Analytical reasoning just isn't our strong suit. We're great on hunches, though—and we've got great memories."

"You'd have to, to remember all these standard responses that you don't understand."

Yorick nodded. "I can remember damn near anything that ever happened to me."

"How about who taught you English?"

"Oh, sure! That's . . ." Then Yorick gelled, staring. After a minute, he tried the sickly grin again. "I, uh, didn't want to get to that, uh, quite so soon."

"Yes, but we did." Rod smiled sweetly. "Who did teach you?"

"Same guy who gave me my name," Yorick said hopefully.

"So he had a little education—and definitely wasn't from a medieval culture."

Yorick frowned. "How'd you make so much out of just one fact?"

"I manipulated a symbol. What's his name?"

"The Eagle," Yorick sighed. "We call him that 'cause he looks like one."

"What? He's got feathers?" Rod had a sudden vision of an avian alien, directing a secondhand conquest of a Terran planet.

"No, no! He's human, all right. He might deny it—but he is. Just got a nose like a beak, always looks a little angry, doesn't have much hair—*you* know. He taught us how to farm."

"Yeah." Rod frowned. "Neanderthals never got beyond a hunting-and-gathering culture, did you?"

"Not on our own, no. But this particular bunch of Neanderthals never would've gotten together on their own anyway. The Eagle gathered us up, one at a time, from all over Europe and Asia."

Rod frowned. "Odd way to do it. Why didn't he just take a tribe that was already together?"

"Because he didn't want a tribe, milord. He wanted to save a bunch of innocent victims."

"Victims?" Rod frowned. "Who was picking on you?"

"Everybody." Yorick spread his arms. "The Flatfaces, for openers—like you, only bigger. They chipped flint into tools, same as we do—only they're a lot better at it."

"The Cro-Magnons," Rod said slowly. "Are your people the last Neanderthals?"

"Oh, nowhere near! That was our problem, in fact—all those other Neanderthals. They'd've rather'd kill us than look at us."

Suddenly, Rod could place Yorick—he was paranoid. "I thought it worked the other way around."

"What—that we'd as soon kill them as look at them?"

"No—that you'd kill them *when* you looked at them."

Yorick looked uncomfortable. "Well, yes, the Evil-Eye thing—that was the problem. I mean, you *try* to cover it up as best you can; you *try* to hide it—but sooner or later somebody's gonna haul off and try and whack you with a club."

"Oh, come on! It wasn't inevitable, was it?"

"Haven't lived with Neanderthals, have you?"

"Oh." Rod cocked his head. "Not very civilized, were you?"

"We lived like cavemen," Yorick confirmed.

"Oh. Right." Rod glanced away, embarrassed. "Sorry—I forgot."

"Great." Yorick grinned. "That's a compliment."

"I suppose it is," Rod said slowly. "But how come your quarrels had to turn violent?"

Yorick shrugged. "What can I tell you? No lawyers. Whatever the reason, we do tend to clobber—and you can't help yourself then; you *have* to freeze him in his tracks."

"Purely in self-defense, of course."

"Oh yeah, purely! Most of us had sense enough not to hit back at someone who was frozen—and the ones who didn't, couldn't; it takes some real concentration to keep a man frozen. There just ain't anything left over to hit with."

"Well, maybe." Rod had his doubts. "But why would he want to kill you, when you hadn't hurt him?"

"That made it worse," Yorick sighed. "I mean, if I put the freeze on you, you're gonna feel bad enough . . ."

The clanking and rustling behind Rod told him that his soldiers had come to the ready. Beside him Tuan murmured, "'Ware, beastman!"

Yorick plowed on, unmindful of them. "But if I *don't* clobber you, you're gonna read it as contempt, and hate me worse. Still, it wasn't the person who got frozen who was the problem —it was the spectators."

"What'd you do—sell tickets?"

Yorick's mouth tightened with exasperation. "You know how hard it is to be alone in these small tribes?"

"Yeah . . . I suppose that would be a problem."

"Problem, hell! It was murder! Who wants you around if you can do *that* to them? And there's one way to make sure you won't be around. No, we'd have to get out of the village on our own first. Usually had a lot of help. . . ."

"It's a wonder any of you survived." Then something clicked in Rod's mind. "But you would, wouldn't you? If anyone got too close, you could freeze him."

"Long enough to get away, yes. But what do you do when you've gotten away?"

"Survive." Rod stared off into the sky, imagining what it would be like. "Kind of lonely . . ."

Yorick snorted. "Never tried to make it on your own in a wilderness, have you? Loneliness is the least of it. A rabbit a day keeps starvation away—but a sabertooth has the same notion about you. Not to mention dire wolves or cave bears."

Rod nodded thoughtfully. "I can see why you'd want to form a new tribe."

"With what?" Yorick scoffed. "We weren't exactly over-populated, you know. It was a long way between tribes—and not very many Evil-Eye espers in any one of 'em. You might have one in a hundred square miles—and do you know how long a hundred miles is, on foot in rough country?"

"About two weeks." But Rod was really thinking about Yorick's choice of word—he'd said "esper," not "witch" or "monster." "This is where your 'Eagle' came in?"

Yorick nodded. "Just in time, too. Picked us up one by one and brought us to this nice little mountain valley he'd picked out. Nice 'n' high up, plenty of rain, nice 'n' cool all year 'round...."

"*Very* cool in winter—I should think."

"You should, 'cause it wasn't. Pretty far south, I suppose—'cause it never got more than brisk. 'Course, there wasn't enough game for the whole four thousand of us."

"Four thousand? A hundred miles or more apart? What'd he do—spend a lifetime finding you all?"

Yorick started to answer, then caught himself and said very carefully, "He knew how to travel fast."

"*Very* fast, I should think—at least a mile a minute." Rod had a vision of a ground-effect car trying to climb a forty-five-degree slope. "And how did he get you up to that mountain valley? Wings?"

"Something like that," Yorick confessed. "And it wasn't all that big a valley. He taught us how to use bows and arrows, and we had a whee of a time hunting—but the Eagle knew that could only last just so long, so he got us busy on planting. And, just about the time game was getting scarce, our first maize crop was getting ready to harvest."

"*Maize?*" Rod gawked. "Where the hell'd he get that?"

"Oh, it wasn't what you think of as maize," Yorick said quickly. "Little bitty ears, only about four inches long."

"In 50,000 B.C. maize was just a thickheaded kind of grass," Rod grated, "like some parties I could mention. And it only grew in the New World. Neanderthals only grew in the Old."

"Who says?" Yorick snorted. "Just because we weren't obliging enough to go around leaving fossils doesn't mean we weren't there."

"It doesn't mean you were, either," Rod said, tight-lipped, "and you've got a very neat way of not answering the question you're asked."

"Yeah, don't I?" Yorick grinned. "It takes practice, let me tell you."

"Do," Rod invited. "Tell me more about this 'Eagle' of yours. Just where did he come from, anyway?"

"Heaven sent him in answer to our prayers," Yorick said piously. "Only we didn't just call him 'Eagle' anymore—we called him the 'Maize King.' That way, we could stay cooped up in our little mountain valley and not bother anybody."

"A laudable ideal. What happened?"

"A bunch of Flatfaces bumped into us," Yorick sighed. "Pure idiot chance. They came up to the mountains to find straight fir trees for shafts, and blundered into our valley. And, being Flatfaces, they couldn't leave without trying a little looting and pillaging."

"Neanderthals never do, of course."

Yorick shook his head. "Why bother? But they just had to try it—and most of 'em escaped, too. Which was worse—because they came back with a whole horde behind 'em."

Rod was still thinking about the "most." "You're not going to try to tell me your people were *peaceful*?"

"Were," Yorick agreed. "Definitely 'were.' I mean, with five hundred screaming Flatfaces charging down on us, even the most pacifistic suddenly saw a lot of advantages in self-defense. And the Eagle had taught us how to use bows, but the Flatfaces hadn't figured out how to make them yet; so we mostly survived."

Again, "most." "But the Eagle decided he hadn't hidden you well enough?"

"Right." Yorick bobbed his head. "Decided we couldn't be safe anywhere on Earth, in fact—so he brought us here. Or to Anderland, anyway." He jerked his head toward the west. "Over that way."

"The mainland," Rod translated. "Just—brought you."

"Right."

"How!?"

"I dunno." The Neanderthal shrugged. "He just took us to this great big square thing and marched us through, and . . . here we were!" He grinned. "Just like that!"

"Just like that." It was strange, Rod reflected, how drastically Yorick's IQ could change when he wanted it to. From the sound of it, the Neanderthals had walked through a time machine. Dread gnawed at Rod's belly—was this Eagle one of the futurian totalitarians who had staged the rebellion two years ago? Or one of the futurian anarchists, who had tried to stage a coup d'etat?

Or somebody else from the future, trying to horn in on Gramarye?

Why not? If there were two time-traveling organizations, why not a third? Or a fourth? Or a fifth? Just how many time machines were hidden away on this planet, anyway? Could Gramarye be *that* important?

But it could be, he admitted silently to himself. He'd learned from a renegade Futurian that Gramarye would eventually become a democracy, and would supply the telepaths that were vital to the survival of an interstellar democracy. That meant that the futurian anarchists and totalitarians were doomed to failure—unless they could subvert Gramarye into dictatorship, or anarchy. The planet was a nexus, a pivotal element in the history of humanity—and if it was the pivot, Rod was its bearing.

The Eagle was obviously a futurian—but from which side? Rod certainly wasn't going to find out from Yorick. He could try, of course—but the Neanderthal was likely to turn into a clam. Rod decided not to press the point—let Yorick finish talking; just sit back and listen. That way, Rod would at least learn everything the Neanderthal *was* willing to say. First get the basic information; then dig for the details. Rod forced a grin and said, "At least you were safe from Flatfaces . . . I mean, Cro-Magnons."

"We sure were. In fact, things were really hunky-dory, for a while. We chased out the dinosaurs, except for the ones who couldn't run fast enough. . . ."

"How'd you handle them?"

"With a knife and fork. Not bad, with enough seasoning. Especially if you grind 'em up and sprinkle it on top of some cornbread, with some cheese sauce."

"I, uh, think we can, uh, delay that tangent." Rod swallowed hard against a queasy stomach. "But I'm sure the regimental cook would love to hear your recipes." There was a gagging sound from the soldiers behind him, and Tuan swallowed heavily. Rod changed the subject. "After you took care of the wildlife, I assume you cleared the underbrush?"

"And the overbrush; made great little houses. Then we put in a crop and practiced fishing while we wa.ched it grow."

"Catch anything?"

"Just coelacanths, but they're not half bad with a little . . ."

"How about the farming?" Rod said quickly.

"Couldn't be better. Grew real fast, too, and real big; nice soil you've got here."

"A regular Garden of Eden," Rod said drily. "Who was the snake?"

"A bright-eyed boy, eager to make good."

Rod had been getting bored, but he suddenly gained interest. "A boy?"

"Well, okay, so he was about forty. And the brightness in his eye was pure greed—but you couldn't call him grown-up, really. Still couldn't tell the difference between reality and fantasy. He decided he was a magician and a priest all rolled into one, and went around telling everybody they should worship the Elder God."

Rod frowned. "Who is the 'Elder God'?"

" 'What' would be more like it. Nobody's ever seen it, mind you . . ."

"That's the way it is with most gods."

"Really? From all the stories I hear, it's just the other way around. But this shaman drew pictures of him for us; it was a huge bloated grotesque thing, with snakes for hair and little fires for eyes. Called him the Kobold." Yorick shuddered. "Gives me the creeps, just to think about it."

"Not the type to inspire confidence," Rod agreed. "And he was hoping to win converts with this thing?"

Yorick nodded. "Didn't get 'em, though—at least, until his buddy Atylem got lost at sea."

"His buddy got lost. This made people think his god was true?"

"No, it was because Atylem came back."

"Oh—the Slain and Risen One."

"Not really. Atylem had been out fishing, see, and he hadn't come back. But finally he did, two weeks later—and he said he'd found a whole new land five days across the water. And it was just chock-full of Flatfaces!"

"Oh." Rod lifted his head slowly, eyes losing focus. "So. Your people decided the Eagle was wrong, eh?"

"You're quick, milord."

"And that meant the Kobold was right."

Yorick nodded. "Doesn't really make sense, does it?"

Rod shrugged. "That's the way people think. I mean, we're talking about public opinion, not logic."

"Sure." Yorick spread his hands. "Put yourself in their place. Why would the Eagle bring you so close to your old enemies if he were really powerful and wise?"

"But they were all the way across the water," Rod said reasonably, "a day's journey."

"That's what we all said." Yorick nodded toward his friends. "We were Eagle's leadership cadre, you see. I was his right-hand man—and Gachol over there was his left-hand."

"And the rest were the fingers?"

"You got it. Anyway, we all said the Flatfaces couldn't bother us much—not with all that water to cross. But one day we looked up, and there was a Flatface floating in the sky."

Rod stiffened, galvanized. Toby, on his spy mission! But hadn't Yorick left something out? A little matter of a raid?

But the Neanderthal plowed on. "Well! The fat was in the fire, I can tell you! That shaman—Mughorck was his name—he was out and about the village before the Flatface was out of the sky, shouting about how Eagle had betrayed us and now the Flatfaces were gonna come over like a ton of devilfish and knock us all into the gizzard!"

"Didn't anybody argue with him?"

"A few of us did try to point out that one Flatface does not an army make—nor a navy, for that matter. But, I mean, this Flatface was *flying*! Everybody was panicking. Some of them were so scared, they actually started digging themselves holes to crawl into! I mean, they were talking magic, and they were talking sorcery—and Eagle had made a big point of telling them that he *wasn't* magical, and he *wasn't* a sorcerer. Not that anybody believed him, of course, but . . ."

"But it laid the egg of doubt," Rod inferred. "I should be so lucky!"

The apeman frowned. "How's that again?"

"Uh, nothing," Rod said hastily. "I take it the people began to believe him, at just the wrongest time?"

"Right. After all, there was Mughorck the shaman, running around telling people that he *was* magical, and *was* a sorcerer—and that his god, the Kobold, could make them strong enough to defeat the Flatfaces, and, well . . . people don't think too clearly when they're scared stiff. First thing you knew, everybody was yelling and shouting that the shaman was right, and the Kobold had to be a true god, after all."

"Didn't you begin to get the feeling that the climate was turning unhealthy?"

"Just about then, yeah. We"—Yorick jerked his head toward his companions—"began to feel the wind shifting. So we headed up to the High Cave, to tell the Eagle to fly."

"I hope he listened to you."

"Listened! He was ahead of us—as usual. He had our knapsacks all packed. While we were slinging our packs onto our backs, he slapped our bows into our hands. Then he told us to disappear into the jungle and build a raft."

"Raft?" Rod frowned.

Yorick nodded. "We had some really thick trees, with really thick bark, and they floated really well. He told us not to worry about where we were going—just to paddle it out into the ocean and hang on. Oh, and he told us to bring plenty of food and lots of drinking water, 'cause we might be on that raft for a long time."

"Without a sail or oars, it must've been." Rod noted silently that the Eagle, whether or not he was a wizard, obviously knew the odd bit about science—which he should have, if he'd been running a time machine. It seemed that he knew about the Beastland-Gramarye current. "Did he tell you where'd you'd land?"

"Yeah—the Land of the Flatfaces. But he told us not to worry about it, because *these* Flatfaces were *good* people, like him." He clapped his hand over his mouth, eyes wide.

The slip, Rod decided, had been a little too obvious. "Didn't you want me to know he was good?"

"Uh . . . yeah." Yorick took his hand away, bobbing his head eagerly, grinning. "Yeah, sure. That he was good, that's all."

"Thought so. I mean, you couldn't've been worried about letting me know he was a Flatface—that's been pretty obvious all along."

"Oh." Yorick's face fell. "You guys *are* good at manipulating symbols, aren't you?"

But how could a Neanderthal realize that words were symbols? His education was showing again. "So you built your raft and paddled out into the ocean—and the current brought you here."

"Yeah." Yorick eyed the wall of spearpoints that hedged him in. "And I don't mind telling you that, for a while there, we thought maybe the Eagle had been wrong about you."

Rod shrugged. "Can you blame them? Some of these men are locals; and your boys hit a village not far from here a few days ago. They turned it into toothpicks and meatloaf—and some of my soldiers had relatives there."

"They *what*?" Yorick stared at him in stark horror. Then he whirled to his own men, pouring out a furious cascade of gutturals and barks. His companions' heads came up; they stared in horror. Then their faces darkened with anger. They answered Yorick in growls of rage. He turned back to Rod. "I don't mean to sound callous, milord—but are you sure about this?"

Rod nodded, fighting to keep his face expressionless. Yorick and his men were either actually surprised and shocked by the news—or very good actors. "They hit a village up north, too. I was there; I saw it. Most of the villagers got away, but they carved up my soldiers like hams at a family reunion."

Yorick's face worked for a moment; then he turned his head and spat. "That skinny, catbait Mughorck! He's got to be behind it somehow!"

"Didst thou, then, know nothing of this?" Tuan demanded.

Yorick shook his head. "No one in the village did."

"There were five score of men at least aboard that long ship," Tuan said. "Many in your village must have known of it."

"If they did, they did a real good job of keeping the secret," Yorick growled. Then he pursed his lips. " 'Course, nobody really would've noticed, with that epidemic going on."

"Epidemic?" Rod perked up his ears. "What kind?"

"Oh, nothing really serious, you understand—but enough so that people had to take to their beds for a week or two with chills and fever. You'll understand we were a little preoccupied."

"I'll understand they were goldbricking," Rod snapped. "This fever didn't happen to affect only single men, did it?"

Yorick gazed off into space. "Now that you mention . . ."

"Simple, but effective," Rod said to Tuan. "If anybody came knocking and didn't get any answer, they'd figure the guy was sleeping, or too sick to want to be bothered." He turned back to Yorick. "Nobody thought to stop in to check and see if they wanted anything, I suppose?"

Yorick shrugged. "Thought, yes—but you don't go into somebody's house without being invited. We left food at the door every night, though—and it was always gone the next morning."

"I'll bet it was—and your shaman's friends had extra rations."

"You've got a point." Yorick's face was darkening. "But we never thought to check on the sick ones—we trusted each other. You don't know how great it is, when you've been alone all your life, to suddenly have a whole bunch of people like yourself. And we wouldn't stop in just to say hello when we were pretty sure the person was feeling rotten; nobody wanted to catch it."

Rod nodded grimly. "Simple. Despicable, but simple." He turned back to Tuan. "So we got hit with private enterprise—a bunch of buckoes out for their own good, without regard to how much harm it might do their neighbors."

"So that louse Mughorck was sending out secret commando raids to get you Flatfaces angry," Yorick growled. "No wonder you sent a spy."

"Wouldn't you?" Rod countered. His eyes narrowed. "Come to think of it, maybe you have."

"Who, us?" Yorick stared, appalled. "Make sense, milord! This is like walking in on a hibernating cave bear and kicking him awake! Do you think we'd take a chance like this if we had any choice?"

"Yes," Rod said slowly. "I don't think you're short on courage. But you wouldn't be dumb enough to come walking in without a disguise, either—especially since at least one of you speaks good Terran English."

Beside him, Tuan nodded heavily. "I think they are what they seem, Lord Warlock—good men who flee an evil one."

"I'm afraid I'd have to say so too," Rod sighed. "But speaking of good men—what happened to the Eagle?"

Yorick shrugged. "All he said was that he was going to hide."

"And take his gadgets with him, I hope," Rod said grimly. "The enemy has entirely too many time machines already."

" 'Enemy'?" Tuan turned to him, frowning. "There is naught here but an upstart hungry for power, Lord Gallowglass."

"Yeah, one who thinks Gramarye looks like a delicious dessert! If that's not 'the enemy,' what is?"

"The futurian totalitarians," Fess murmured through the earphone implanted in Rod's mastoid, right behind his ear, "and the futurian anarchists."

"But you know my devious mind," Rod went on, ostensibly to Tuan. "I always have to wonder if there's a villain behind the villain."

Tuan smiled, almost fondly. "If this suspicion will aid thee to guard us as thou hast in the past, why, mayst thou ever see a bear behind each bush!"

"Well, not a bear—but I usually do see trouble bruin."

"Optimists have more fun, milord," Yorick reminded him.

"Yeah, because pessimists have made things safe for 'em. And how do we make things safe when we never know where the enemy's gonna strike next?"

Yorick shrugged. "Mughorck can only field a thousand men. Just put five hundred soldiers every place they might hit."

"*Every* place?" Rod asked with a sardonic smile. "We've got three thousand miles of coastline, and we'd need those five hundred soldiers at *least* every ten miles. Besides, five hundred wouldn't do it—not when the enemy can freeze 'em in their tracks. We'd need at least a couple of thousand at each station."

Yorick shrugged. "So, what's the problem?"

Rod felt anger rise, then remembered that Neanderthals couldn't manipulate symbols—including simple multiplication. "That'd be about six hundred thousand men, and we've . . ."

Yorick stopped him with a raised palm. "Uh . . . I have a little trouble with anything more than twenty. If it goes past my fingers and toes . . ."

"Just take my word for it; it's a lot more men than we have available. Medieval technology doesn't exactly encourage massive populations."

"Oh." Yorick seemed crestfallen. Then he brightened. "But you could post sentries."

"Sure—and we did. But there's still the problem of getting the army to where the raiders are in time to meet them."

"It can't be all *that* hard!"

Rod took a deep breath. "Look—we have to move at least as many men as your whole village."

"What for—to fight just a lousy thousand?"

"I don't think you realize just how much of an advantage

that Evil Eye gives your men," Rod said sourly.

"Not all that much. I mean, one man can only freeze one other man. Maybe two, if he pushes it—but not very well."

Rod stared at him for a moment.

Then he said, "One boatload of your men held a small army of ours totally frozen."

"What!?"

Rod nodded. "That'd be about, uh, two hands of my men for every one of yours."

Yorick stared at his outspread fingers and shook his head. "Can't be. No way. At all."

Rod gazed at him, then shrugged his shoulders. "Apparently, somebody found a way to do it." He remembered what Gwen had said about the lightning.

"Then figure out a way to *un*do it," Yorick said promptly. "You Flatfaces are good at that kind of thing. We can show you how the Freeze—what'd you call it, the Evil Eye?—we can show you how it works."

"That might help . . ."

"Sure it will! You gotta be able to figure out something from that!"

"Oh, I do, do I? How come?"

"Because," Yorick said, grinning, "you can manipulate symbols."

Rod opened his mouth to answer—but he couldn't really think of anything, so he closed it again. That's what set him apart from ordinary men. He just smiled weakly and said, "Manipulating symbols doesn't *always* produce miracles, Yorick."

"I'll take a chance on it. You just tell us what we can do, and we'll do it."

"Might they not be of some value with our force?" Tuan inquired.

Rod turned to him, frowning. "Fighting side by side with our soldiers? They'd get chopped up in the first battle by our own men."

"Not if we were to employ them to slip ahead of our main force to reconnoiter the enemy's forces. Let us train them in the use of longbow, crossbow, and lance, and send them ahead to wreak havoc ere we arrive."

Rod shook his head. "The nearest knight would charge them in a second. They're not exactly inconspicuous, you know." Suddenly his eyes widened; he grinned. "Oh!"

"Oh?" Tuan said warily.

"Yeah. If they stand out too much to do any good here —then we should use them someplace where they won't!"

Tuan's face slowly cleared into a beatific smile. "Aye, certes! Train them well, and send them back to Beastland. Then they can attack this Mughorck's men unbeknownst!"

"Well, not quite. Just because they all look alike to us doesn't mean they look alike to one another. But they *could* hide out in the bush and recruit some others from among the disaffected, and . . ."

"Aye! Build up a small army!"

"Well, I wasn't thinking on that scale. . . ."

"Couldn't manage an army." Yorick shook his head. "Fifty men, though, I might be able to get—but that's fifty, tops." He glanced back at his colleagues, then up at Rod. "That's all our hands together—right?"

"Right." Rod fought down a grin. "But put 'em in the right place, at the right time . . ."

"Aye, fifty men who know the lay of the land." Tuan's eyes kindled. " 'Twould be well done indeed, Master Beastman."

" 'Yorick' is good enough," the Neanderthal said with a careless wave of his hand. "Fifty, I think I could get. Yeah. We could hide out in the jungle on the other side of the cliffs from the village. no more than fifty, though. Most of the men have wives and children. That makes a man cautious."

Rod nodded toward the other Neanderthals. "How about your guys?"

Yorick shook his head. "All bachelors. We wondered why the Eagle didn't choose any of the married men for his cadre—and I don't mind telling you, some of the ladies were pretty upset about it."

"Don't worry—it was nothing compared to how they would've squawked the first time their husbands had to work late." Rod thought of Gwen with a gush of gratitude. "So they thought Eagle was a misogynist?"

"No; he turned handsprings anytime anyone married. And if one of the Inner Circle got spliced, he was even happier. Kicked 'em into the Outer Circle, of course—but he always said the guy was being promoted, to husbandry."

"Odd way to look at it." Rod mulled it over. "Maybe accurate, though. . . ."

"It *is* a job, all by itself," Yorick agreed. "But the lack of dependents sure came in handy when we had to leave town in a hurry."

"Think the Eagle had that in mind all along?"

"I'm sure of it—now. So, we'll get bachelors for this guerrilla force, for you—but what do you want us to do with them?"

"Thou must needs assault them from their rear, whilst we storm in from the ocean," Tuan answered. "Then, mayhap, we can bring thine Eagle from his aerie."

"Or wherever he's hiding." Yorick nodded. "Sounds like a great idea."

"Then, it's a deal." Rod held out a hand—carefully, it must be admitted.

Yorick frowned at Rod's hand for a moment. Then he grinned. "Oh, yeah! Now I remember!" He grabbed Rod's hand in both of his and pumped it enthusiastically. "Allies, huh?"

"Allies," Rod confirmed. "By the way, ally . . ."

"Anything, milord," Yorick said expansively.

"Viking gear."

"Huh?"

"Viking gear," Rod said again. He was glad to see the phrase had meant absolutely nothing to the Neanderthal. "Your shaman's raiders came decked out in Viking gear—you know, horned helmets, round shields . . ."

"Yeah, yeah, I know what Vikings were," Yorick said in annoyance. "Dragon ships too?"

Rod nodded. "Any idea why?"

"Well, nothing very deep—but I'll bet it scared hell out of the locals."

Rod stared at him for a second.

"Makes sense, if you're trying to adapt terrorism to a medieval culture," Yorick explained.

"Too much sense," Rod agreed. "Come on, let's get back to Runnymede—we've got to start a military academy for you."

The train headed northward with a squad of spearmen leading; then Rod and Tuan; then the Neanderthals, à la carte—or à la wagon, anyway, commandeered from the nearest farmer (the Neanderthals had never even thought of riding horses; eating, maybe . . .); and well-surrounded by spearmen and archers. The soldiers and the beastmen eyed each other warily through the whole trip.

"I hope your wife doesn't mind surprise guests," Rod cautioned Tuan.

"I am certain she will be as hospitable as she ever is," Tuan replied.

"That's what I was afraid of. . . ."

"Come, Lord Warlock! Certes, thou'lt not deny my gentle wife's goodness!"

"Or your good wife's gentleness," Rod echoed. "We'll just have to hope these cavemen know what a bed and a chair are."

"I doubt not we'll have to teach them the uses of many articles within our castle," Tuan sighed, "save, perhaps, their captain Yorick. He doth seem to have acquired a great deal of knowledge ere this."

"Oh, yeah! He's a regular wise guy! But I'm not so much worried about *what* he's learned, as who he learned it from."

Tuan glanced at him keenly. "Dost thou speak of the Eagle?"

"I dost," Rod confirmed. "What'd you get out of our little cross-examination?"

"I was cross that we had so little opportunity to examine. The fellow hath a deliberate knack for turning any question to the answer he doth wish to give."

"Nicely put," Rod said judiciously. It was also unusually perceptive, for Tuan. "But I think I did figure out a few items he didn't mean to tell us. What did you hear between his bursts?"

Tuan shrugged. "I did learn that the Eagle is a wizard."

"Yeah, that was pretty obvious—only I'd say he was *my* kind of wizard. He does his magic by science, not by, uh, talent."

Tuan frowned, concerned. "How much of this 'science' hath he taught to Yorick?"

"None. He couldn't have; it depends on mathematics. The basic concepts, maybe—but that's not enough to really *do* anything with. He has taught Yorick some history, though, or the big lug wouldn't've known what the Vikings were. Which makes me nervous—what *else* did the Eagle teach Yorick, and the rest of his people, for that matter?"

Tuan waved away the issue. "I shall not concern myself with such matters, Lord Warlock. These beastmen, after all, cannot have sufficient intelligence to trouble us—not these five alone—when they cannot truly learn our language."

"I . . . wouldn't . . . quite . . . say . . . that. . . ." Rod took a deep breath. "I will admit that not being able to encode and analyze does limit their ability to solve problems. But they've got as much gray matter between their ears as you and I do."

Tuan turned to him, frowning. "Canst thou truly believe that they may be as intelligent as thyself or myself?"

"I truly can—though I have to admit, it's probably a very strange sort of intelligence." He glanced back over his shoulder at the group of Neanderthals. The spearmen surrounding them happened to lean toward the outside at that moment, affording Rod a glimpse of Yorick's face. He turned back to the front. "*Very* strange."

Gwen snuggled up to him afterward and murmured, "Thou hast not been away so long as *that*, my lord."

"So now I need a reason?" Rod gave her an arch look.

"No more than thou ever hast," she purred, burrowing her head into the hollow between his shoulder and his jaw.

Suddenly Rod stiffened. "Whazzat?"

"Hm?" Gwen lifted her head, listening for a moment. Then she smiled up at him. " 'Twas naught but a tree branch creaking without, my lord."

"Oh." Rod relaxed. "Thought it was the baby. . . . You *sure* he's snug in his crib?"

"Who may say, with an infant warlock?" Gwen sighed. "He may in truth be here—yet he might as easily be a thousand miles distant." She was still for a moment, as though she were listening again; then she relaxed with a smile. "Nay, I hear his dream. He is in his crib indeed, my lord."

"And he won't float out, with that lid on it." Rod smiled. "Who would ever have thought I'd have a lighter-than-air son?"

"Dost thou disclaim thine own relative?"

Rod rolled over. "*That* comment, my dear, deserves . . ." He jerked bolt-upright. "Feel that?"

"Nay," she said petulantly, "though I wish to."

"No, no! Not *that*! I meant that puff of wind."

"Of wind?" Gwen frowned. "Aye, there was . . ." Then her eyes widened. "Oh."

"Yeah." Rod swung his legs over the side of the bed and

pulled on his robe. "There's a warlock within." He raised his voice, calling, "Name yourself!"

For answer, there was a knock on the front of the cave.

"Of all the asinine hours of the night to have company calling," Rod grumbled as he stamped down the narrow flight of stairs to the big main room.

A figure stood silhouetted against the night sky in the cave mouth, knocking.

"Wait a minute." Rod frowned. "We don't have a door. What're you knocking on?"

"I know not," the shadow answered, "yet 'tis wood, and 'tis near."

"It's a trunk," Rod growled. "Toby?"

"Aye, Lord Warlock. How didst thou know of mine arrival?"

"When you teleported in you displaced a lot of air. I felt the breeze." Rod came up to the young warlock with a scowl. "What's so important that I have to be called out at this time of night? I just got back! Have our, ah, 'guests' escaped?"

"Nay, Lord Warlock. They are snug in their dunge . . . ah, guest room. Still, His Majesty summons thee."

"What's the matter? Did the cook leave the garlic out of the soup again? I keep telling him this isn't vampire country!"

"Nay," Toby said, his face solemn. " 'Tis the Queen. She is distraught."

The guard saw Rod coming, and stepped through the door ahead of him. Rod stamped to a halt, chafing at the bit. He could hear the sentry murmuring; then the door swung open. Rod stepped through—and almost slammed into Tuan. The young King held him off with a palm, then lifted a finger to his lips. He nodded his head toward the interior of the room. Rod looked and saw Catharine seated in a chair by the hearth, firelight flickering on her face. Her eyes reflected the flames, but they were cold, in a face of granite. As he watched she bent forward, took a stick from the hearth, and broke it. "Swine, dog, and offal!" She spat. "All the land knows the Queen for a half-witch, and this motley half-monk hath bile to say. . . ." She hurled the broken stick into the fire, and the flames filled her eyes as she swore, "May he choke on the cup of his own gall and die!"

Rod murmured to Tuan, "What's got her so upset?"

"She rode out about the countryside, with heralds before

her and guardsmen after, to summon all who might have any smallest touch of witch-power within them to come to the Royal Coven at Runnymede.''

Rod shrugged. "So she was recruiting. Why does that have her ready to eat sand and blow glass?''

Catharine looked up. "Who speaks?''

" 'Tis the Lord Warlock, my love.'' Tuan stepped toward her. "I bethought me he'd find thine news of interest.''

"Indeed he should! Come hither, Lord Warlock! Thou wilt rejoice exceedingly in the news I have to tell, I doubt not!''

Rod could almost feel his skin wither under her sarcasm. He stepped forward with a scowl. "If it has anything to do with witches, I'm all ears. I take it your people didn't exactly give you a warm reception?''

"I would have thought 'twas the dead of winter!'' Catharine snapped. "My heralds told me that, ere my coach came in view, they felt 'twas only the royal arms on their tabards saved them from stoning.''

"Not exactly encouraging—but not exactly new, either. Still, I had been hoping for a change in public attitude toward our espers . . . uh, witches.''

"So had I also, and so it might have happed—had there not been a voice raised against them.''

"Whose?'' Rod's voice held incipient murder.

"A holy man.'' Catharine made the words an obscenity.

Rod's mouth slowly opened, then snapped shut. He straightened, a touch of disgust in his face. "I should have known.''

" 'Tis a renegade friar,'' said the Queen, toying with her ring, "or seems to be. I ha' spoke with Milord Abbot, and he disclaims all knowledge of the recreant.''

"A self-appointed Jonah.'' Rod smiled, with acid. "Lives in a cave in the hills on berries and bee-stings, calling himself a holy hermit and a prophet, and sanctifying his flesh by never sullying it with the touch of water.''

"He doth preach against me,'' said Catharine, her hand tightening on the glass, "and therefore against the King also. For I gather the witches to me here in our castle, and therefore am I unworthy of my royal blood, and mine husband of his crown, though he be annointed sovereign of Gramarye; for mine own slight witchcraft, saith this preacher, is the work of the devil.''

Progress, Rod noted silently. Two years ago, she wouldn't

have admitted to her own telepathic powers, rudimentary though they were.

"And therefore," said the Queen, "are we agents of Satan, Tuan and I, and unfit to rule. And, certes, all witches in our land must die." She released her wineglass, striking the table with her fist.

Catharine let her head drop into her hands, massaging the temples with her fingertips. "Thus is all our work, thine, mine, and Tuan's, our work of two years and more, brought low in a fortnight; and this not by armies, nor knights, but by one unclean, self-ordained preacher, whose words spread through the land faster than ever a herald might ride. It would seem there is no need of battles to unseat a King; rumor alone is enough."

"I think," Rod said slowly, "that this is one little virus that had better be quarantined and eliminated, but fast."

"Fear not that," Tuan growled. "Sir Maris hath even now dispatched men throughout the kingdom to listen for word of this monster. When we find him he will be in our dungeons ere the sun sets."

The words sent a cold chill down Rod's spine. Sure, when *he* said it, it sounded okay—but when it came from the King, it had the full iron ring of censorship in its worst form. For the best of reasons, of course—but it was still censorship.

That was about when he began to realize that the real danger here was Gramarye's reaction to attack, not the raids themselves.

"I'm not so sure it'd do much good to lock up just one man," he said slowly.

" 'Just one'?" Catharine looked up, her eyes wild. "What dost thou say?"

"There could be several." Rod chose his words carefully. "When you have beastmen attacking from the outside, and you suddenly discover enemies inside . . ."

"Aye, I should have thought!" Tuan's fist clenched. "They would be in league, would they not?"

"We call them 'fifth columnists,' where I come from." Rod stared at the flames. "And now that you mention it, Tuan, the thought occurs to me . . ."

"The enemy behind the enemy again?" Tuan breathed.

Rod nodded. "Why couldn't it be the same villain behind both enemies?"

"Of what dost thou speak?" Catharine demanded.

"The beastmen's king be o'erthrown, sweet chuck." Tuan stepped up behind her, clasping her shoulder. "Their king, whom they call the Eagle. He hath been ousted by one whom they name Mughorck the shaman. Mughorck is his name; and by 'shaman,' they mean some mixture of priest, physician, and wizard."

"A priest again!" Catharine glared up at her husband. "Methinks there is too much of the religious in this."

"They can be very powerful tools," Rod said slowly.

"They can indeed. Yet, who wields these tools?"

"Nice question. And we may need the answer FESSter then we can get it."

Behind his ear, Fess's voice murmured, "Data cannot yet support an accurate inference."

Well, Rod had to admit the truth of it; there wasn't any real evidence of collusion. On the way back north, he'd pretty much decided that the shaman was probably backed by the futurian totalitarians. Might even be one himself; never ignore the wonders of plastic surgery. What he'd effected was, essentially, a palace revolt with popular support, bearing an uncomfortable resemblance to the October Revolution in Russia in 1917, back on old Terra.

But that was quite another breed from the witch-hunt the Gramaryan preachers were mounting, which wasn't the kind of movement that lent itself well to any really effective central control. A single voice could start it, but it tended to get out of hand very quickly. A central power could direct its broad course but couldn't determine the details. It was an anarchist's technique, destroying the bonds of mutual trust that bound people together into a society—and it could lay the groundwork for a warlord.

Of course, if a warlord took over a whole nation, the distinction between warlord and dictator became rather blurry; but the anarchist's technique was to keep several warlords fighting, and increase their number as much as possible.

"Dost thou truly believe," Tuan asked, "that both are prongs of one single attack?"

Rod shook his head. "Can't be sure; they could just as easily be two independent efforts, each trying to take advantage of the other. But for all practical purposes, we're fighting two separate enemies, and have to split our forces."

"Then," said Tuan with decision, "the wisest course is to carry the fight to one enemy, and maintain a guard against the other." He looked down at Catharine. "We must double the size of our army, at least, my love; for, some must stay here to guard whilst some go overseas to the beastmen's domain."

"Thou dost speak of war, mine husband—of war full and bloody."

Tuan nodded gravely.

Catharine squeezed her eyes shut. "I had feared it would come to this pass. Eh, but I have seen men in battle ere now—and the sight did not please me."

That, Rod decided, was another huge improvement.

Catharine looked up at Tuan again. "Is there no other way?"

He shook his head heavily. "There cannot be, sweet chuck. Therefore must we gather soldiers—and shipwrights."

Tuan, Rod guessed, was about to invent a navy.

All Rod had said was, "Take me to the beastmen." He hadn't asked for a tour of the dungeons.

On second thought, maybe he had.

The sentry who guided him turned him over to a fat warder with a bunch of huge keys at his belt. Then the soldier turned to go. Rod reached out and caught his arm. "Hold on. The beastmen're supposed to be our guests, not our captives. What're they doing down here?"

The sentry's face hardened. "I know not, Lord Warlock. 'Tis as Sir Maris commanded."

Rod frowned; that didn't sound like the old knight. "Fetch me Sir Maris forthwith—uh, that is, give him my compliments and tell him I request his presence down here." Then he turned to follow the warder while the sentry clattered off angrily.

Rod lost track of his whereabouts very quickly; the dungeon was a virtual maze. Probably intentionally. . . .

Finally the warder stopped, jammed a one-pound key into a porthole lock in a door that was scarcely wider than he was. He turned it with both hands, and the key grated through a year or two's worth of rust. Then the warder kicked the door open, revealing a twenty-foot-square chamber with a twelve-foot ceiling and five glowering beastmen who leaped to their feet, hands reaching for daggers that weren't there any more. Then the flickering light of the warder's torch showed them who their visitor was, and they relaxed—or at least Yorick did, and the others followed suit.

Rod took a breath to start talking, then had to shove his face back into the hall for a second one. Braced against aroma, he stepped through the doorway, looking around him, his nose wrinkling. "What in the name of Heaven do you call *this*?"

"A dungeon," Yorick said brightly. "I thought that's where we were."

"This is an insult!"

Yorick nodded slowly. "Yeah . . . I'd say that was a good guess. . . ."

Rod spun about, glaring at the warder. "These men are supposed to be our guests!"

"Men?" the warder snorted. Then he squelched his feelings under an occupational deadpan. "I but do as I am bid, Lord Warlock."

"And what's *this*?" Rod reached out a foot to nudge a wooden bowl next to Yorick's foot.

"Gruel," Yorick answered.

Rod felt his gorge rise. "What's in it?"

"They didn't bother telling us," Yorick said. "But let me guess—an assortment of grains from the bottom of the bin. *You* know—the ones that fell out of the bag and spilled on the floor. . . ."

"I hope you didn't eat any of it!"

"Not really." Yorick looked around. "To tell you the truth, it's not what's *in* it that bothers me. It's how *old* it is."

Rod scowled. "I thought that was a trick of the light."

"No." Yorick jerked his head up at a window set high in the wall—barred, of course. "We took it over into the sunshine while there still was some. It really *is* green. Made great bait, though."

"Bait?" Rod looked up with foreboding.

"Yeah. We've been holding a rat-killing contest." Yorick shrugged. "Not much else to do with the time." He jerked his head toward a pile of foot-long corpses. "So far, Kroligh's ahead, seven to four."

Against his better judgment, Rod was about to ask who had the four when the warder announced, "Comes Sir Maris."

The old knight stepped through the door, his head covered with the cowl of his black robe; but the front was open, showing chain mail and a broadsword. "Well met, lord Warlock."

That's debatable, Rod thought; but he had always respected and liked the old knight, so he only said, "As are you, Sir Maris." He took a deep breath to hold down the anger that threatened to spill over now that it had a logical target. "Why are these men housed within a prison?"

Sir Maris blinked, surprised at the question. "Why—His Majesty bade me house them according to their rank and station!"

Rod let out a huge, gusty breath. "But, Sir Maris—they are not criminals! And they are not animals, either."

"Assuredly they cannot be much more!"

"They can—*vastly* more!" Rod's anger drowned under the need to make the old knight understand. "It's the soul that matters, Sir Maris—not intelligence. Though they've enough of that, Lord knows. And their souls are every bit as human as ours. Just as immortal too, I expect." Rod didn't mention that there were two ways of interpreting that statement. "Their appearance may differ from ours, and they may wear only the skins of beasts; but they are free, valiant warriors—yeomen, if you will. And, within their own land and nation, the least of *these* is the equal of a knight."

Sir Maris's eyes widened, appalled; but Yorick had a complacent smile. "A little thick, maybe, milord—but gratifying. Yes, gratifying. We *are* refugees, though."

Rod clasped Sir Maris's shoulder. "It'll take a while to understand, I know. For the time being, take my word for it: the King would be appalled if he knew where they were. Take them up to a tower chamber where they may climb up to the roof for air."

"To walk the *battlements*, my Lord Warlock?" Sir Maris cried in outrage. "Why, they might signal the enemy!"

Rod closed his eyes. "The enemy has never come closer than the coast, Sir Maris—hundreds of miles away. And these men are *not* the enemy—they've *fled* from the enemy!" He glanced back at the Neanderthals. "And, come to that—please give them back their knives."

"Arms!?" the old knight gasped. "Lord Warlock—hast thou thought what they might *do* with them?"

"Kill rats," Rod snapped. "Which reminds me—give them rations fit for a fighting man. Bread, Sir Maris—and meat!"

The old knight sighed, capitulating. "It shall be as thou hast . . ."

"Dada!" Rod's shoulder suddenly sagged under twenty pounds of baby. He reached up in a panic to catch Magnus's arm, then remembered that, for Magnus at least, falling was scarcely a danger. He let out a sigh of relief, feeling his knees turn to jelly. "Don't *do* that to me, Son!"

"Da'y, s'ory! Tell s'ory!"

"A story? Uh—not just now, Son." Rod lifted the baby from his shoulder and slung him in front of his stomach. "I'm a little busy."

The beastmen stared, then began muttering apprehensively to one another.

"Uh—they're saying that baby's gotta be a witch," Yorick advised gently.

"Huh?" Rod looked up, startled. "No, a warlock. That's the male term, you know."

Yorick stared at him for a beat, then nodded deliberately. "Right." He turned and said something to the other Neanderthals. They looked up, their faces printed with fear of the supernatural. Yorick turned back to Rod. "They're not what I'd call 'reassured,' milord."

So, it started that early, Rod noted. He shrugged. "They'll get used to it. It's endemic around here." He looked directly into Yorick's eyes. "After all, we're not exactly used to your instant freeze, either, are we? I mean, fair is fair."

"Well, yeah, but the Evil Eye isn't witch-power, it's . . ." Yorick held up a finger, and ran out of words. He stared at Rod for a second, then nodded his head. "Right." He turned back to the beastmen to try to explain it.

"No, no time for a story." Rod bounced Magnus against his belt. "Go ask Mommy."

"Mommy *gone*." The baby glowered.

Rod froze.

Then he said, very quietly, "Oh." And, "Is she?"

Magnus nodded. "Mommy gone *away!*"

"Really!" Rod took a deep breath. "And who's taking care of you while she's gone?"

"Elf." The baby looked up, grinning. "Elf slow."

Rod stared at him. Then he nodded slowly. "But elf catch up with Baby."

The child's smile faded.

"Baby naughty to run away from elf," Rod pursued, punching the moral of the story.

Magnus hunkered down with a truculent look.

"Baby *stay* with the nice elf," Rod advised, "or Daddy spank." Rod tried not to look too severe.

Magnus sighed, took a deep breath, and squeezed his eyes shut.

"No, no! Don't go back quite yet!" Rod squeezed the kid a little tighter.

Magnus opened his eyes in surprise.

"Let's get back to Mommy for a second," Rod said casually. "Where . . . did Mommy . . . *go*?"

"Dunno." The baby shook his head, wide-eyed. "Mommy say . . ."

"There thou art, thou naughty babe!" A miniature whirlwind burst through the door and up to Rod, where it screeched to a halt and resolved itself into the form of an eighteen-inch-high elf with a broad mischievous face and a Robin Hood costume. At the moment, he looked definitely chagrined. "Lord Warlock, my deepest apologies! He did escape me!"

"Yes, and I've scolded him for it." Rod kept a stern eye on Magnus. The baby tried to look truculent again, but began to look a little tearful instead. "I think he'll stay with you this time, Puck," Rod went on, smiling. The baby saw, and tried a tentative smile himself. Rod tousled his hair, and he beamed. Rod eyed the elf sideways. "Did Gwen tell you where she was going?"

"Aye, Lord Warlock. When the Queen did return from her progress of the province, she did summon thy wife to tell her what ill luck she had had in seeking out witches to swell the ranks of the Royal Coven—and spoke unto her the why of it, too."

"The hedge priest." Rod nodded grimly. "I've heard about him. I take it she wasn't happy?"

"Indeed she was not. But thy wife was never one to think of revenge."

Remembering some of the things Rod had seen Gwen do, he shuddered. "Lucky for him."

"It is indeed. Yet she did not think of what he had done; she thought only of other ways to gain more witches for the Royal Coven."

"Oh?" Rod felt dread creeping up over the back of his skull. "*What* ways?"

"Why—she did believe the surest way now would be to seek out the ancient witches and warlocks who have hidden away in the forests and mountains, for they care not what the people think or say."

The dread gained territory. "Yeah, but—I thought they

were supposed to be sour and bitter, as likely to hex you as help you.''

"They are indeed," Puck acknowledged. "E'en so, if aught can bring them to give aid, 'twould be thy sweet Gwendylon's cajoling.''

"Yeah, provided they don't hex her first." Rod whirled to plop Magnus into Puck's arms. Puck stared at the baby in surprise, but held him easily—even though Magnus was at least as big as he.

"Where'd she go?" Rod snapped. "Which witch?"

"Why, the most notorious," Puck answered, surprised, "the one whose name all folk do know, who comes first to mind when mothers tell their babes witch tales. . . ."

"The champion horror-hag, eh?" Sweat sprang out on Rod's brow. "What's her name? Quick!"

"Agatha, they call her—Angry Aggie. She doth dwell high up in the Crag Mountains in a cave, noisome, dark, and dank.''

"Take care of the kid!" Rod whirled toward the door.

Air boomed out and Toby was there, right in front of him. "Lord Warlock!"

The beastmen shrank back, muttering fearfully to one another. Yorick spoke soothingly to them—or it would've been soothingly if his voice hadn't shaken.

"Not *now,* Toby!" Rod tried to step around him.

But the young warlock leaped in front of him again. "The beastmen, Lord Warlock! Their dragon ships approach the coast! And three approach where formerly there was but one!"

"Tell 'em to wait!" Rod snapped, and he leaped out the door.

Being a robot, Fess could gallop much faster than a real horse when he wanted to; and right now Rod wanted every ounce of speed the black horse could give him. Fess had been reluctant to go faster than twenty miles per hour until Rod had had an oversized knight's helmet outfitted with webbing, making it an acceptable crash helmet; but he still wouldn't ride with the visor down.

"But don't you dare try to get me to wear the rest of the armor!"

"I would not dream of it, Rod." Which was true; being a machine, Fess did not dream. In fact, he didn't even sleep. But he did do random correlations during his off hours, which served the same function. "However, I would appreciate it if you would strap yourself on."

"Whoever heard of a saddle with a seat belt?" Rod griped; but he fastened it anyway. "You shouldn't have to stop that fast, though. I mean, what do you have radar for?"

"Precisely." Fess stepped up the pace to sixty miles per hour. "But I must caution you, Rod, that such breakneck speed on a horse will not diminish your reputation as a warlock."

"We'll worry about public relations later. Right now, we've got to get to Gwen before she runs into something fatal!"

"You have a singular lack of confidence in your wife, Rod."

"*What?*" Rod's double take was so violent, he almost knocked himself off the saddle. "I'd trust her with my life, Fess!"

"Yes, but not with hers. Do you really think she would have gone on this mission alone if she thought there were any real danger?"

"Of course I do! She's not a coward!"

"No, but she has a baby and a husband who need her. She would no longer be willing to risk her life quite so recklessly."

"Oh." Rod frowned. "Well—maybe you've got a point." Then his sense of urgency returned. "But she could be underestimating them, Fess! I mean, that sour old witch has been up in those hills for probably forty years, at least! Who knows what kind of deviltry she's figured out by now?"

"Probably Gwendylon does. Your wife *is* a telepath, Rod."

"So's Agatha. And what Gwen can read, maybe Agatha can block! Come *on,* Fess! We've got to *get* there!"

Fess gave the static hiss that was a robot's sigh, and stepped up the pace. Drowsy summer fields and tidy thatched cottages flew by.

"She's up *there?*" Rod stared up at an almost sheer wall of rock towering into the sky above him, so close that it seemed to snare laggard clouds.

"So said the peasant we asked, Rod. And I think he was too terrified by our speed to have prevaricated."

Rod shrugged. "No reason for him to lie, anyway. How do we get up there, Fess?"

"That will not be so difficult." The robot eyed the uneven

surfaces of the cliff face. "Remember, Rod—lean into the climb." He set hoof on the beginning of a path Rod hadn't even noticed before.

"If that peasant is watching, he's going to go under for good now," Rod sighed. "Who ever saw a horse climbing a mountain before?"

"Everything considered," Fess said thoughtfully as he picked his way along a ledge a little narrower than his body, "I believe it would have been faster to have replaced my brain-case into the spaceship and flown here."

"Maybe, but it would've been a lot harder to explain to the peasantry—*and* the lords, for that matter." Rod eyed the sheer drop below, and felt his stomach sink. "Fess, I don't suppose this body was built with a few antigravity plates in it?"

"Of course it was, Rod. Maxima designers consider all eventualities." Fess was a little conceited about the planetoid where he'd been manufactured.

"Well, it's a relief to know that, if we fall, we won't hit too hard. But why don't we just float up to the cave?"

"I thought you were concerned about our passage's effect on observers."

"A point," Rod sighed. "Onward and upward, Rust Rider. *Excelsior!*"

Ahead and to their left, a cave-mouth yawned—but it was only six feet high. Rod eyed it and pronounced, "Not quite high enough for both of us."

"I agree. Please dismount with caution, Rod—and be careful to stay against the rock wall."

"Oh, don't worry—I won't stray." Rod slid down between Fess and the cliff-face, trying to turn himself into a pancake. Then he eased past the great black horse and sidled along the ledge toward the black emptiness of the cave-mouth. He edged up to it, telling himself that a real witch couldn't possibly look like the ones in the fairy tales; but all the cradle epics came flooding back into his mind as he oozed toward the dank darkness of the witch's lair. The fact that Angry Aggie was mentioned by name in the Gramarye versions of most of those stories, in a featured, popular, but not entirely sympathetic role, did not exactly help to calm him. A comparison of the relative weights of logic and childhood conditioning in determining the mature human's emotional reactions makes a fascinating study in theory; but firsthand observation of the practical aspects can be a trifle uncomfortable.

A wild cackle split the air. Rod froze; the cackle faded, slackened, and turned into sobbing. Rod frowned and edged closer to the cave. . . . Gwen's voice! He could hear her murmuring, soothing. Rod felt his body relax; in fact, he almost went limp. He hadn't realized he'd been *that* worried. But if Gwen was doing the comforting, well . . . she couldn't be in *too* much danger. Could she?

Not at the moment, at least. He straightened and took a firm step forward to stride into the cave—but the testy crackle of the old woman's voice froze him in his tracks.

"Aye, I know, they are not *all* villains. They could not be, could they? Yet I would never guess it from my own life!"

Gwen, Rod decided, was amazing. She couldn't have been here more than half an hour ahead of him, and already she had the old witch opened up and talking.

Gwen murmured an answer, but Rod couldn't make it out. He frowned, edging closer to the cave—just in time to hear old Agatha say, "Rejoice, lass, that thou dost live in the new day which has dawned upon us—when the Queen protects those with witch-power, and a witch may find a warlock to wed her."

"In that, I know I am fortunate, reverend dame," Gwen answered.

Rod blushed. He actually blushed. This was going too far. He was eavesdropping for certain now. He straightened his shoulders and stepped into the cave. "Ahem!" It was very dim. He could scarcely make out anything—except two female figures seated in front of a fire. The older one's head snapped up as she heard him. Her face was lit by the firelight below, which made it look unearthly enough; but even by itself, it was a hideous, bony face.

For a second, she stared at him. Then the face split into a gargoyle grin, with a huge cackle. "Eh, what have we here? Can we not even speak of men without their intruding upon us?"

Gwen looked up, startled. Then her face lit with delighted surprise. "My lord!" She leaped to her feet and came toward him.

The old woman's face twisted into a sneer. She jerked her head toward Rod. "Is it thine?"

"It is." Gwen caught Rod's hands; her body swayed toward

him for a moment, then away. Rod understood; public display of affection can be offensive, especially to those who don't have any. But her eyes said she was flattered and very glad of his support.

Her lips, however, said only, "Why dost thou come, husband?"

"Just a little worried, dear. Though I see it was foolish of me."

"Not so foolish as thou might have thought," the witch grated. "Yet thou art lately come, to be of aid." She frowned in thought. "Nay, but mayhap thou'rt timely come also; for, an thou hadst been with her when first she had appeared in my cave-mouth, I doubt not I would have sent thee both packing."

Rod started to add, "If you could," then thought better of it. "Uh. Yeah. Sorry to intrude."

"Think naught of it," Agatha said acidly, "no other man has." She transferred her gaze to Gwen. "Thou'rt most excellent fortunate, to be sure."

Gwen lowered her eyes, blushing.

"Yet, I doubt thou knowest the true extent of thy fortune." The witch turned back to the fireplace, jammed a paddle into a huge cauldron, and stirred. "There was no tall young wizard for me, but a horde of plowboys from mountain villages, who came by ones and by fives to me for a moment's pleasure, then come threescore all together, with their mothers and sisters and wives and their stern village clergy, to flog me and rack me and pierce me with hot needles, crying, 'Vile witch, confess!' till I could contain it no longer, till my hatred broke loose upon them, smiting them low and hurling them from out my cave!"

She broke off, gasping and shuddering. Alarmed, Gwen clasped Agatha's hands in her own, and paled as their chill crept up to her spine. She had heard the tale of how, long years ago, the witch Agatha had flung the folk of five villages out of her cave, how many had broken their heads or their backs on the slopes below. No witch in Gramarye, in all the history of that eldritch island, had been possessed of such power. Most witches could lift only two, or perhaps three, at a time. And as for hurling them about with enough force to send them clear of a cave—why, that was flatly impossible.

Wasn't it?

Therefore, if a witch had indeed performed such a feat,

why, obviously she must have had a familiar, a helping spirit. These usually took the form of animals; but Agatha had kept no pets. Therefore—why, there still had to be a familiar, but it must have been invisible.

" 'Twas then," panted the witch, "that I came to this cavern, where the ledge without was so narrow that only one man could enter at once, and so that in my wrath I might never injure more than a few. But those few . . ."

The scrawny shoulders slackened, the back bowed; the old witch slumped against the rough table. "Those few, aie! Those few . . ."

"They sought to burn thee," Gwen whispered, tears in her eyes, "and 'twas done in anger, anger withheld overlong, longer than any man might have contained it! They debased thee, they tortured thee!"

"Will that bring back dead men?" Agatha darted a whetted glance at Gwen.

Gwen stared at the ravaged face, fascinated. "Agatha . . ." She bit her lip, then rushed on. "Dost thou wish to make amends for the lives thou hast taken?"

"Thou dost speak nonsense!" The witch spat. "A life is beyond price; thou canst not make amends for the taking of it!"

"True," Rod said thoughtfully, "but there is restitution."

The whetted glance sliced into him, freezing almost as effectively as the Evil Eye.

Then, though, the gaze lightened as the witch slowly grinned. "Ah, then!" She threw her head back and cackled. It was a long laugh, and when it faded Agatha wiped her eyes, nodding. "Eh! I had pondered the why of thy coming; for none come to old Agatha lest they have a wish, a yearning that may not be answered by any other. And this is thine, is it not? That the folk of the land be in danger; they stand in need of old Agatha's power! And they have sent thee to beg me the use of it!"

Her gaunt body shook with another spasm of cackling. She wheezed into a crooning calm, wiping her nose with a long bony finger. "Eh, eh! Child! Am I, a beldam of threescore years and more, to be cozened by the veriest, most innocent child? Eh!" And she was off again.

Rod frowned; this was getting out of hand. "I wouldn't exactly call it 'cozening.' "

The witch's laughter chopped off. "Wouldst thou not?" she spat. "But thou wilt ask aid of me, aye! And wilt seek to give me no recompense, nay!" She transferred her gaze to Gwen. "And thou wilt do as he bids thee, wilt thou not?"

"Nay!" Gwen cried, affronted. "I have come of my own, to beg of thee . . ."

"Of thine own!" The witch glared. "Hast thou no stripes to thy back, no scars to thy breasts where their torturers have burned thee? Hast thou not known the pain of their envy and hate, that thou shouldst come, unforced, uncajoled, to beg help for them?"

"I have." Gwen felt a strange calm descend over her. "Twice I was scourged, and thrice tortured, four times bound to a stake for the burning; and I must needs thank the Wee Folk, my good guardians, that I live now to speak to thee. Aye, I ha' known the knotted whip of their fear; though never so deeply as thou. Yet . . ."

The old witch nodded, wondering. "Yet, you pity them."

"Aye." Gwen lowered her eyes, clasping her hands tight in her lap. "Indeed, I do pity them." Her eyes leaped up to lock with Agatha's. "For their fear is the barbed thong that lashes us, their fear of the great dark that stands behind such powers as ours, the dark of unknown, and the unguessable fate that we bring them. 'Tis they who must grope for life and for good in midnightmare, they who never ha' known the sound of love-thoughts, the joy of a moonlit flight. Ought we not, then, to pity them?"

Agatha nodded slowly. Her old eyes filmed over, staring off into a life now distant in time. "So I had thought once, in my girlhood. . . ."

"Pity them, then," said Gwen, sawing hard at the reins of her eagerness. "Pity them, and . . ."

"And forgive them?" Agatha snapped back to the present, shaking her head slowly, a bitter smile on her gash of a mouth. "In my heart, I might forgive them. The stripes and the blows, the burning needles, the chains and the flaming splinters under my nails—aye, even this might I forgive them. . . ."

Her eyes glazed, gazing back down the years. "But the abuse of my body, my fair, slender girl's body and my ripe-blossomed woman's body, all the long years, my most tender flesh and the most intimate part of my heart, the tearing and rending of that heart, again and again, to feed them, their craving, insensible hunger . . . no!" Her voice was low and guttural, gurgling acid, a black-diamond drill. "No, nay! That, I may never forgive them! Their greed and their lust, their slavering hunger! Forever and ever they came, to come in and take me, and hurl me away; to come for my trembling flesh—then spurn me away, crying, 'Whore!' Again and again, by one and by five, knowing I would not, could not, turn them away; and therefore they came and they came. . . . Nay! That, I may never forgive them!"

Gwen's heart broke open and flowed; and it must have shown in her face, for Agatha transfixed her with a shimmering glare. "Pity them if you must," she grated, "but never have pity for me!"

She held Gwen's eyes for a moment, then turned back to the caldron, taking up her paddle again. "You will tell me that this was no fault of theirs," she muttered, "any more than it was of mine, that their hunger forced them to me as truly as mine constrained me to welcome them."

Her head lifted slowly, the eyes narrowing. "Or didst thou not know? Galen, the wizard of the Dark Tower. He it was who should have answered my hunger with his own. The greatest witch and the greatest warlock of the kingdom together, is it not fitting? But he alone of all men would never come to me, the swine! Oh, he will tell you he hath too much righteousness to father a child into a Hell-world like this; yet the truth of it is, he fears the blame of that child he might father. Coward! Churl! Swine!"

She dug at the caldron, spitting and cursing. "Hell-spawned, thrice misbegotten, bastard mockery of a man! Him"—she finished in a harsh whisper—"I hate most of all!"

The bony, gnarled old hands clutched the paddle so tight it seemed the wood must break.

Then she was clutching the slimy wooden paddle to her sunken dried breast. Her shoulders shook with dry sobs. "My child," she murmured. "O my fair, unborn, sweet child!"

The sobs diminished and stilled. Then, slowly, the witch's eyes came up again. "Or didst thou not know?" She smiled harshly, an eldritch gleam in her rheumy yellowed eye. "He it is who doth guard my portal, who doth protect me—my unborn child, Harold, my son, my familiar! So he was, and so he will ever be now—a soul come to me out of a tomorrow that once might have been."

Gwen stared, thunderstruck. "Thy familiar . . . ?"

"Aye." The old witch's nod was tight with irony. "My familiar and my son, my child who, because he once might have been, and should have been, bides with me now, though he never shall be born, shall never have flesh grown out of my own to cover his soul with. Harold, most powerful of wizards, son of old Galen and Agatha, of a union unrealized; for the Galen and Agatha who sired and bore him ha' died in us long ago, and lie buried in the rack and mire of our youth."

She turned back to the caldron, stirring slowly. "When first he came to me, long years ago, I could not understand."

Frankly, Rod couldn't either—although he was beginning to suspect hallucinations. He wondered if prolonged loneliness could have that effect in a grown person—developing an imaginary companion.

But if Agatha really believed in this "familiar," maybe the hallucination could focus her powers so completely that it would dredge up every last ounce of her potential. That could account for the extraordinary strength of her psi powers. . . .

Agatha lifted her head, gazing off into space.

"It seemed, lo, full strange to me, most wondrous strange; but I was lonely, and grateful. But now"—her breath wheezed like a dying organ—"now I know, now I understand." She nodded bitterly. " 'Twas an unborn soul that had no other home, and never would have."

Her head hung low, her whole body slumped with her grief.

After a long, long while, she lifted her head and sought out Gwen's eyes. "You have a son, have you not?"

There was a trace of tenderness in Agatha's smile at Gwen's nod.

But the smile hardened, then faded; and the old witch shook her head. "The poor child," she muttered.

"Poor child!" Gwen struggled to hide outrage. "In the name of Heaven, old Agatha, why?"

Agatha gave her a contemptuous glance over her shoulder. "Thou hast lived through witch-childhood, and thou hast need to ask?"

"No," Gwen whispered, shaking her head; then, louder, "No! A new day has dawned, Agatha, a day of change! My son shall claim his rightful place in this kingdom, shall guard the people and have respect from them, as is his due!"

"Think thou so?" The old witch smiled bitterly.

"Aye, I believe it! The night has past now, Agatha, fear and ignorance have gone in this day of change. And never again shall the folk of the village pursue them in anger and fear and red hatred!''

The old witch smiled sourly and jerked her head toward the cave-mouth. "Hear thou that?"

Rod saw Gwen turn toward the cave-mouth, frowning. He cocked his ear and caught a low, distant rumble. He realized it had been there for some time, coming closer.

The heck with the cover. "Fess! What's that noise?"

" 'Tis these amiable villager folk of thine," said old Agatha with a sardonic smile, "the folk of twelve villages, gathered together behind a preacher corrupted by zeal, come to roust old Agatha from her cave and burn her to ashes, for once and for all."

"Analysis confirmed," Fess's voice said behind Rod's ear.

Rod leaped to the cave-mouth, grabbed a rocky projection, and leaned out to look down.

Halfway up the slope, a churning mass filled the stone ledges.

Rod whirled back to face the women. "She's right—it's a peasant mob. They're carrying scythes and mattocks."

A sudden gust blew the mob's cry more loudly to them.

"Hear!" Agatha snorted, nodding toward the cave-mouth. Her mouth twisted with bitterness at the corners. "Hear them clamoring for my blood! Aye, when an unwashed, foaming madman drives them to it!"

She looked down at the swarming mob climbing ledge by ledge toward them. Steel winked in the sun.

Gwen felt the clammy touch of fear; but fear of what, she did not know. "Thou speakest almost as though thou hadst known this beforehand . . ."

"Oh, to be certain, I did." The old witch smiled. "Has it not come often upon me before? It was bound to be coming again. The time alone I did not know; but what matter is that?"

The ledges narrowed as the horde surged higher. Gwen could make out individual faces now. "They come close, Agatha. What must we do against them?"

"Do?" The old witch raised shaggy eyebrows in surprise. "Why, nothing, child. I have too much of their blood on my hands already. I am tired, old, and sick of my life; why then should I fight them? Let them come here and burn me. This time, at least, I will not be guilty of the blood of those I have saved."

Agatha turned away from the cave-mouth, gathering her shawl about her narrow old shoulders. "Let them come here and rend me; let them set up a stake here and burn me. Even though it come in the midst of great torture, death shall be sweet."

Rod stared, appalled. "You've got to be joking!"

"Must I, then?" Agatha transfixed him with a glare. "Thou shalt behold the truth of it!" She hobbled over to a scarred chair and sat down. "Here I rest, and here I stay, come what will, and come who will. Let them pierce me, let them burn me! I shall not again be guilty of shedding human blood!"

"But we *need* you!" Rod cried. "A coven of witches scarcely out of childhood needs you! The whole land of Gramarye needs you!"

"Wherefore—the saving of lives? And to save their lives, I must needs end these?" She nodded toward the roaring at the cave-mouth. "I think not, Lord Warlock. The very sound of it echoes with evil. Who saves lives by taking lives must needs be doing devil's work."

"All right, so don't kill them!" Rod cried, exasperated. "Just send them away."

"And how shall we do that, pray? They are already halfway up the mountain. How am I to throw them down without slaying them?"

"Then, do not slay them." Gwen dropped to her knees beside Agatha's chair. "Let them come—but do not let them touch thee."

Rod's eyes glowed. "Of course! Fess's outside on the ledge! He can keep them out!"

"Surely he is not!" Gwen looked up, horrified. "There must be an hundred of them, at the least! They will pick him up and throw him bodily off the cliff!"

Rod's stomach sank as he realized she was right. Not that it would hurt Fess, of course—he remembered that antigravity plate in the robot's belly. But it wouldn't keep the peasants out, either.

"What is this 'Fess' thou dost speak of?" Agatha demanded.

"My, uh, horse," Rod explained. "Not exactly . . . a horse. I mean, he looks like a horse, and he sounds like a horse, but . . ."

"If it doth appear to be an horse, and doth sound like to an horse, then it must needs be an horse," Agatha said with asperity, "and I would not have it die. Bring it hither, within the cave. If it doth not impede them, they will not slay it."

Loose rock clattered, and hooves echoed on stone as Fess walked into the cave. Behind Rod's ear his voice murmured, "Simple discretion, Rod."

"He's got very good hearing," Rod explained.

"And doth understand readily too, I wot," Agatha said, giving Fess a jaundiced glance. Then her eye glittered and she looked up, fairly beaming. "Well-a-day! We are quite cozy, are we not? And wilt thou, then, accompany me to my grave?"

Gwen froze. Then her shoulders straightened, and her chin lifted. "If we must, we will." She turned to Rod. "Shall we not, husband?"

Rod stared at her for a second. Even in the crisis, he couldn't help noticing that he had been demoted from "my lord" to "husband." Then his mouth twisted. "Not if I can help it." He stepped over to the black horse and fumbled in a saddlebag. "Fess and I have a few gimmicks here . . ." He pulled out a small compact cylinder. "We'll just put up a curtain of fire halfway back in the cave, between us and them. Oughta scare 'em outa their buskins. . . ."

"It will not hold them long!" Agatha began to tremble. "Yet, I see thou dost mean it. Fool! Idiot! Thou wilt but madden them further! They will break through thy flames; they will tear thee, they will rend thee!"

"I think not." Gwen turned to face the cave-mouth. "I will respect thy wishes and not hurl them from the ledge; yet, I can fill the air with a rain of small stones. I doubt me not an that will afright them."

"An thou dost afright them, they will flee! And in their flight, they will knock one another from the ledge, a thousand feet and more down to their deaths!" Agatha cried, agonized. "Nay, lass! Do not seek to guard me! Fly! Thou'rt young, and a-love! Thou hast a bairn and a husband! Thou hast many years left to thee, and they will be sweet, though many bands like to this come against thee!"

Gwen glanced longingly at her broomstick, then looked up at Rod. He met her gaze with a somber face.

"Fly, fly!" Agatha's face twisted with contempt. "Thou canst not aid a sour old woman in the midst of her death throes, lass! Thy death here with me would serve me not at all! Indeed, it would deepen the guilt that my soul is steeped in!"

Rod dropped to one knee behind a large boulder and leveled his laser at the cave-mouth. Gwen nodded and stepped behind a rocky pillar. Pebbles began to stir on the floor of the cave.

"Nay!" Agatha screeched. "Thou must needs be away from this place, and right quickly!" Turning, she seized a broomstick and slammed it into Gwen's hands; her feet lifted off the floor. Rod felt something pick him up and throw him toward Gwen. He shouted in anger and tried to swerve aside, but he landed on the broomstick anyway. It pushed up underneath him, then hurtled the two of them toward the cave-mouth—and slammed into an invisible wall that gave under them, slowed them, stopped them, then tossed them back toward old Agatha. They jarred into each other and tumbled to the floor.

"Will you make up your *mind*!" Rod clambered to his feet, rubbing his bruises. "Do you want us out, or don't . . ." His voice trailed off as he saw the look on the old witch's face. She stared past his shoulder toward the cave-mouth. Frowning, he turned to follow her gaze.

The air at the cave-mouth shimmered.

The old witch's face darkened with anger. "Harold! Begone! Withdraw from the cave-mouth, and quickly; this lass must be away!"

The shimmering intensified like a heat haze.

A huge boulder just outside the cave-mouth stirred.

"Nay, Harold!" Agatha screeched. "Thou shalt not! There ha' been too much bloodshed already!"

The boulder lifted slowly, clear of the ledge.

"Harold!" Agatha screamed, and fell silent.

For, instead of dropping down onto the toiling peasants below, the boulder lifted out and away, rising swiftly into the sky.

It was twenty feet away from the cave when a swarm of arrows spat out from the cliff above, struck the boulder, and rebounded, falling away into the valley below.

The old witch stood frozen a long moment, staring at the heat haze and the boulder arcing away into the forest.

"Harold," she whispered, "arrows . . ."

She shook her head, coming back to herself. "Thou must not leave now."

"He ha' saved our lives." said Gwen, round-eyed.

"Aye, that he hath; there be archers above us, awaiting the flight of a witch. Mayhap they thought I would fly; but I never have, I ha' always stayed here and fought them. It would seem they know thou'rt with me. A yard from that ledge now, and thou wouldst most truly resemble two hedgehogs.''

Agatha turned away, dragging Gwen with her toward the back of the cave. ''Thou, at least, must not die here! We shall brew witchcraft, thou and I, for a storm of magic such as hath never been witnessed in this land! Harold!'' she called over her shoulder to the heat haze. ''Guard the door!''

Rod started to follow, then clenched his fists, feeling useless.

Agatha hauled a small iron pot from the shelf and gasped as its weight plunged against her hands. She heaved, thrusting with her whole body to throw it up onto a small tripod that stood on the rough table. ''I grow old,'' she growled as she hooked the pot onto the tripod, ''old and weak. Long years it ha' been since I last stewed men's fates in this.''

''Men's fates . . . ?'' Gwen was at her elbow. ''What dost thou, Agatha?''

''Why, a small cooking, child.'' The old witch grinned. ''Did I not say we would brew great magic here?''

She turned away and began pulling stone jars from the shelf. ''Kindle me a fire, child. We shall live, lass, for we must; this land hath not yet given us dismissal.''

A spark fell from Gwen's flint and steel into the tinder. Gwen breathed on the resulting coal till small flames danced in the kindling. As she fed it larger and larger wood scraps, she ventured, ''Thou art strangely joyous for a witch who ha' been deprived of that which she wanted, old Agatha.''

The old witch cackled and rubbed her thin, bony hands. ''It is the joy of a craftsman, child, that doth his work well, and sees a great task before him, a greater task than ever his trade yet ha' brought him. I shall live, and more joyous and hearty than ever before; for there is great need of old Agatha, and great deeds a-doing. The undoing of this war thou hast told me of will be old Agatha's greatest work.''

She took a measure from the shelf and began ladling powders from the various jars into the pot, then took a small paddle and began stirring the brew.

Gwen flinched at the stench that arose from the heating-pot. ''What is this hideous porridge, Agatha? I have never known a witch to use such a manner of bringing magic, save in child's tales.''

Agatha paused in her stirring to fasten a pensive eye on

Gwen. "Thou art yet young, child, and know only half-truths of witchery."

She turned back to stirring the pot. "It is true that our powers be of the mind, and only of the mind. Yet true it also is that thou hast never used but a small part of thy power, child. Thou knowest not the breadth and the width of it, the color and the warp and the woof of it. There be deep, unseen parts of thy soul thou hast never uncovered; and this deep power thou canst not call up at will. It lies too far buried, beyond thy call. Thou must needs trick it into coming out, direct it by ruse and gin, not by will." She peered into the smoking, bubbling pot. "And this thou must do with a bubbling brew compounded of things which stand for the powers thou doth wish to evoke from thy heart of hearts and the breadth of thy brain. Hummingbird's feathers, for strength, speed, and flight; bees, for their stings; poppyseed, for the dulling of wits; lampblack, for the stealth and silence of night; woodbine, to bind it to the stone of the cliffs; hearth-ash, for the wish to return to the home."

She lifted the paddle; the mess flowed slowly down from it into the pot. "Not quite thick enow," the old witch muttered, and went back to stirring. "Put the jars back on the shelves, child; a tidy kitchen makes a good brew."

Gwen picked up a few jars, but as she did she glanced toward the cave-mouth. The clamor was much louder. "Old Agatha, they come!"

The first of the villagers stormed into the cave, brandishing a scythe.

"Their clamor shall but help the brew's flavor," said the old witch with a delightedly wicked grin. She bent over the pot, and crooned.

The peasant slammed into the invisible haze barrier, and rebounded, knocking over the next two behind him. The fourth and fifth stumbled over their fallen comrades, adding nicely to the pile. The stack heaved as the ones on the bottom tried to struggle to their feet. The top layers shrieked, leaped up, and fled smack-dab into the arms of their lately-come reinforcements. The resulting frantic struggle was somewhat energetic, and the ledge was only wide enough for one man at a time; the peasants seesawed back and forth, teetering perilously close to the edge, flailing their arms for balance and squalling in terror.

" 'Tis a blessing the ledge is so narrow, they cannot come

against me more than one at a time." Agatha wrapped a rag around the handle of the pot and hefted it off the hook, strands of muscle straining along her arms. "Quickly, child," she grated, "the tripod! My son Harold is summat more than a man, but he cannot hold them long, not so many! Quickly! Quickly! We must prepare to be aiding him!"

She hobbled into the entryway. Gwen caught up the tripod and ran after her.

As she set down the tripod and Agatha hooked the pot on it again, two sticks of wood thudded against the ledge, sticking two feet up above the stone.

"Scaling ladders!" gasped Agatha. "This was well-planned, in truth! Quickly, child! Fetch the bellows!"

Gwen ran for the bellows, wishing she knew what old Agatha was planning.

As she returned—handing the bellows to Agatha where she crouched over the pot in the middle of the entryway—a tall, bearded figure appeared at the top of the ladder, clambering onto the ledge. The man leveled his dark, polished staff at the cave-mouth. The staff gave a muted clank as he set its butt against the stone.

"An iron core!" Agatha pointed the bellows over the pot at the preacher and began pumping them furiously. "That staff must not touch my son!"

But the forward end of the staff had already touched the heat haze. A spark exploded at the top of the staff. Skolax howled victory and swung his staff to beckon his forces. The peasants shouted and surged into the cave.

"Bastard!" Agatha screamed. "Vile Hell-fiends! Murrain upon thee! Thou hast slain my son!"

She glared furiously, pumping the bellows like a maniac. The steam from the pot shot forward toward the mob.

They stopped dead. A deathly pallor came over their faces. Little red dots began appearing on their skins. They screamed, whirling about and flailing at their comrades, swatting at something unseen that darted and stung them.

For a moment, the crowd milled and boiled in two conflicting streams at the cave-mouth; then the back ranks screamed and gave way as the phantom stings struck them too, and the mob fled back along the ledge, away from the cave.

Only the preacher remained, struggling against the flock of phantom bees, his face swelling red with ghost-stings.

The old witch threw back her head and cackled shrill and

long, still pumping the bellows. "We have them, child! We have them now!" Then she bent grimly over the pot, pumping harder, and spat, "Now shall they pay for his death! Now shall my Eumenides hie them home!"

With a titanic effort, Skolax threw himself forward, his staff whirling up over the witch's head. Gwen leaped forward to shield her; but the staff jumped backward, jerking the preacher off his feet and throwing him hard on the stone floor. Agatha's triumphant cry cut through his agonized bellow: "He lives! My son Harold lives!"

But the preacher lifted his staff as though it were a huge and heavy weight, his face swelling with ghost-stings and rage. "Hearken to me! Hearken to Skolax! Tear them! Rend them! They cannot stand against us! Break them—*now*!" And he lurched toward his victims with a roar.

Rod leaped forward, grabbing the staff, yanking it out of the preacher's hands with a violent heave. But the whole crowd surged in after him, screaming and shouting. Fingers clawed at the witches; scythes swung. . . .

Then light, blinding light, a sunburst, a nova—silent light, everywhere.

And silence, deep and sudden, and falling, falling, through blackness, total and unrelieved, all about them, and cold that drilled to their bones. . . .

2

And something struck his heels, throwing him back. Something hard, heels, hips, and shoulders, and he tucked his chin in from reflex.

And fire burned in the blackness.

A campfire, only it burned in a small iron cage, black bars slanting up to a point.

Rod's eyes fastened on that cage for the simple reassurance of solid geometry in a world suddenly crazy. It was a tetrahedron, a fire burning inside a tetrahedron.

But what the hell was it doing here?

And for that matter, where was "here"?

Rephrase the question; because, obviously, the fire and cage belonged here. So . . .

What was Rod doing here?

Back to Question Number Two: Where was "here"?

Rod started noticing details. The floor was stone, square black basalt blocks, and the fire burned in a shallow circular well, surrounded by the basalt. The walls were distant, hard to see in the dim light from the fire; they seemed to be hung with velvet, some dark deep color, not black. Rod squinted—it looked to be a rich maroon.

The hell with the curtains. Gwen . . .

A sudden, numbing fear pervaded Rod. He was scarcely able to turn his head, was afraid to look, for fear she might not be there. Slowly, he forced his gaze around the darkened chamber, slowly . . .

A great black form lay about ten feet from him: Fess.

Rod knelt and felt for broken bones, taking things in easy stages. Satisfied that he didn't have to be measured in fractions, he clambered carefully to his feet and went over to the horse.

Fess was lying very still, which wasn't like him; but he was also very stiff, each joint locked, which was like him when he had had a seizure. Rod didn't blame him; being confronted with that journey, he could do with a seizure himself—or at least a mild jolt; bourbon, for instance. . . .

He groped under the saddlehorn and found the reset switch.

The black horse relaxed, then slowly stirred, and the great head lifted. The eyes opened, large, brown, and bleary. Not for the first time, Rod wondered if they could really be, as the eye-specs claimed, plastic.

Fess turned his head slowly, looking as puzzled as a horse-hair-over-metal face can, then turned slowly back to Rod.

"Di-dye . . . chhhab a . . . zeizure, RRRRRodd?"

"A seizure? Of course not! You just decided you needed a lube job, so you dropped into the nearest grease station." Rod tactfully refrained from mentioning just how Fess had "dropped in."

"I . . . fffai-led you innn . . . duhhh . . . momenduv . . ."

Rod winced at the touch of self-contempt that coated the vodered words and interrupted. "You did all you could; and since you've saved my life five or six times before, I'm not going to gripe over the few times you've failed." He patted Fess between the ears.

The robot hung his head for a moment, then surged to his feet, hooves clashing on the stone. His nostrils spread; and Rod had a strange notion his radar was operating, too.

"We arrre inna gread chall," the robot murmured; at least when he had seizures, he made quick recoveries. "It is stone, hung with maroon velvet curtains; a fire burns in the center in a recessed well. It is surrounded by a metal, latticework tetrahedron. The metal is an alloy of iron containing nickel and tungsten in the following percentages . . ."

"Never mind," Rod said hastily. "I get the general idea." He frowned suddenly, turning away, brooding. "I also get the idea that maybe my wife isn't dead; if she was, her body would have been there. So they've kidnapped her?''

"I regret . . ."

" 'That the data is insufficient for . . .' " Rod recited with him. "Yeah, yeah. Okay. So how do we find her?"

"I regret. . . ."

"Skip it. I've got to find her." He struck his forehead with his fist. "Where is she?"

"In the next room," boomed a deep, resonant voice. "She is unharmed and quite well, I assure thee. Agatha is there also."

A tall old man with long white hair streaming down over his shoulders and a long white beard down his chest, in a long, dark-blue monk's robe with the hood thrown back, stood by the fire. His robe was sprinkled with silver zodiac signs; his arms were folded, hands thrust up the wide, flaring sleeves. His eyes were surrounded by a network of fine wrinkles under white tufts of eyebrows; but the eyes themselves were clear and warm, gentle. He stood tall and square-shouldered near the fire, looking deep into Rod's eyes as though he were searching for something.

"Whoever you are," Rod said slowly, "I thank you for getting me out of a jam and, incidentally, for saving my life. Apparently I also owe you my wife's life, and for that I thank you even more deeply."

The old man smiled thinly. "You owe me nothing, Master Gallowglass. None owe me ought."

"And," Rod said slowly, "you owe nothing to anyone. Hm?"

The wizard's head nodded, almost imperceptibly.

Rod chewed at the inside of his cheek and said, "You're Galen. And this is the Dark Tower."

Again the old man nodded.

Rod nodded too, chewing again. "How come you saved me? I thought you ignored the outside world."

Galen shrugged. "I had an idle moment."

"So," said Rod judiciously, "you saved two witches, my horse, and my humble self, just to kill time."

"Thou art quick to comprehend," said Galen, hiding a smile deep in his beard. "I had no pressing researches at the moment."

"Rod," Fess's voice murmured, "an analysis of vocal patterns indicates he is not telling the whole truth."

"For this I need a computer?" Rod muttered dryly.

Galen tilted his head closer, with a slight frown. "Didst thou speak?"

"Oh, uh—just an idle comment about the physical aspects of thought."

"Indeed." The old wizard's head lifted. "Dost thou, then, concern thyself with such problems?"

Rod started to answer, then remembered that he was talking to a wizard who had locked himself away for forty years and had gained power continually throughout that time—and it wasn't because he'd been fermenting. "Well, nothing terribly deep, I'm afraid—just the practical side of it."

"All knowledge is of value," the wizard said, eyes glittering. "What bit of knowledge hast thou gained?"

"Well . . . I've just been getting some firsthand experience in the importance of the prefrontal lobes." Rod tapped his forehead. "The front of the brain. I've just had a demonstration that it acts as a sort of tunnel."

"Tunnel?" Galen's brows knit. "How is that?"

Rod remembered that the original Galen had authored the first definitive anatomy text back at the dawn of the Terran Renaissance. Had to be coincidence—didn't it? "There seems to be a sort of wall between concept and words. The presence of the concept can trigger a group of sounds—but that's like someone tapping on one side of a wall and someone on the other side taking the tapping as a signal to, oh, let's say . . . play a trumpet."

Galen nodded. "That would not express the thought."

"No, just let you know it was there. So this front part of the brain"—Rod tapped his forehead again—"sort of makes a hole in that wall and lets the thought emerge as words."

Galen slowly nodded. "A fascinating conjecture. Yet, how could one verify its accuracy?"

Rod shrugged. "By being inside the mind of someone who doesn't have prefrontal lobes, I suppose."

Galen lost his smile, and his eyes lost focus. "Indeed we could—an we could find such a person."

Rod couldn't help a harsh bark of laughter. "We've got 'em, Master Wizard—more than we want. Much more! The peasants call 'em 'beastmen,' and they're raiding our shores." He remembered the alarm, and guilt gnawed at him. "Raiding 'em right now, come to think of it."

"Truly?" The old wizard actually seemed excited. "Ah,

then! When I finish my current tests I will have to let my mind drift into one of theirs!"

"Don't rush 'em," Rod advised. "But please do rush *me*! I'm needed at the home front to help fight your test group—and I'd kinda like to take my wife back with me."

"As truly thou shouldst." Galen smiled. "Indeed, there is another here whom thou must also conduct away from this Dark Tower."

"Agatha? Yeah, I want her too—but not for the same reasons. Would you happen to know where they are?"

"Come," said Galen, turning away, "thy wife is without the chamber."

Rod stared after him a moment, surprised at the old man's abruptness; then he shrugged and followed, and Fess followed Rod.

The wizard seemed almost to glide to the end of the cavernous room. They passed through the maroon hangings into a much smaller room—the ceiling was only fifteen feet high. The walls were hung with velvet drapes, cobalt blue this time, and one huge tapestry. The floor boasted an Oriental carpet, with a great black carven wood chair at each corner. Roman couches, upholstered in burgundy plush, stood between the chairs. A large round black wood table stood in the center of the room before a fair-sized fireplace. Six huge calf-bound volumes lay open on the table.

Rod didn't notice the splendor, though; at least, not the splendor of the furnishings. The splendor of his wife was something else again.

Her flame-red hair didn't go badly with the cobalt-blue drapes, though. She stood at the table, bent over one of the books.

She looked up as they came in. Her face lit up like the aurora. "My lord!" she cried, and she was in his arms, almost knocking him over, wriggling and very much alive, lips glued to his.

An eternity later—half a minute, maybe?—anyway, much too soon, a harsh voice grated, "Spare me, child! Pity on a poor old hag who never was one tenth as fortunate as thou!"

Gwen broke free and spun about. "Forgive me, Agatha," she pleaded, pressing back against her husband and locking his arms around her waist. "I had not thought . . ."

"Aye, thou hadst not," said the old witch with a grimace that bore some slight resemblance to a smile, "but such is the way of youth, and must be excused.''

"Bitter crone!" Galen scowled down at her from the dignity of his full height. "Wouldst deny these twain their rightful joy for no reason but that it is joy thou never knew? Hath the milk of love so curdled in thy breast that thou canst no longer bear . . .''

"Rightful!" the witch spat in a blaze of fury. "Thou darest speak of 'rightful,' thou who hast withheld from me . . .''

"I ha' heard thy caterwauls afore," said Galen, his face turning to flint. "Scrape not mine ears again with thy cant; for I will tell thee now, as I ha' told thee long agone, that I am no just due of thine. A man is not a chattel, to be given and taken like a worn, base coin. I am mine own man to me alone; I never was allotted to a woman, and least of all to thee!"

"Yet in truth thou wast!" Agatha howled. "Thou wert accorded me before thy birth or mine and, aye, afore the world were formed in God's own mind. As sure as night was given day, wert thou allotted me; for thou art, as I am, witch-blood, and of an age together with me! Thy hates, thy joys, are mine. . . .''

"Save one!" the wizard grated.

"Save none! Thine every lust, desire, and sin are each and all alike to mine, though hidden deep within thy heart!"

Galen's head snapped up and back.

Agatha's eyes lit with glee. She stalked forward, pressing her newfound advantage. "Aye, thy true self, Galen, that thou secretest veiled within thy deepest heart, is like to me! The lust and body weakness that ever I made public thou hast in private, mate to mine! Thus thou hast hid for threescore years thy secret shame! Thou hast not honesty enow to own to these, thy covered, covert sins of coveting! Thou art too much a coward. . . .''

"Coward?" Galen almost seemed to settle back, relaxing, smiling sourly. "Nay, this is a cant that I ha' heard afore. Thou wanest, Agatha. In a younger age, thou wouldst not so soon have slipped back upon old argument."

"Nor do I now," the witch said, "for now I call thee coward of a new and most unmanly fear! Thou who cry heedlessness of all the world without the walls of thy Dark Tower; thou, who scornest all the people, fearest their opinion! Thou wouldst have them think thee saint!"

Galen's face tightened, eyes widening in glare.

"A saint!" Agatha chortled, jabbing a finger at him. "The

Saint of Hot and Heaving Blood! A saint, who hast as much of human failing as ever I did have, and great guilt! Greater! Aye, greater, for in thy false conceit thou hast robbed me of mine own true place with thee! For thou art mine by right, old Galen; 'twas thou whom God ordained to be my husband, long before thy mother caught thy father's eye! By rights, thou shouldst be mine; but thou hast held thyself away from me in cowardice and pompousness!"

Galen watched her a moment with shadowed eyes; then his shoulders squared, and he took a breath. "I receive only the curse that I have earned."

Agatha stared for a moment, lips parting. "Thou wilt admit to it!"

Then, after a moment she fixed him with a sour smile. "Nay. He means only that he hath saved mine life six times and more; and thus it is his fault that I do live to curse him."

She lifted her head proudly, her eyes glazing. "And in this thou mayst know that he is a weakling; for he cannot help himself but save us witches. It is within his nature, he who claims to care naught for any living witch or plowman. Yet he is our guardian and our savior, all us witches; for, if one of us should die when he might have prevented it, his clamoring conscience would batter down the weakness of a will that sought to silence it, and wake him in the night with haunted dreams. Oh, he can stand aloof and watch the peasant and the noble die, for they would gladly burn him; but a witch, who has not hurt him, and would render him naught but kindness—had he the courage or the manhood to be asking it—these he cannot help but see as part and parcel like him; and therefore must he save us, as he ha' done a hundred times and more."

She turned away. "Thou mayst credit him with virtue and compassion if thou wishest; but I know better."

" 'Tis even as she saith," said the old man proudly. "I love none, and none love me. I owe to none; I stand alone."

Old Agatha gave a hoot of laughter.

"Uh . . . yes," said Rod. The fight seemed to have reached a lull, and Rod was very eager to be gone before it refueled.

And since Galen's brow was darkening again, it behooved Rod to make haste.

"Yes, well, uh, thanks for the timely rescue, Galen," he said. "But now, if you'll excuse us, we really gotta be getting back to Runnymede, uh—don't we, Gwen?"

He paused suddenly, frowning at the old wizard. "I don't, uh, suppose you'd consider coming back with us?"

Agatha's head lifted slowly, fire kindling in her eye.

"I thank thee for thy kindness in offering of hospitality," said the old wizard in a voice rigid with irony. "Yet greatly to my sorrow, I fear that I cannot accept."

"Oh, to thy sorrow, to be sure!" spat Agatha. "Indeed, thou art the sorriest man that e'er I knew, for thou hast brought me sorrow deep as sin!"

She spun toward Rod and Gwen. "And yet, fear not; thy folk shall not go all unaided! There lives, at least, still one old witch of power threescore-years-and-ten in learning, who will not desert her countrymen in this time of need! There lives still one, aye, be assured; though this old gelding"—she jerked her head toward Galen—"will idly stand and watch thy folk enslaved, a power strong as his will guard thy land!" She stretched out her hand. "Come take me with thee, get us gone, for my stomach crawls within me at his presence! He thinks of naught but himself."

"And thou dost not?" Galen grated, glaring at the old witch. "Is this aught but a sop to thy thwarted wish for mothering of a child thou never hadst?"

Agatha flinched almost visibly and turned, hot words on her tongue; but Galen raised an imperious hand and intoned:

"Get thee hence, to Runnymede!"

White light flared, burning, blinding.

When the afterimages faded, Rod could see, as well as feel, Gwen in his arms, which feeling had been very reassuring while the sun went nova.

He could dimly make out Agatha too, leaning shaken against a wall, a gray granite wall.

And a high timbered ceiling, and a knot of young witches and warlocks gathered around them, staring, eyes and mouths round.

Their voices exploded in clamoring questions.

Yep, home, Rod decided. It was obviously the Witches' Tower in the King's Castle at Runnymede.

He wondered what would happen if Galen ever got mad enough to tell someone to go to Hell.

One young warlock's face thrust closer as he dropped to one knee. "Lord Warlock! Where has thou been?"

"Galen's Dark Tower," Rod croaked, and was rewarded

with a huge communal gasp. He looked around at eyes gone round as wafers. "And as to how we got here—well, he sent us home."

The teenagers exchanged glances. "We can wish ourselves from place to place," said one of the warlocks, "but none of us can do it to another."

"Yeah, well, Galen's a little older than you, and he's learned a few more tricks." Privately, Rod wondered—that did amount to a new kind of psi power, didn't it? Well, he was prepared for constant surprises. "Your name's Alvin, isn't it?"

"Thus am I called, Lord Warlock."

Rod rubbed a hand over his eyes. "I seem to remember, before I lit out to find Gwen, something about the beastmen attacking?"

"Aye, milord. Their three long ships were only the vanguard. Behind them, their fleet did darken the waters."

"Fleet?" Rod snapped completely out of his grogginess. "How many of them were there?"

"An army," a girl answered from behind Alvin. "Thou couldst not call it less."

Rod staggered to his feet, looking around. He saw the great black horse standing stiff-legged, head hanging low. Rod stumbled over to him and slid a hand under the head. It lifted, turning to look at him. Rod frowned. "No seizure, huh?"

"Indeed I did not," the robot's voice said in his ear only, "since I had experienced it once, and knew it to be possible. It thus did not cause great enough anxiety to trigger a seizure."

"So," Rod said carefully, "you were awake during the whole thing."

The horsehead lifted higher. "I was. I . . . recorded it . . . all. . . . I must play it back . . . very slowly . . . later . . . later. . . ."

"Just offhand, what would you say . . . happened? Just at a guess."

"A preliminary analysis would indicate that we passed through another dimension." Fess's body shuddered. "At least, I hope that is what I will decide happened."

"Yeah." Rod swallowed. "Uh. Well . . . decide it later, okay?" He set his foot in the stirrup and swung up onto the saddle. "We've got to get to the coast. Where'd you say they landed, Alvin?"

"At the mouth of the River Fleuve, milord. We wait as

reserve, yet have heard no call.''

Rod took a more thorough look at the handful left in the room and realized there wasn't a one over fourteen. Small wonder they hadn't been called. If they had been, things would have been *really* desperate. Rod nodded. "The Fleuve isn't too far. I might still get in on the action." He leaned down from his saddle to plant a quick kiss on Gwen. "Keep the home fires burning, dear. Come help pick up the pieces when you've got your strength back." He swung back upright and kicked his heels against Fess's sides. The black horse started trotting toward the doorway, protesting, "Rod, the lintels are too low."

"So I'll duck. Upward and onward, Steel Steed! Ho, and away!"

"You forgot the 'horse and hattock,' " Fess reminded.

Fess swept down the road to the south in the easy, tireless, rocking-chair gait possible only to electric horses. Rod sat back in the saddle and enjoyed the ride.

"Of course," he was saying, "it's possible this revivalist is just what he seemed to be, nothing more—just a neurotic, unordained religious nut. But somehow I find myself able to doubt it."

"Coincidence is possible," Fess agreed, "though scarcely probable."

"Especially since his activities are weakening the war effort very nicely—nicely for the beastmen, that is. And why else would he start operating at just this particular time? He must have begun preaching a week or two before Catharine began recruiting; otherwise we would have had at least a *few* volunteers."

"We may assume, then, that there is some correlation between the two phenomena—the war and the preacher," Fess opined.

"Correlation, Hell! He's working for 'em, Fess! How else could you explain it?"

"I do not have an alternate theory prepared," the robot admitted. "Nonetheless, the probability of direct collusion is extremely low."

"Oh, come off it!"

"Examine the data, Rod. The Neanderthals and the preacher are separated by approximately a hundred miles of ocean. Moreover, there is no physiological resemblance apparent from the reports we have received."

"A point," Rod admitted. "Still, I say . . ."

"Pardon the interruption," Fess said suddenly, "but . . . you are aware that I am using radar . . ."

"I should hope so, when we're going sixty miles an hour!"

"Two flying objects have just passed overhead."

Rod's stomach sank. "Just a couple of birds, right?"

"I'm afraid not, Rod."

Rod darted a glance at the sky. There they were, already dwindling in the distance—two broomsticks, with women attached. "They didn't!"

"I fear they did, Rod. I estimate their equivalent ground speed in excess of one hundred miles per hour. And, of course, they can fly in a direct, straight line."

"They're gonna get to the battlefield before us!" Rod glared after the ladies, then heaved a sigh and relaxed. "Well . . . I suppose I should be glad they'll be there in time to help out. . . . Gwen will have enough sense to keep them both up in the sky, won't she?"

"I trust not, since she will need to be able to concentrate all her powers in fighting the Evil Eye."

"Yeah . . . I'd forgotten about that. Well!" Rod sighed and sat back. "That's a relief!"

"I should think it would cause greater anxiety, Rod." Fess actually sounded puzzled.

"No—because she'll probably settle down wherever the Royal Witchforce is stationed—and Tuan'll have 'em very well guarded." Rod grinned. "She'll be safe in spite of herself. But just in case . . . step up the pace, will you?"

"Then did the Foemen fall upon us in endless waves. Their long ships were myriad, a plague of Dragons clawing up out of the ocean onto the beach, vomiting forth beastmen in their thousands. Tall, they were, and fanged, with their heads beneath their shoulders, and Murder in their eyes. Our doughty soldiers blanched and fell back; but the King exhorted them, and they held their places. Then did the High Warlock rise up before them, and Thunder smote the air, and Lightning blasted the ground about him. In a voice like unto a trumpet, he swore unto the soldiers that his Witches would ward the Evil Eye away from them; therefore he bade them march forth to meet and best the foemen, for the sakes of their Wives and Daughters and Sweethearts. Courage flowed from him to the heart of every soldier, and they began their march.

But the beastmen then had formed their line, and the lightning glittered from their shields and helms. They roared with bestial Lust and set forth against King Tuan's army.

With a shout, the soldiers charged; yet each beastman caught the eyes of two among them, or mayhap three, then half a dozen, and froze them where they stood. Then did the beastmen laugh—a hideous, grating Noise—and 'gan to stride forward to make Slaughter.

But the High Warlock cried out to his Witchfolk there on the hill from whence they watched the battle, and they joined hands in prayer, speeding forth the greatest of their Powers, grappling with the beastmen's darkling Strength, and freeing the minds of all the soldiers from its Spell. The army then cried out in anger, striding forth with pikes upraised; but Thunder crashed, and Lightning smote the land, leaping up into the beastmen's eyes, to freeze the soldiers there again within their tracks; and on their hill, the Witchfolk lay in a swoon, like unto Death —for the power of the demon Kobold had seared their minds.

And the beastmen grunted laughter and swung huge war axes, laying low the soldiers of the King.

The High Warlock cried out then in his Rage, and did ride down upon them on his steed of Night, laying about him with a sword of Fire, hewing through the beastmen's line; while his wife and an ancient Hag of the Hills did hear his cry, and sped unto the battle. There they joined hands, and bent their heads in prayer, and did betwixt them what all the King's Witchfolk together had done— grappled with the Kobold's power, and lifted its spell from off our soldiers' minds. Yet too many amongst them had fallen already; they could defend themselves but little more.

Then did the High Warlock again charge the beastmen's line, chanting high his ancient War Song, and the soldiers heard it and took heart. They gave ground then, step by step, and laid waste such beastmen as were fool-hardy enough to come nigh them; thus King Tuan brought them away from that cursed beach whereon so many of their Comrades did lie slain; thus he brought them up into the hills—battered, bruised, yet an army still—and bade them rest themselves and bind their wounds, assuring them their Time would come again.

And the High Warlock turned unto his wife upon the Hill, to consider how they might yet confound the beast-men; and they left the monsters to number their dead, and dig themselves deep Holes to hide in."

—Chillde's *Chronicles of the Reign of Tuan and Catharine*

Fess trotted up to the crest of the hill, and Rod stared down at the most miserable collection of teenage warlocks and witches he'd ever seen. They lay or sat on the ground, heads hanging, huddling inside blankets. Brother Chillde wove his way among them, handing out steaming mugs. Rod wondered what was in them—and wondered even more if the Lord Abbot knew that Brother Chillde was actually helping witchfolk. The little monk seemed, to say the least, unorthodox.

Then Rod realized that one of the blanketed ones was his wife.

"Gwen!" He leaped off Fess's back, darting down to kneel by her side. "Are you . . . did you . . ." He gave up on words and gathered her into his arms, pressing her against his chest. "You *feel* okay. . . ."

"I am well enough, my lord," she said wearily; but she didn't try to pull away. "Thou shouldst have greater care for these poor children—and for poor old Agatha."

"Have care for thyself, if thou must," spat the old crone. "I am nearly restored to full energy." But she seemed just as droopy as the kids.

"What happened?" Rod grated.

Gwen pushed a little away from him, shaking her head. "I scarce do know. When we came, Toby and all his witchlings and warlocks lay senseless on the ground, and our soldiers stood like statues on the beach. The beastmen passed among them, making merry slaughter. Therefore did Agatha and I join hands to pool our power against the beastmen's Evil Eye—and, oh, my lord!" She shuddered. "It was as though we heaved our shoulders up under a blackened cloud that lay upon us like unto some great, soft . . ." She groped for words. " 'Twas like the belly of a gross fat man, pushing down upon us—dark and stifling. Seemly it could soak up all the force that we could throw unto it; yet we heaved up under, Agatha and I; we did lift it off our soldiers' minds so that they could, at least, defend themselves—though scarcely more; they were sorely outnumbered. Then lightning rent the sky, and that huge, dark bank fell down upon us, smothering." She shook her head, eyes closed. " 'Tis all that I remember."

"Yet 'twas enow."

Rod looked up; Brother Chillde stood near them, his eyes glowing. "Thy wife, milord, and her venerable crone held off the beastmen's power long enow."

"Long enough for what?"

"For King Tuan to retreat back up this slope with the remnant of his soldiers, far enough so that the beastmen durst not follow. Nay, they stayed below, and began to dig their graves."

"Theirs or ours?" Rod grated. He surged to his feet, giving Gwen's hand a last squeeze, and strode to the brow of the hill.

A hundred feet below, the river-mouth swept into a long, gentle curve—a bow; and the beastmen were stringing that bow. They were digging, but not graves—a rampart, a fortress-line. Already, it was almost complete. Rod looked down and swore; they'd have a hell of a time trying to dig the beastmen out of *that*!

Then he saw what lay on the near side of the rampart—a jumbled row of bloody bodies, in the royal colors.

Rod swore again. Then he spat out, "They had to be planning it. They just had to. Somebody had to have put the idea into Gwen's mind—the idea to go see old Agatha; somebody had to have told that nutty preacher to attack Agatha's cave right then. *Right* then, so I'd be pulled away and couldn't be here! Damn!"

"Do not berate thyself so severely, Lord Warlock," Tuan said wearily behind him. " 'Twas not thy absence that defeated us."

"Oh?" Rod glared up at him. "Then what was it?"

Tuan sighed. "The power of their Kobold, like as not!"

"Not!" Rod whirled away to glare down at the beach. "Definitely 'not'! That Kobold of theirs can't be anything but a wooden idol, Tuan! It's superstition, sheer superstition!"

"Have it as thou wilt." Tuan shrugged his shoulders. "It was the beastmen's Evil Eye, then. We did not think its power would be so great, yet it blasted our witches' minds and froze our soldiers in their tracks. Then the beastmen slew them at their leisure.''

" 'Twas the lightning,'' Agatha grated in a hollow voice.

Tuan turned toward her, frowning. "What goodly beldam is this, Lord Warlock? Our debt to her is great, yet I wot me not of her name.''

"That's just 'cause you haven't been introduced. She's, uh, well . . . she's kinda famous, in her way.''

Agatha grimaced, squinting against a throbbing headache. "Temporize not, Lord Warlock. Be direct, e'en though it may seem evil. Majesty, I am called 'Angry Agatha.' '' And she inclined her head in an attempt at a bow.

Tuan stared, and Rod suddenly realized that the King was young enough to have heard some nasty nursery tales himself. But Tuan was never short on courage; he forced a smile, took a deep breath, squared his shoulders, and stepped up to the old lady. "I must needs thank thee, revered dame, for without thee, my men and I had been naught but butcher's meat.''

Agatha peered up at him through narrowed eyes; then slowly she smiled. "Mine head doth split with agony, and I ache in every limb; yet would I do this service again for so handsome a thanking.'' The smile faded. "Aye, or even without it; for I think that I have saved some lives this day, and my heart is glad within me.''

Tuan stood, gazing down at her for a moment.

Then he cleared his throat and turned to Rod. "What manner of hill-hag is this, Lord Warlock? I had thought the ancients 'mongst the witches were all sour and bitter and hated all of humankind.''

"Not this one, it turns out,'' Rod said slowly. "She just hated the way people treated her. . . .''

"Oh, still thy prattle!'' Agatha snapped. "I do hate all men, and all women, too, Majesty—unless I'm near them.''

Tuan turned back to her, nodding slowly with glowing eyes. "Now, God save thee! For hypocrisy such as thine would confound the very Devil! Praise Heaven thou wert here!''

"And curse me that I wasn't!'' Rod snapped, turning to glower down at the entrenched beastmen.

"Again thou hast said it!'' Tuan cried, exasperated. "What ails thee, Lord Warlock? Why dost thou say that thou wert absent, when thou wert here in truth, and fought as bravely as any—aye, and more!''

Rod froze.

Then he whirled about. *"What!"*

"Thou wast here, indeed." Tuan clamped his jaw shut. "Thou wert here, and the beastmen could not freeze thee."

"I' truth, they could not!" Brother Chillde cried, his face radiant. "Thou didst sweep across their line, Lord Warlock, like unto a very tempest, laying about thee with thy sword of flame. Five at a time thou didst grapple with, and conquer! Their whole line thou didst confound and craze! And 'twas thou who didst give heart unto our soldiers, and didst prevent their retreat from becoming a rout."

"But . . . that's impossible! I . . ."

" 'Tis even as he doth say, my lord." Gwen's voice was low, but it carried. "From this hilltop did I see thee far below; and 'twas thou who didst lead, even as this good friar saith."

Rod stared at her, appalled. If *she* didn't know him, who did?

Then he turned away, striding down the back of the hill.

"Hold, Lord Warlock! What dost thou seek?" Tuan hurried to keep pace with him.

"An on-the-spot witness," Rod grated. "Even Gwen could be mistaken from a distance."

He skidded to a stop beside a knot of soldiers who huddled under the protection of a rocky overhang. "You there, soldier!"

The soldier lifted his tousled blond head, holding a scrap of cloth to a long rent in his arm.

Rod stared, amazed. Then he dropped to one knee, yanking the cloth off the wound. The soldier yelled, galvanized. Rod glanced up and felt his heart sink; surely that face belonged to a boy, not a man! He turned back to the wound, inspecting it. Then he looked up at Tuan. "Some brandywine."

" 'Tis here," the young soldier grated.

Rod looked down and saw a bottle. He poured a little on the cut and the soldier gasped, long and with a rattle, his eyes nearly bulging out of his head. Rod tore open his doublet and tore a strip of cloth from his singlet. He held the wound closed and began to wrap the bandage around it. "There's a lot of blood, but it's really just a flesh wound. We'll have to put some stitches in it later." He looked up at the young ranker. "Know who I am?"

"Aye," the young man gasped. "Thou'rt the Lord High Warlock."

Rod nodded. "Ever seen me before?"

"Why, certes! Thou didst stand beside me in the melee! Thou wert then no farther from me than thou art now!"

Rod stared up at him. Then he said, "Are you *sure*? I mean, *absolutely* sure?"

"Nay, be sure that I am! Had it not been for the sight of thee, I'd ha' turned and fled!" Then his eyes widened and he glanced quickly at his companions, flushing; but they only nodded somber agreement.

"Take heart." Tuan slapped his shoulder. "Any would have fled such a battle, an they could have."

The young soldier looked up, finally realized the King himself stood near, and almost fainted.

Rod grasped his shoulder. "You saw me, though. You really did see me."

"Truly, my lord." The young man's eyes were wide. "I' truth, I did." He lowered his eyes, frowning. "And yet—'tis strange."

"Strange?" Rod frowned. "Why?"

The young soldier bit his lip; then the words spilled out. "Thou didst seem taller in the battle—by a head or more! I could have sworn thou didst tower above all soldiers there! And thou didst seem to glow. . . ."

Rod held his eyes for a moment longer.

Then he went back to wrapping the bandage. "Yeah, well, you know how it is during a battle. Everything seems bigger than it really is—especially a man on a horse."

"Truth," the young soldier admitted. "Thou wast astride."

"Right." Rod nodded. "Big roan horse."

"Nay, milord." The young soldier frowned. "Thy mount was black as jet."

"Calm down, Rod," Fess's voice murmured, "you are beside yourself."

"I am?" Rod looked around in a panic.

"It was a figure of speech," the robot assured him. "Lower your anxiety level—you are quite definitely a singular personality."

"I'd like to be sure of that." Rod frowned down at the soldiers around him. He was walking through the camp, surveying what was left of Tuan's army. Whether he'd been there during the battle or not, the mere sight of him was putting heart back into them. Personally, he felt sheepish, even guilty; but . . .

"Your presence is good for morale, Rod," Fess murmured.

"I suppose," Rod muttered. Privately, he wondered if he wasn't "showing himself" to reassure himself that he was indeed himself. "I mean, the phenomenon is totally impossible, Fess. You do understand that, don't you?"

Soldiers stared up at him in awe. Rod ground his teeth; he knew the rumor would fly through the camp that the Lord Warlock had been talking to his "familiar."

"Certainly, Rod. Attribute it to mass hysteria. During the battle, they needed the reassurance that the Lord High Warlock stood by them, to oppose the beastmen's magic. Then one soldier, in the heat of the fight, mistook some other knight for yourself, and doubtless cried out, 'Behold the High Warlock!' And all his fellows, in the gloom of a lightning-lit battle, also imagined that they saw you."

Rod nodded, a little reassured. "Just a case of mistaken identity."

"Lord Warlock?"

"Um?" Rod turned, looked down at a grizzled old sergeant who sat in the mud. "What's the matter, ancient?"

"My boys hunger, Lord Warlock." The ancient gestured to a dozen men in their young twenties, who huddled near him. "Will there be food?"

Rod stared down at him.

After a moment, he said, "Yeah. It'll just take a little while. Rough terrain, and wagons—you know."

The ancient's face relaxed. "Aye, milord."

As Rod turned away, he heard a soldier say, "Surely he will not." The man beside him shrugged. "A king is a king. What knows he of a common man-at-arms? What matters it to him if we are slain and frozen?"

"To King Tuan, it matters greatly," the other said indignantly. "Dost not recall that he was King of Beggars ere he was King of Gramarye?"

"Still . . . he is a lord's son. . . ." But the other seemed to doubt his own prejudice. "How could a lordling care for the fate of common men!"

"Assuredly thou'lt not believe he wastes his soldiers' lives?"

"And wherefore should I not?"

"Because he is a most excellent general, if for no reason other!" the first cried, exasperated. "He'll not send us to our

deaths unheeding; he is too good a soldier! For how shall he
win a battle if he has too small an army?''

His mate looked thoughtful.

"He'll husband us as charily as any merchant spends his
gold." The first soldier leaned back against a hillock. "Nay,
he'll not send us 'gainst the foe if he doth not believe that most
of us will live, and triumph.''

The other soldier smiled. "Mayhap thou hast the truth of
it—for what is a general that hath no army?''

Rod didn't wait for the answer; he wandered on, amazed by
Tuan's men. They weren't particularly worried about the Evil
Eye. Dinner, yes; being sent against the beastmen with the
odds against them, yes; but, magic? No. Not if Tuan waited
till he had the proper counterspell. "Put the average Terran in
here," he muttered, "put him against an Evil Eye that really
works, and he'd run so fast you wouldn't see his tracks. But
the way these guys take it, you'd think it was nothing but a
new kind of crossbow.''

"It is little more, to them," Fess's voice murmured behind
his ear. He stood atop the cliff, far above, watching Rod walk
through the camp. "They have grown up with magic, Rod—as
did their fathers, and their grandfathers, and their ancestors
—for twenty-five generations. The phenomena do not frighten
them—only the possibility that the enemy's magic might prove
stronger.''

"True." Rod pursed his lips, nodding. Looking up, he saw
Brother Chillde winding a bandage around an older soldier's
head. The man winced, but bore the pain philosophically. Rod
noticed several other scars; no doubt the man was used to the
process. Rod stepped up to the monk. "You're all over the
field, good friar.''

Brother Chillde smiled up at him. "I do what I may, Lord
Warlock." His smile didn't have quite the same glow it had
had earlier.

"And a blessing it is for the men—but you're only human,
Brother. You need some rest yourself.''

The monk shrugged, irritated. "These poor souls do need
mine aid far more, milord. 'Twill be time enough for rest
when the wounded rest as easily as they may." He sighed and
straightened, eyeing the bandaged head. "I've eased the pass-
ing of those who had no hope, what little I could. 'Tis time to
think of the living." He looked up at Rod. "And to do what

we can to ensure that they remain alive.''

"Yes," Rod said slowly, "the King and I were thinking along the same lines."

"Indeed!" Brother Chillde perked up visibly. "I am certain thou dost ever do so—yet what manner of aiding dost thou have a-mind?"

The idea crystallized. "Witches—more of 'em. We managed to talk one of the older witches into joining us this time."

"Aye." Brother Chillde looked up at the hilltop. "And I did see that she and thy wife, alone, did hold off the beast-men's Evil Eye the whiles our soldiers did retreat. Indeed, I wrote it in my book whilst yet the battle raged."

Rod was sure he had—in fact, that's why he'd told the monk. He seemed to be the only medieval equivalent to a journalist available, there being no minstrels handy.

Brother Chillde turned back to Rod. "Thy wife must needs be exceeding powerful."

Rod nodded. "Makes for an interesting marriage."

Brother Chillde smiled, amused, and the old soldier chuckled. Then the monk raised an eyebrow. "And this venerable witch who did accompany her—she, too, must have powers extraordinary."

"She does," Rod said slowly. "Her name's 'Angry Agatha.' "

The old soldier's head snapped up. He stared; and two or three other soldiers nearby looked up too, then darted quick glances at each other. Fear shadowed their faces.

"She decided it's more fun to help people than to hurt them," Rod explained. "In fact, she's decided to stay with us."

Every soldier within hearing range began to grin.

" 'Tis wondrous!" Brother Chillde fairly glowed. "And dost thou seek more such ancient ones?"

Rod nodded. "A few more, hopefully. Every witch counts, Brother."

"Indeed it doth! Godspeed thine efforts!" the monk cried. And as Rod turned away, Brother Chillde began to bandage another damaged soldier, chattering, "Dost'a hear? The High Warlock doth seek to bring the ancient wizards and the hill-hags to aid us in our plight!"

Rod smiled to himself; just the effect he'd wanted! By evening, every soldier in the army would know that they were fighting fire with blazing enthusiasm—and that the witches were going out for reinforcements.

He stopped, struck by another thought. Turning, he looked back up the hillside. Tuan stood, silhouetted against a thundercloud, arms akimbo, surveying the devastation below him.

You shouldn't lie to your army. That'd just result in blasted morale—and, after a while, they'd refuse to fight, because they couldn't be sure what they'd be getting into, that you wouldn't be deliberately throwing their lives away.

Rod started back up the hill. He'd promised the rank and file more witch-power; he'd better convince Tuan.

Tuan's head lifted as Rod came up to the brow of the hill; he came out of his brown study. "An evil day, Rod Gallowglass. A most evil day."

"Very." Rod noticed the use of his name, not his title; the young King was really disturbed. He stepped up beside Tuan and gazed somberly down at the valley with him. "Nonetheless, it could have been worse."

Tuan just stared at him for a moment. Then, understanding, relaxed his face; he closed his eyes and nodded. "I' truth, it could have. Had it not been for thy rallying of the troops . . . and thy wife, and Angry Agatha . . . i' truth, all the witches . . ."

"And warlocks," Rod reminded. "Don't forget the warlocks."

Tuan frowned. "I trust I will not."

"Good. Then you won't mind seeking out some more of them."

"Nay, I surely will not," Tuan said slowly. "Yet where wilt thou discover them?"

Rod sighed and shook his head. "The ladies had the right idea, Tuan. We should've gone out recruiting."

Tuan's mouth twisted. "What young witch or warlock will join us now, with this crazed preacher raising the whole of the land against them?"

"Not too many," Rod admitted. "That's why I've realized Gwen had the right idea."

Tuan's frown deepened in puzzlement. "Of what dost thou speak?"

"The old ones, my liege—starting with Galen."

For the first time since Rod had known him, he saw fear at the back of Tuan's eyes. "Rod Gallowglass—dost thou know whereof thou dost speak?"

"Yeah—a *grown* wizard." Rod frowned. "What's so bad

about that? Don't we *want* a little more mystical muscle on our side?"

"Aye—if he's on our side i' truth!"

"He will not be," croaked Agatha from a boulder twenty feet away. "He doth care for naught but himself."

"Maybe." Rod shrugged, irritated. "But we've got to try, don't we?"

"My lord," Gwen said softly, "I ha' told thee aforetime, 'tis the lightning that lends them their strength—and not even old Galen can fight 'gainst a thunderbolt."

Rod turned slowly toward her, a strange glint coming into his eye. "That's right, you did mention that, didn't you?"

Gwen nodded. "We did free our soldiers from the Evil Eye—but the lightning flared, and the witches lay unconscious. 'Twas then the soldiers froze, and the beastmen mowed them like hay in summer."

"Lightning," Rod mused.

He turned away, slamming his fist into his palm. "That's the key, isn't it? The lightning. But how? Why? The answer's there somewhere, if only I could find it and FESSten to it."

"Here, Rod," his mentor murmured.

"Why would the Evil Eye be stronger right after a lightning flash?" Rod seemed to ask of no one in particular.

The robot hesitated a half-second, then answered. "Directly prior to a lightning flash, the resistance of the path the bolt will follow lowers tremendously, due to ionization, thus forming a sort of conductor between the lithosphere and the ionosphere."

Rod frowned. "So?"

Tuan frowned, too. "What dost thou, Lord Warlock?"

"Just talking to myself," Rod said quickly. "A dialogue with my alter ego, you might say."

Fess disregarded the interruption. "The ionosphere is also capable of functioning as a conductor, though the current passed would have to be controlled with great precision."

Rod's lips formed a silent O.

Gwen sat back with a sigh. She had long ago acquired the wifely virtue of patience with her husband's eccentricities. He would've been patient with hers as well, if he could find any (he didn't think of esper powers as eccentric).

Fess plowed on. "The ionosphere is thus capable of functioning as a conductor between any two points on earth —though it would tend toward broadcast; to avoid loss of power some means of beaming would need to be developed. There are several possibilities for such limiting. Signals may thus travel via the ionosphere rather than by the more primitive method of . . ."

"Power, too," Rod muttered. "Not just signals. Power."

Gwen looked up, startled and suddenly fearful.

"Precisely, Rod," the robot agreed, "though I doubt that more than a few watts would prove feasible."

Rod shrugged. "I suspect psi powers work in milliwatts anyway."

Tuan frowned. "Milling what?"

"That's right. You wouldn't need much for a psionic blast."

Tuan eyed him warily. "Rod Gallowglass . . ."

"All that would be needed," said Fess, "is a means of conducting the power to ground level."

"Which is conveniently provided by the ionization of the air just before the lightning bolt, yes! But how do you feed the current *into* the ionosphere?"

Tuan glanced at Gwen; they both looked apprehensive.

Old Agatha grated, "What incantation's this?"

"That," said Fess virtuously, "is *their* problem, not ours."

Rod snorted. "I thought you were supposed to be logical!"

Tuan's head came up in indignation. "Lord Warlock, be mindful to whom you speak!"

"Huh?" Rod looked up. "Oh, not you, Your Majesty. I was, uh . . . talking to my, uh, familiar."

Tuan's jaw made a valiant attempt to fraternize with his toes. Rod could, at that moment, have read a gigantic increase in his reputation as a warlock in the diameters of Tuan's eyes.

"So." Rod touched his pursed lips to his steepled fingertips. "Somebody overseas lends the beastmen a huge surge of psionic power—in electrical form, of course; we're assuming psionics are basically electromagnetic. The beastmen channel the power into their own projective telepathy, throw it into the soldier's minds—somehow, eye contact seems to be necessary there . . ."

"Probably a means of focusing power. Unsophisticated minds would probably need such a mental crutch, Rod," Fess conjectured.

"And from the soldiers' minds, it flows into the witches', immediately knocking out anyone who's tuned in! Only temporarily, thank Heaven."

"An adequate statement of the situation, Rod."

"The only question now is: Who's on the other end of the cable?"

"Although there is insufficient evidence," mused the robot, "that which is available would seem to indicate more beast-men as donors."

"Maybe, maybe." Rod frowned. "But somehow this just doesn't seem like straight ESP. . . . Oh, well, let it pass for the moment. The big question is not where it comes from, but how we fight it."

Tuan shrugged. "Thou hast said it, Lord Warlock—that we must seek out every witch and wizard who can be persuaded to join us."

"We tried that, remember?" But Rod smiled, a light kindling in his eyes. "Now that we've got some idea about how the Evil Eye gains so much power so suddenly, we should be able to make better use of the available witch-power."

The phrase caught Tuan's military attention. A very thoughtful look came over his face. "Certes . . ." He began to smile himself. "We must attack."

"What!?"

"Aye, aye!" Tuan grinned. "Be not concerned, Lord Warlock—I have not gone brain-sick. Yet, consider—till now, it has not been our choice whether to attack or not. Our enemy came in ships; we could only stand and wait the whiles they chose both time and place. Now, though, the place is fixed —by their earthworks." He nodded contemptuously toward the riverbank below. "We do not now seek a single long ship in the midst of a watery desert—we have a camp of a thousand men laid out before us! We can attack when we will!"

"Yeah, and get chopped to pieces!"

"I think not." Tuan grinned with suppressed glee. "Not if we fight only when the sky is clear."

A slow smile spread over Rod's face.

Tuan nodded. "We will make fray whilst the sun shines."

"You must admit that the idea has merit, Rod," Fess said thoughtfully. "Why not attempt it full-scale, immediately?"

"Well, for one thing, those earthworks *are* a major barrier." Rod sat astride the great black robot-horse on top of the cliffs in the moonlight. "And for another, well . . . we're *pretty* sure it'll work, Fess, but . . ."

"You do not wish to endanger your whole army. Sensible, I

must admit. Still, logic indicates that . . ."

"Yes, but Finagle's Law indicates caution," Rod interrupted. "If we made a full-scale frontal attack by day, we'd *probably* win—but we'd lose an awful lot of men. We *might* be defeated —and Tuan only bets on a sure thing, if he has a choice."

"I gather he is not the only one who favors caution. Allow me to congratulate you, Rod, on another step towards maturity."

"Great thanks," Rod growled. "A few more compliments like that, and I can hold a funeral for my self-image. How old do I have to be before you'll count me grown-up—an even hundred?"

"Maturity is mental and emotional, Rod, not chronological. Still, would it seem more pleasant if I were to tell you that you are still young at heart?"

"Well, when you put it *that* way . . ."

"Then, I will," the robot murmured. "And to do you justice, Rod, you have never been a reckless commander."

"Well . . . thanks." Rod was considerably mollified. "Anyway, that's why we're just gonna try a raid first. We'll hit 'em under a clear sky where they're weak."

A dark shadow moved up beside them, about even with Rod's stirrup. "The moon will set in an hour's time, Rod Gallowglass."

"Thanks, Your Elfin Majesty." Rod looked down at Brom. "Any particular point in the earthworks that's weaker than the others?"

"Nay. Yet should we spring up the riverbanks to attack them, then would they fall back amazed and confused, and elves might hap upon them and trip them in flight."

Rod grinned. "While our men relieve their camp of everything portable, eh? Not such a bad idea."

"I shall be amused," Brom rumbled.

"*You* shall? *They'll* just die laughing."

The moon set, and Tuan gave the signal. A picked band of soldiers (all former foresters) clambered into the small boats Rod had hurriedly requisitioned from the local fishermen and rowed toward the beastmen's camp with feathered oars.

But the advance party was already at work.

The sky was clear, the stars drifted across the hours; but there was no moon this night. The Neanderthal camp lay deep in gloom.

There are superstitions holding that the dark of the moon is a time conducive to magical, and not always pleasant, events. They are justified.

Watchfires dotted the plain locked within the semicircle of cliffs. Groups of beastmen huddled around the fires while sentries paced the shore. In the center of the camp, a large long hut announced the location of the chiefs.

The beastmen were to remember this night for a long time, wishing they could forget. Looking back, they would decide the defeat itself wasn't all that bad; after all, they fought manfully and well, and lost with honor.

It was the prelude to the battle that would prove embarrassing. . . .

While one of the small groups gathered around one of the fires were companionably swiping gripes as soldiers always have, a diminutive shadow crept unseen between two of them, crawled to the fire, and threw something in. Then it retreated, fast.

The beastmen went on grumbling for a few minutes; then one stopped abruptly and sniffed. "Dosta scent summat strange?" he growled.

The beastman next to him sniffed—and gagged—gripping his belly.

The smell reached the rest of the group very quickly, and quite generously. They scrambled for anywhere, as long as it was away, gagging and retching.

Closer to the center of the camp, a dark spherical object hurtled through the air to land and break open in the center of another group of beastmen. With an angry humming sound, tiny black flecks filled the air. The beastmen leaped up and ran howling and swatting about them with more motivation than effect. Little red dots appeared on their skins.

At another group, a series of short, violent explosions from the fire sent the beastmen jumping back in alarm.

At still another fire, a beastman raised his mug to his lips, tilted his head back, and noticed that no beer flowed into his mouth. He scowled and peered into the mug.

He dropped it with an oath as it landed on his toe, and jumped back with notable speed, holding one foot and hopping on the other as a small human figure scampered out of the mug with a high-pitched, mocking laugh.

The elf howled in high glee and scampered on through the camp.

Another beastman swung after him, mouthing horrible oaths as his huge club drove down.

A small hand swung out of the shadows and clipped through his belt with a very sharp knife.

The loincloth, loosened, wobbled a little.

In another two bounds, it had decidedly slipped.

The elf scampered on through the camp, chuckling, and a whole squad of beastmen fell in after him, bellowing, clubs slamming the ground where the elf had just been.

A small figure darted between them and the fugitive, strewing something from a pouch at its side.

The Neanderthals lunged forward, stepped down hard, and jumped high, screaming and frantically jerking leprechaun shoe-tacks out of their soles.

The fleeing elf, looking over his shoulder to laugh, ran smack into the ankles of a tall, well-muscled Neanderthal—a captain who growled, swinging his club up for the death-blow.

A leprechaun popped up near his foot and slammed him a wicked one on the third toe.

The captain howled, letting go of his club (which swung on up into the air, turning end over end) as he grabbed his hurt foot, hopping about.

He hopped up, and the club fell down and the twain met with a very solid and satisfying thunk.

As he went down, the fleeing elf—Puck—scampered away chortling.

He skipped into a tent, shouting, "Help! Help! Spies, traitors, spies!"

Three beastmen dashed in from the nearest campfire, clubs upraised and suspicions lowered, as the tent's occupants swung at Puck and missed him. Outside, a score of elves with small hatchets cut through the tent ropes.

The poles swayed and collapsed as the tent fabric enfolded its occupants tenderly. The beastmen howled and struck at the fabric, and connected with one another.

Chuckling, Puck slipped out from under the edge of the tent. Within twenty feet, he had another horde of beastmen howling after him.

But the beastmen went sprawling, as their feet shot out from under them, flailing their arms in a losing attempt at keeping their balances—which isn't easy when you're running on marbles. They scrambled back to their feet somehow, still on precarious balance, whirling about, flailing their arms, and in a moment it was a free-for-all.

Meanwhile, the captain slowly sat up, holding his ringing head in his hands.

An elf leaned over the top of the tent and shook something down on him.

He scrambled up howling, slapping at the specks crawling over his body—red ants can be awfully annoying—executed a beautiful double-quick goose step to the nearest branch of the river and plunged in over his head.

Down below, a water sprite coaxed a snapping turtle, and the snapper's jaws slammed into the captain's already swollen third toe.

He climbed out of the water more mud than man, and stood up bellowing.

He flung up his arms, shouting, and opened his mouth wide for the hugest bellow he could manage, and with a *splock,* one large tomato, appropriately overripe, slammed into his mouth.

Not that it made any difference, really; his orders weren't having too much effect anyway, since his men were busily clubbing at one another and shouting something about demons. . . .

Then the marines landed.

The rowboats shot in to grate on the pebbles, and black-cloaked soldiers, their faces darkened with ashes, leaped out of the boats, silent in the din. Only their sword-blades gleamed. For a few minutes. Then they were red.

An hour later, Rod stood on the hilltop, gazing down. Below him, moaning and wailing rose from the beastmen's camp. The monk sat beside him, his face solemn. "I know they are the foe, Lord Gallowglass—but I do not find these groans of pain to be cause for rejoicing."

"Our soldiers think otherwise." Rod nodded back toward the camp and the sounds of low-keyed rejoicing. "I wouldn't say they're exactly jubilant—but a score of dead beastmen has done wonders for morale."

Brother Chillde looked up. "They could not use their Evil Eye, could they?"

Rod shook his head. "By the time our men landed, they didn't even know where the enemy was, much less his eyes. We charged in; each soldier stabbed two beastmen; and we ran out." He spread his hands. "That's it. Twenty dead Neanderthals—and their camp's in chaos. We still couldn't storm in

there and take that camp, mind you—not behind those earthworks, not with a full army. And you may be very sure they
won't come out unless it's raining. But we've proved they're
vulnerable." He nodded toward the camp again. "That's
what they're celebrating back there. They know they can
win."

"And the beastmen know they can be beaten." Brother
Chillde nodded. " 'Tis a vast transformation, Lord Warlock."

"Yes." Rod glowered down at the camp. "Nasty. But
vast."

"Okay." Rod propped his feet up on a camp stool and took
a gulp from a flagon of ale. Then he wiped his mouth and
looked up at Gwen and Agatha. "I'm braced. Tell me how
you think it worked."

They sat inside a large tent next to Tuan's, the nucleus of a
village that grew every hour around the King's Army.

"We've got them bottled up for the moment," Rod went
on, "though it's just a bluff. Our raids are keeping them
scared to come out because of our 'magic'—but as soon as
they realize we can't fight the Evil Eye past the first thunderclap, they'll come boiling out like hailstones."

The tassels fringing the tent doorway stirred. Rod noted it
absently; a breeze would be welcome—it was going to be a
hot, muggy day.

"We must needs have more witches," Gwen said firmly.

Rod stared at her, appalled. "Don't tell me you're going to
go recruiting among the hill-hags again! Uh—present company excepted, of course."

"Certes." Agatha glared. The standing cup at her elbow
rocked gently. Rod glanced at it, frowning; surely the breeze
wasn't *that* strong. In fact, he couldn't even feel it. . . .

Then his gaze snapped back to Agatha's face. "Must
what?"

"Persuade that foul ancient, Galen, to join his force here
with ours," Agatha snapped. "Dost thou not hearken? For,
an thou dost not, why do I speak?"

"To come up with any idea that crosses your mind, no matter how asinine." Rod gave her his most charming smile. "It's
called 'brainstorming.' "

"Indeed, a storm must ha' struck thy brain, if thou canst
not see the truth of what I say!"

The bowl of fruit on the table rocked. He frowned at it, tensing. Maybe a small earthquake coming . . .?

He pulled his thoughts together and turned back to Agatha. "I'll admit we really need Galen. But how're you going to persuade him to join us?"

"There must needs be a way." Gwen frowned, pursing her lips.

An apple shot out of the bowl into the air. Rod rocked back in his chair, almost overturning it. "Hey!" Then he slammed the chair forward, sitting upright, frowning at Gwen, hurt. "Come on, dear! We're talking serious business!"

But Gwen was staring at the apple hanging in the air; an orange jumped up to join it. "My lord, I did not . . ."

"Oh." Rod turned an exasperated glare on Agatha. "I might have known. This's all just a joke to you, isn't it?"

Her head pulled back, offended. "What dost thou mean to say, Lord Warlock?"

A pear shot out of the bowl to join the apple and the orange. They began to revolve, up and around, in an intricate pattern.

Rod glanced up at them, his mouth tightening, then back to Agatha. "All right, all right! So we know you can juggle—the hard way, no hands! Now get your mind back to the problem, okay?"

"I?" Agatha glanced at the spinning fruits, then back to Rod. "Surely thou dost not believe 'tis *my* doing!"

Rod just stared at her.

Then he said carefully, "But Gwen said *she* wasn't doing it—and she wouldn't lie, would she?"

Agatha turned her head away, disgusted, and ended looking at Gwen. "How canst thou bear to live with one so slow to see?"

"Hey, now!" Rod frowned. "Can we keep the insults down to a minimum, here? What am I supposed to be seeing?"

"That if I have not done it, and she hath not done it, then there must needs be another who *doth* do it," Agatha explained.

"Another?" Rod stared up at the fruit, his eyes widening as he understood. He felt his hackles trying to rise. "You mean . . ."

"My son." Agatha nodded. "Mine unborn son." She waved a hand toward the spinning fruits. "He must needs fill the idle hour. Dost'a not know that young folk have not great patience? Yet is he good-hearted withal, and will not wreak any true troubles. Dismiss him from thy mind and care. We spake, just now, of the wizard Galen . . ."

"Uh . . . yeah." Rod turned back to the two ladies, trying very hard to ignore the fruit bobbing above him. "Galen. Right. Well, as I see it, he's a true isolate, a real, bona fide, died-in-the-haircloth hermit. Personally, I can't think of a single thing that could persuade him to join us."

"I fear thou mayest have the truth of it," Gwen sighed. "Certes, I would not say that he is amenable."

Air popped and a baby was sitting in her lap, clapping his hands. "Momma, Momma! Pa'y cake! Pa'y cake!"

Gwen stiffened, startled. Then a delighted smile spread over her face. "My bonny babe!" Her arms closed around Magnus and squeezed.

Rod threw up his hands and turned away. "Why bother trying? Forget the work! C'mere, son—let's play catch."

The baby chortled with glee and bounced out of Gwen's lap, sailing over to Rod. He caught the boy and tossed him back to Gwen.

"Nay, husband." She caught Magnus and lowered him to the ground, suddenly becoming prim. " 'Tis even as thou sayest—we have matters of great moment in train here. Back to thine elf-nurse, child."

Magnus thrust out his lip in a pout. "Wanna stay!"

Rod bent a stern glance on his son. "Can you be quiet?"

The baby nodded gleefully.

Gwen gave an exasperated sigh and turned away. "Husband, thou wilt have him believing he can obtain aught he doth wish!"

"But just one bit of noise, mind you!" Rod leveled a forefinger at the baby. "You get in the way just one little bit, and home you go!"

The baby positively glowed. He bobbed his head like a bouncing ball.

"Okay—go play." Rod leaned back in his chair again. "Now. Assuming Galen can't be persuaded—what do we do?"

Agatha shrugged. "Nay, if he will not be persuaded, I can not see that we can do aught."

"Just the words of encouragement I needed," Rod growled. "Let's try another tack. Other veterans. Any other magical hermits hiding out in the forests?"

"Magnus, thou didst promise," Gwen warned.

Agatha frowned, looking up at the tent roof. "Mayhap old Elida . . . She is bitter but, I think, hath a good heart withal. And old Anselm . . ." She dropped her eyes to Rod, shaking her head. "Nay, in him 'tis not bitterness alone that doth work, but fear also. There is, perhaps, old Elida, Lord Warlock—but I think . . ."

"Magnus," Gwen warned.

Rod glanced over at his son, frowning. The baby ignored Gwen and went on happily with what he had been doing—juggling. But it was a very odd sort of juggling; he was tossing the balls about five feet in front of him, and they were bouncing back like boomerangs.

Rod turned to Gwen. "What's he doing?"

"Fire and fury!" Agatha exploded. "Wilt thou not leave the bairn to his play? He doth not intrude; he maketh no coil, nor doth he cry out! He doth but play at toss-and-catch with my son Harold, and is quiet withal! He maketh no bother; leave the poor child be!"

Rod swung about, staring at her. "He's doing *what*?"

"Playing toss-and-catch," Agatha frowned. "There's naught so strange in that."

"But," Gwen said in a tiny voice, "his playmate cannot be seen."

"Not by us," Rod said slowly. "But, apparently, Magnus sees him very well indeed."

Agatha's brows knitted. "What dost thou mean?"

"How else would he know where to throw the ball?" Rod turned to Agatha, his eyes narrowing. "Can *you* see your son Harold?"

"Nay, I cannot. Yet what else would return the apples to the child?"

"I was kinda wonderin' about that." Rod's gaze returned to his son. "But I thought you said Harold was an unborn spirit."

"Summat of the sort, aye."

"Then, how can Magnus see him?" Gwen lifted her head, her eyes widening.

"I did not say he had not been born," Agatha hedged. She stared at the bouncing fruit, her gaze sharpening. "Yet I ha' ne'er been able to see my son aforetimes."

"Then, how come Magnus can?" Rod frowned.

"Why, 'tis plainly seen! Thy son is clearly gifted with more magical powers than am I myself!''

Rod locked gazes with Gwen. Agatha was the most powerful old witch in Gramarye.

He turned back to Agatha. "Okay, so Magnus is one heck of a telepath. But he can't see a body if there's none there to see.''

"My son ha' told me that he did have a body aforetime," Agatha said slowly. " 'Twould seem that he doth send outward from himself his memory of his body's appearance.''

"A projective telepath," Rod said slowly. "Not a very strong one, maybe, but a projective. Also apparently a telekenetic. But I thought that was a sex-linked trait. . . .''

Agatha shrugged. "Who can tell what the spirit may do when it's far from its body?''

"Yes—his body," Rod said softly, eyes locked on the point where the fruit bounced back toward Magnus. "Just where *is* this body he remembers?''

Agatha sighed and leaned back in her chair, closing her eyes and resting her head against the high back. "Thou dost trouble me, Lord Warlock; for I cannot understand these matters that Harold doth speak of.''

"Well, maybe Gwen can." Rod turned to his wife. "Dear?''

But Gwen shook her head. "Nay, my lord. I cannot hear Harold's thoughts.''

Rod just stared at her.

Then he gave himself a shake and sat up straighter. "Odd." He turned back to Agatha. "Any idea why you should be able to hear him, when Gwen can't?''

"Why, because I am his mother.'' Agatha smiled sourly.

Rod gazed at her, wondering if there was something he didn't know. Finally, he decided to take the chance. "I didn't know you'd ever borne children.''

"Nay, I have not—though I did yearn for them.''

Rod gazed at her while his thoughts raced, trying to figure out how she could be barren and still bear a son. He began to build an hypothesis. "So," he said carefully, "how did you come by Harold?''

"I did not.'' Her eyes flashed. "He came to me. 'Tis even as he doth say—he is my son, and old Galen's.''

"But, Galen . . .''

"Aye, I know.'' Agatha's lips tightened in bitterness. "He is the son that Galen and I *ought* to have had, but did not, for reason that we ne'er have come close enough to even touch.''

"Well, I hate to say this—but . . . uh . . .'' Rod scratched behind his ear, looking at the floor. He forced his eyes up to meet Agatha's. "It's, uh, very difficult to conceive a baby if, uh, you never come within five feet of one another.''

"Is't truly!'' Agatha said with withering scorn. "Yet, e'en so, my son Harold doth say that Galen did meet me, court me, and wed me—and that, in time, I did bear him a son, which is Harold.''

"But that's impossible.''

"The depth of thy perception doth amaze me,'' Agatha said drily. "Yet Harold is here, and this is his tale. Nay, further—he doth say that Galen and I reared him, and were ever together, and much a-love.'' Her gaze drifted, eyes misting, and he could scarcely hear her murmur: "Even as I was used to dream, in the days of my youth . . .''

Rod held his silence. Behind him, Gwen watched, her eyes huge.

Eventually, Agatha's attention drifted back to them. She reared her head up to glare at Rod indignantly. "Canst thou truly say there is no sense to that? If his body has not been made as it should have been, canst thou be amazed to find his spirit here, uncloaked in flesh?''

"Well, yes, now that you mention it.'' Rod leaned back in his chair. "Because, if his body was never made—where did his spirit come from?''

"There I can thresh no sense from it,'' Agatha admitted. "Harold doth say that, when grown, he did go for a soldier. He fought, and bled, and came away, and this not once, but a score of times—and rose in rank to captain. Then, in his final battle, he did take a grievous wound, and could only creep away to shelter in a nearby cave. There he lay him down and fell into a swoon—and lies there yet, in a slumber like to death. His body lies like a waxen effigy—and his spirit did drift loose from it. Yet could it not begin that last adventure, to strive and toil its way to Heaven . . .'' She shuddered, squeezing her eyes shut. "And how he could be eager for such a quest is more than I can tell. Yet indeed he was''—she looked back up at Rod, frowning—"yet could he not; for though his body lay in a sleep like unto death, yet 'twas *not* death—no, not quite. Nor could the spirit wake that body neither.''

"A coma.'' Rod nodded. "But let it alone long enough, and

the body'll die from sheer starvation.''

Agatha shrugged impatiently. "He's too impatient. Nay, he would not wait; his spirit did spring out into the void, and wandered eons in a place of chaos—until it found me here." She shook her head in confusion. "I do not understand how aught of that may be."

"A void . . ." Rod nodded his head slowly.

Agatha's head lifted. "The phrase holds meaning for thee?"

"It kind of reminds me of something I heard of in a poem—'the wind that blows between the worlds.' I always did picture it as a realm of chaos. . . ."

Agatha nodded judiciously. "That hath the ring of rightness to it. . . ."

"That means he came from another universe."

Agatha's head snapped up, her nostrils flaring. "Another universe? What tale of cock-and-bull is this, Lord Warlock? There is only this world of ours, with sun and moons and stars. *That* is the universe. How could there be another?"

But Rod shook his head. " 'How' is beyond my knowledge —but the, uh, 'wise men' of my, uh, homeland, seem to pretty much agree that there *could* be other universes. Anyway, they can't prove there aren't. In fact, they say there may be an infinity of other universes—and if there are, then there must also be universes that are almost exactly like ours, even to the point of having—well—another Agatha, and another Galen. Exactly like yourselves. But their lives took—well, a different course."

"Indeed they did." Agatha's eyes glowed.

"But, if Harold's spirit went looking for help—why didn't it find the Agatha in that other universe?"

"Because she lay dead." Agatha's gaze bored into Rod's eyes. "She had died untimely, of a fever. So had her husband. Therefore did Harold seek out through the void, and was filled with joy when he did find me—though at first he was afeard that I might be a ghost."

Rod nodded slowly. "It makes sense. He was looking for help, and he recognized a thought-pattern that he'd known in his childhood. Of course he'd home in on you. . . . Y'know, that almost makes it all hang together."

"I' truth, it doth." Agatha began to smile. "I ne'er could comprehend this brew of thoughts that Harold tossed to me; yet what thou sayest doth find a place for each part of it, and fits it all together, like to the pieces of a puzzle." She began to nod. "Aye. I will believe it. Thou hast, at last, after a score of years, made sense of this for me." Suddenly, she frowned. "Yet his soul is here, not bound for Heaven, for reason that his body lies in sleeping death. How could it thus endure, after twenty years?"

Rod shook his head. "Hasn't been twenty years—not in the universe he came from. Time could move more slowly there than it does here. Also, the universes are probably curved—so, *where* on that curve he entered our universe could determine what time, what year, it was. More to the point, he could reenter his own universe just a few minutes after his body went into its coma."

But Agatha had bowed her head, eyes closed, and was waving in surrender. "Nay, Lord Warlock! Hold, I prithee! I cannot ken thine explanations! 'Twill satisfy me, that thou dost."

"Well, I can't be *sure*," Rod hedged. "Not about the why of it, at least. But I can see how it fits in with my hypothesis."

"What manner of spell is that?"

"Only a weak one, till it's proved. Then it becomes a theory, which is much more powerful indeed. But for Harold, the important point is that he needs to either kill his body, so he can try for Heaven—or cure it and get his spirit back into it."

"Cure it!" Agatha's glare could have turned a blue whale into a minnow. "Heal him or do naught! I would miss him sorely when his spirit's gone to its rightful place and time— but, I will own, it must be done. Still, I'd rather know that he's alive!"

"Well, I wasn't really considering the alternative." Rod gazed off into space, his lips pursed.

Agatha saw the look in his eyes and gave him a leery glance. "I mistrust thee, Lord Warlock, when thou dost look so fey."

"Oh, I'm just thinking of Harold's welfare. Uh, after the battle—a while after, when I was there and you'd recovered a bit—didn't I see you helping the wounded? You know, by holding their wounds shut and telling them to think hard and believe they were well?"

"Indeed she did." Gwen smiled. "Though 'tis somewhat more than that, husband. Thou must needs think at the wound thyself, the whiles the wounded one doth strive to believe himself well; for the separate bits of meat and fat must be welded back together—which thou canst do by making them move amongst one another with thy mind.''

"*You* can, maybe." Inwardly, Rod shuddered. All he needed was for his wife to come up with one more major power—all corollaries of telekinesis, of course; but the number of her variations on the theme was stupefying.

He turned back to Agatha. "Uh—did you think up this kind of healing yourself?"

"Aye. I am the only one, as far as I can tell—save thy wife, now that I've taught her." Agatha frowned, brooding. "I came to the knowing of it in despair, after I'd thrown aside a lad who sought to hurt me. . . ."

Rod had to cut off that kind of train of thought; the last thing he wanted was for Agatha to remember her hurts. "So. You can help someone 'think' themselves well—telekinesis on the cellular level."

Agatha shook her head, irritated. "I cannot tell thy meaning, with these weird terms of thine—'tele-kine'? What is that—a cow that ranges far?"

"Not quite, though I intend to milk it for all it's worth." Rod grinned. "Y'know, when we were at Galen's place, he told me a little about his current line of research."

Agatha snorted and turned away. " 'Researches?' Aye—he will ever seek to dignify his idle waste of hours by profound words."

"Maybe, but I think there might be something to it. He was trying to figure out how the brain itself, that lumpy blob of protoplasm, can create this magic thing called 'thought.' "

"Aye, I mind me an he mentioned some such nonsense," Agatha grated. "What of it?"

"Oh, nothing, really." Rod stood up, hooking his thumbs in his belt. "I was just thinking, maybe we oughta go pay him another visit."

The dark tower loomed before them, then suddenly tilted alarmingly to the side. Rod swallowed hard and held on for dear life; it was the first time he'd ever ridden pillion on a broomstick. "Uh, dear—would you try to swoop a little less sharply? I'm, uh, still trying to get used to this. . . ."

"Oh! Certes, my lord!" Gwen looked back over her shoulder, instantly contrite. "Be sure, I did not wish to afright thee."

"Well, I wouldn't exactly say I was *frightened* . . ."

"Wouldst thou not?" Gwen looked back at him again, wide-eyed in surprise.

"Watch where you're going!" Rod yelped.

Gwen turned her eyes back to the front as her broomstick drifted sideways to avoid a treetop. "Milord," she chided, "I knew it was there."

"I'm glad somebody did," Rod sighed. "I'm beginning to think I should've gone horseback after all—even though it would've been slower."

"Courage, now." Gwen's voice oozed sympathy. "We must circle this Dark Tower."

Rod took a deep breath and squeezed the shaft.

The broomstick began to swing around the tower, following Agatha's swoop ahead of them. Rod's stomach lurched once before he forgot it, staring in amazement at the Tower. They were sixty feet up, but it soared above them, a hundred feet high and thirty wide, the top corrugated in battlements. Altogether, it was an awesome mass of funereal basalt. Here and there, arrow-slits pierced the stones—windows three feet high, but only one foot wide.

"I wouldn't like to see his candle bill," Rod grunted. "How do you get *in*?"

The whole bottom half of the Dark Tower reared unbroken and impregnable, pierced by not so much as a single loophole.

"There *has* to be a door."

"Wherefore?" Gwen countered. "Thou dost forget that warlocks do fly."

"Oh." Rod frowned. "Yeah, I did kinda forget that, didn't I? Still, I don't see how he gets in; those loopholes are mighty skinny."

"Yonder." Gwen nodded toward the top of the Tower, and her broomstick reared up.

Rod gasped and clung for dear life. "He *would* have to have a heliport!"

Agatha circled down over the battlements and brought her broomstick to a stop in the center of the roof. She hopped off nimbly; Gwen followed suit. Rod disentangled himself from the broom straws and planted his feet wide apart on the roof, grabbing the nearest merlon to steady himself while he waited for the floor to stop tilting.

"Surely, 'twas not so horrible as that." Gwen tried to hide a smile of amusement.

"I'll get used to it," Rod growled. Privately, he planned not to have the chance to. "Now." He took a deep breath, screwed up his courage, and stepped forward. The stones seemed to tilt only slightly, so he squared his shoulders, took a deep breath, and took another step. "Okay. Where's the door?"

"Yonder." Agatha pointed.

Right next to a merlon and its crenel, a trapdoor was set flush with the roof. Rod stepped over to it—carefully—and frowned down, scanning the rough planks. "I don't see a doorknob."

"Why would there be one?" Agatha said beside him. "Who would come up here, other than the ancient cockerel himself? And when he doth, I doubt not he doth ope' this panel from below."

"And just leaves it open? What does he do about rain?"

Agatha shook her head. "I misdoubt me an he would come up during foul weather."

"True," Rod said judiciously. "He probably only comes up to stargaze—so why bother, when there aren't any stars?"

He drew his dagger and dropped to one knee. "Gotta be careful about this—it's good steel, but it *could* break." He jabbed the tip into the wood and heaved up. The trap rose an inch; he kicked his toe against it to hold it, pulled the dagger out, and dropped it, then caught the wood with his fingertips and heaved again—with a whine of pain; the maneuver certainly didn't do his manicure any good. But he hauled it up enough to get his boot-toe under, then caught it with his fingers properly and swung it open. "Whew! So much for basic breaking-and-entering!"

"Well done!" Agatha said, mildly surprised.

"Not exactly what I'd call a major effort." Rod dusted off his hands.

"Nor needful," the old witch reminded him. "Either thy wife or myself could ha' made it rise of its own."

"Oh." Rod began to realize that, with very little persuasion, he could learn to hate this old biddy. In an attempt to be tactful, he changed the subject. "Y'know, in a culture where so many people can fly, you'd think he'd've thought to use a lock."

At his side, Gwen shook her head. "Few of the witchfolk would even dare to come here, my lord. Such is his reputation."

That definitely was not the kind of line to inspire confidence in a hopeful burglar. Rod took a deep breath, stiffened his muscles to contain a certain fluttering in the pit of his stomach, and started down the stairs. "Yes. Well—I suppose we really should have knocked . . ." But his head was already below the level of the roof.

The stairs turned sharply and became very dark. Rod halted; Agatha bumped into his back. "Mmmmf! Wilt thou not give warning when thou'rt about to halt thy progress, Lord Warlock?"

"I'll try to remember next time. Darling, would you mind? It's a little dark down here."

"Aye, my lord." A ball of luminescence glowed to life on Gwen's palm. She brushed past him—definitely too quickly for his liking—and took up the lead, her will-o'-the-wisp lighting the stairway.

At the bottom, dark fabric barred their way—curtains overlapping to close out drafts. They pushed through and found themselves in a circular chamber lit by two arrow-slits. Gwen extinguished her fox fire, which darkened the chamber; outside, the sky was overcast, and only gray light alleviated the gloom. But it was enough to show them the circular worktable that ran all the way around the circumference of the room, and the tall shelf-cases that lined the walls behind the tables. The shelves were crammed with jars and boxes exuding a mixture of scents ranging from spicy to sour; and the tables were crowded with alembics, crucibles, mortars with pestles, and beakers.

Agatha wrinkled her nose in distaste. "Alchemy!"

Rod nodded in slow approval. "Looks as though the old geezer has a little more intellectual integrity than I gave him credit for."

"Thou canst not mean thou dost condone the Black Arts!" Agatha cried.

"No, and neither does Galen, apparently. He's not satisfied with knowing that something works—he wants to know why, too."

"Is't not enough to say that devils do it?"

Rod's mouth tightened in disgust. "That's avoiding the question, not answering it."

Glass tinkled behind him. He spun about.

A jar floated above an alembic, pouring a thin stream of

greenish liquid into it. As Rod watched, the cover sank back onto the jar and tightened in a half-turn as the jar righted itself, then drifted back up onto a shelf.

"Harold!" Agatha warned. "Let be; these stuffs are not thine."

"Uh, let's not be too hasty." Rod watched a box float off another shelf. Its top lifted, and a stream of silvery powder sifted into the alembic. "Let the kid experiment. The urge to learn should never be stifled."

" 'Tis thou who shouldst be stifled!" Agatha glowered at Rod. "No doubt Harold's meddling doth serve some plan of thine."

"Could be, could be." Rod watched an alcohol lamp glow to life under the alembic. "Knocking probably wouldn't have done much good anyway, really. Galen strikes me as the type to be so absorbed in his research that . . ."

"My lord." Gwen hooked fingers around his forearm. "I mislike the fashion in which that brew doth bubble."

"Nothing to be worried about, I'm sure." But Ron glanced nervously at some test tubes on another table, which had begun to dance, pouring another greenish liquid back and forth from one to another. They finally settled down, but . . .

"That vial, too, doth bubble," Agatha growled. "Ho, son of mine! What dost thou?"

Behind them, glass clinked again. They whirled about to see a retort sliding its nose into a glass coil. Flame ignited under the retort, and water began to drip from a hole in a bucket suspended over the bench, spattering on the glass coil.

"My lord," Gwen said nervously, "that brew doth bubble most marvelously now. Art thou certain that Harold doth know his own deeds?"

Rod was sure Harold knew what he was doing, all right. In fact, he was even sure that Harold was a lot more sophisticated, and a lot more devious, than Rod had given him credit for. And suspense was an integral part of the maneuver, pushing it close to the line. . . .

But not this close! He leaped toward the alembic. Gasses being produced in the presence of open flame bothered him.

"What dost thou?"

The words boomed through the chamber, and Galen towered in the doorway, blue robe, white beard, and red face. He took in the situation at a glance, then darted to the alembic to dampen the fire, dashed to seize the test tube and throw it into a tub of water, then leaped to douse the lamp under the retort.

"Thou dost move most spryly," Agatha crooned, "for a dotard."

The wizard turned to glare at her, leaning against the table, trembling. His voice shook with anger. "Vile crone! Art so envious of my labors that thou must needs seek to destroy my Tower?"

"Assuredly, 'twas naught so desperate as that," Gwen protested.

Galen turned a red glower on her. "Nay, she hath not so much knowledge as that—though her mischief could have laid this room waste, and the years of glassblowing and investigating that it doth contain!" His eyes narrowed as they returned to Agatha. "I do see that ne'er should I ha' given thee succor—for now thou'lt spare me not one moment's peace!"

Agatha started a retort of her own, but Rod got in ahead of her. "Uh, well—not really."

The wizard's glare swiveled toward him. "Thou dost know little of this haggard beldam, Lord Warlock, an thou dost think she could endure to leave one in peace."

Agatha took a breath, but Rod was faster again. "Well, y' see—it wasn't really her idea to come back here."

"Indeed?" The question fumed sarcasm. " 'Twas thy good wife's, I doubt me not."

"Wrong again," Rod said brightly. "It was mine. And Agatha had nothing to do with tinkering with your lab."

Galen was silent for a pace. Then his eyes narrowed. "I' truth, I should ha' seen that she doth lack even so much knowledge as to play so learned a vandal. Was it thou didst seek explosion, Lord Warlock? Why, then?"

" 'Cause I didn't think you'd pay any attention to a knock on the door," Rod explained, "except maybe to say, 'Go away.' "

Galen nodded slowly. "So, thou didst court disaster to bring me out from my researches long enough to bandy words with thee."

"That's the right motive," Rod agreed, "but the wrong culprit. Actually, not one single one of us laid a finger on your glassware."

Galen glanced quickly at the two witches. "Thou'lt not have

me believe they took such risks, doing such finely detailed work, with only their minds?''

"Not that they couldn't have," Rod hastened to point out. "I've seen my wife make grains of wheat dance." He smiled fondly, remembering the look on Magnus's face when Gwen did it. "And Agatha's admitted she's healed wounds by making the tiniest tissues flow back together—but this time neither of them did."

"Assuredly, not *thou* . . ."

" 'Twas thy son," Agatha grated.

The laboratory was silent as the old wizard stared into her eyes, the color draining from his face.

Then it flooded back, and he erupted. "What vile falsehood is this? What deception dost thou seek to work now, thou hag with no principle to thy name of repute? How dost thou seek to work on my heart with so blatant a lie? Depraved, evil witch! Thou hast no joy in life but the wreaking of others' misery! Fool I was, to ever look on thy face, greater fool to e'er seek to aid thee! Get thee gone, get thee hence!" His trembling arm reared up to cast a curse that would blast her. *"Get thee to . . ."*

"It's the truth," Rod snapped.

Galen stared at him for the space of a heartbeat.

It was long enough to get a word in. "He's the son of another Galen, and another Agatha, in another world just like this one. You know there are other universes, don't you?"

Galen's arm hung aloft, forgotten; excitement kindled in his eyes. "I had suspected it, aye—the whiles my body did lie like to wood, and my spirit lay open to every slightest impress. Distantly did I perceive it, dimly through chaos, a curving presence that . . . But nay, what nonsense is this! Dost thou seek to tell me that, in one such other universe, I do live again?''

" 'Again' might be stretching it," Rod hedged, "especially since your opposite number is dead now. But that a Galen, just like you, actually did live, yes—except he seems to have made a different choice when he was a youth.''

Galen said nothing, but his gaze strayed to Agatha.

She returned it, her face like flint.

"For there was an Agatha in that other universe, too," Rod said softly, "and they met, and married, and she bore a son.''

Galen still watched Agatha, his expression blank.

"They named the son Harold," Rod went on, "and he grew to be a fine young warlock—but more 'war' than 'lock.' Apparently, he enlisted, and fought in quite a few battles. He survived, but his parents passed away—probably from sheer worry, with a son in the infantry. . . ."

Galen snapped out of his trance. "Do not seek to cozen me, Master Warlock! How could they have died, when this Agatha and I . . ." His voice dwindled and his gaze drifted as he slid toward the new thought.

"Time is no ranker, Master Wizard; he's under no compulsion to march at the same pace in each place he invests. But more importantly, events can differ in different universes—or Harold would never have been born. And if the Galen and Agatha of his universe could marry, they could also die—from accident, or disease, or perhaps even one of those battles that their son survived. I'm sure he'd be willing to tell you, if you asked him."

Galen glanced quickly about the chamber, and seemed to solidify inside his own skin.

"Try," Rod breathed. "Gwen can't hear him, nor can any of the other witches—save Agatha. But if you're the analog of his father, you should be able to. . . ."

"Nay!" Galen boomed. "Am I become so credulous as to hearken to the tales of a stripling of thirty?"

"Thirty-two," Rod corrected.

"A child, scarcely more! I credit not a word of this tale of thine!"

"Ah, but we haven't come to the evidence yet." Rod grinned. "Because, you see, Harold didn't survive one of those battles."

Galen's face neutralized again.

"He was wounded, and badly," Rod pressed. "He barely managed to crawl into a cave and collapse there—and his spirit drifted loose. But his body didn't. No, it lay in a lasting, deathlike sleep; so his spirit had no living body to inhabit, but also had not been freed by death and couldn't soar to seek Heaven. But that spirit was a warlock, so it didn't have to just haunt the cave where its body lay. No, it went adventuring— out into the realm of chaos, seeking out that curving presence you spoke of, searching for its parents' spirits, seeking aid. . . ."

"And found them," Galen finished in a harsh whisper.

Rod nodded. "One, at least—and now he's found the other."

Galen's glances darted around the chamber again; he shuddered, shrinking more tightly into his robes. Slowly then, his frosty glare returned to Rod. "Thou hadst no need to speak of this to me, Lord Warlock. 'Twill yield thee no profit."

"Well, I did think Harold deserved a chance to at least try to meet you—as you became in this universe. Just in case."

Galen held his glare, refusing the bait.

"We have the beastmen bottled up, for the time being," Rod explained, "but they're likely to come charging out any minute, trying to freeze our soldiers with their Evil Eye. Our young warlocks and witches will try to counter it with their own power, feeding it through our soldiers. They wouldn't stand a chance against the beastmen's power by themselves—but they'll have my wife and Agatha to support them."

"Aye, and we're like to have our minds blasted for our pains," Agatha ground out, "for some monster that we wot not of doth send them greater power with each thunderbolt. Though we might stand against them and win, if thou wert beside us."

"And wherefore should I be?" Galen's voice was flat with contempt. "Wherefore should I aid the peasant folk who racked and tortured me in my youth? Wherefore ought I aid their children and grandchildren who, ever and anon all these long years, have marched against me, seeking to tear down my Dark Tower and burn me at the stake? Nay, thou softhearted fool! Go to thy death for the sake of those that hate thee, an thou wishest—but look not for me to accompany thee!"

"Nay, I do not!" Agatha's eyes glittered with contempt. "Yet, there's one who's man enough to do so, to bear up with me under that fell onslaught."

Galen stared at her, frozen.

"Harold's a dutiful son," Rod murmured. "I thought you might like the chance to get acquainted with him." He left the logical consequence unsaid. Could a spirit be destroyed? He hoped he wouldn't find out.

"I credit not one single syllable!" Galen hissed. " 'Tis but a scheme to cozen me into placing all at risk for them who like me not!" He turned back to Rod. "Thou dost amaze me, Lord Warlock; for even here, in my hermitage, I had heard thy repute and I had thought thee lord of greater intellect than this. Canst thou author no stronger scheme to gain mine aid, no subtle, devious chain of ruses?''

''Why bother?'' Rod answered with the ghost of a smile. ''The truth is always more persuasive.''

Galen's face darkened with anger. His arm lifted, forefinger upraised, to focus his powers for teleporting them away. Then, suddenly, his head snapped about, eyes wide in shock for a moment before they squeezed shut in denial.

Agatha winced too, but she grinned. ''Ah, then! That shout did pierce even thy strong shield!''

The wizard turned his glare to her. ''I know not what trickery thou hast garnered to thus simulate another's mind. . . .''

''Oh, aye, 'tis trickery indeed! Oh, I have studied for years to fashion the feel and texture of another's mind, and all for this moment!'' Agatha turned her head and spat. ''Lord Warlock, let us depart; for I sicken of striving to speak sense unto one who doth seek to deafen his own ears!''

''Aye, get thee hence,'' Galen intoned, ''for thy scheme hath failed! Get thee hence, and come not hither again!''

''Oh, all right!'' Rod shuddered at the thought of another broomstick ride. ''I was kinda hoping to catch the express. . . .''

''Thou wilt come to joy in it, husband,'' Gwen assured him, pushing past, ''if thou canst but have faith in me.''

''Faith?'' Rod bleated, wounded. ''I trust you implicitly!''

''Then thou'lt assuredly not fear, for 'tis my power that doth bear thee up.'' Gwen flashed him an insouciant smile.

''All right, all right!'' Rod held his hands up in surrender. ''You win—I'll get used to it. After you, beldam.''

Agatha hesitated a moment longer, trying to pierce Galen's impenetrable stare with her whetted glance, but turned away in disgust. ''Aye, let him remain here in dry rot, sin that he doth wish it!'' She stormed past Rod, through the curtains, and up the stair.

Rod glanced back just before dropping the curtain, to gaze at Galen, standing frozen in the middle of his laboratory, staring off into space, alone, imprisoned within his own invisible wall.

Rod clung to the broomstick for dear life, telling himself sternly that he was *not* scared, that staring at the gray clouds over Gwen's shoulder, hoping desperately for sight of Tuan's tent, was just the result of boredom. But it didn't work; his stomach didn't unclench, and the only object ahead was Agatha, bobbing on her broomstick.

Then, suddenly, there was a dot in the sky two points off Agatha's starboard bow. Rod stared, forgetting to be afraid. "Gwen—do you see what I see?"

"Aye, my lord. It doth wear a human aspect."

It did indeed. As the dot loomed closer, it grew into a teenage boy in doublet and hose, waving his cap frantically.

"Human," Rod agreed. "In fact, I think it's Leonatus. Isn't he a little young to be out teleporting alone?"

"He is sixteen now," Gwen reminded. "Their ages do not stand still for us, my lord."

"They don't stand for much of anything, now that you mention it—and I suppose he is old enough to be a messenger. See how close you can come, Gwen; I think he wants to talk."

Gwen swooped around the youth in a tight hairpin turn, considerably faster than Rod's stomach did. "Hail, Leonatus!" she cried—which was lucky, because Rod was swallowing heavily at the moment. "How dost thou?"

"Anxiously, fair Gwendylon," the teenager answered. "Stormclouds lower o'er the bank of the Fleuve, and the beastmen form their battle-line!"

"I knew there was something in the air!" Rod cried. *Ozone, probably.* "Go tell your comrades to hold the fort, Leonatus! We'll be there posthaste!" Especially since the post was currently air mail.

"Aye, my lord!" But the youth looked puzzled. "What is a 'fort'?"

"A strong place," Rod answered, "and the idea is to catch your enemy between it and a rock."

"An thou dost say it, Lord Warlock." Leonatus looked confused, but he said manfully, "I shall bear word to them," and disappeared with a small thunderclap.

Rod muttered, "Fess, we're coming in at full speed. Meet me at the cliff-top."

"I am tethered, Rod," the robot's voice reminded him.

Rod shrugged. "So stretch it tight. When you're at the end of your tether, snap it and join me."

They dropped down to land at the witches' tent, just as the first few drops of rain fell.

"How fare the young folk?" Agatha cried.

"Scared as hell," Rod called back. "Will they ever be glad

to see you!'' He jumped off the broomstick and caught up his
wife for a brief but very deep kiss.

"My lord!'' She blushed prettily. "I had scarcely expected . . .''

"Just needed a little reminder of what I've got to come
home to.'' Rod gave her a quick squeeze. "Good luck, darling.'' Then he whirled and pounded away through the drizzle.

He halted at the edge of the cliff-top by the river, staring
down. He was just in time to see the first wave of beastmen
spill over their earthworks and lope away up the river valley,
shields high and battle-axes swinging. Rod frowned, looking
around for the Gramarye army. Where was it?

There, just barely visible through the drizzle, was a dark,
churning mass, moving away upstream.

"Fess!''

"Here, Rod.''

Rod whirled—and saw the great black horsehead just two
feet behind him. He jumped back, startled—then remembered
the sheer drop behind him and skittered forward to slam foot
into stirrup and swing up onto the robot-horse's back.
"How'd *you* get here so fast?''

"I do have radar.'' Fess's tone was mild reproof. "Shall we
go, Rod? You are needed upstream.''

"Of course!'' And, as the great black horse sprang into a
canter, "What's going on?''

"Good tactics.'' The robot's tone was one of respect, even
admiration. He cantered down the slope, murmuring, "Perhaps Tuan should explain it to you himself.''

Rod scarcely had time to protest before they had caught up
with the army. Everything was roaring confusion—the clang-
ing clash of steel, the tramping squelch of boots in ground that
had already begun to turn to mud, the bawling of sergeants'
orders, and the whinnies of the knights' horses. Rod looked all
about him everywhere, but saw no sign of panic. Sure, here
and there the younger faces were filled with dread and the
older ones were locked in grim determination and the army as
a whole was moving steadily away from the beastmen—but it
was definitely a retreat, and not a rout.

"Why?'' Rod snapped.

"Tuan has ordered it,'' Fess answered, "and wisely, in my
opinion.''

"Take me to him!''

They found the King at the rear, for once, since that was the part of the army closest to the enemy. "They fall back on the left flank!" he bawled. "Bid Sir Maris speed them; for stragglers will surely become corpses!"

The courier nodded and darted away through the rain.

"Hail, sovereign lord!" Rod called.

Tuan looked up, and his face lit with relief. "Lord Warlock! Praise Heaven thou'rt come!"

"Serves you right for inviting me. Why the retreat, Tuan?"

"Assuredly thou dost jest, Lord Warlock! Dost thou not feel the rain upon thee? We cannot stand against them when lightning may strike!"

"But if we don't," Rod pointed out, "they'll just keep marching as long as it rains."

Tuan nodded. "The thought had occurred to me."

"Uh—this could be a good way to lose a kingdom. . . ."

"Of this, too, I am mindful. Therefore, we *shall* turn and stand—but not until they are certain we're routed."

Rod lifted his head slowly, eyes widening. Then he grinned. "I should've known better than to question your judgment on tactics! But will they really believe we'd just flat-out run, when we've been fighting back for so long?"

"They'll expect some show of resistance, surely," Tuan agreed. "Therefore wilt thou and the Flying Legion ride out against them." He nodded toward the right flank. "They await thee, Lord Warlock."

His commandos raised a cheer when they saw him, and he raised them with quick orders. A minute later, half of them faded into the grass and scrub growth that lined the riverbank. The other half, the ones with the hipboots, imitated Moses and drifted into the bullrushes.

Rod stayed with the landlubbers, easing silently back along the bankside till they reached a place where the beach widened, walled with a semicircle of trees, the spaces between them filled with brush. Ten minutes later, the first scouts from the beastman advance guard came up even with them. Rod waited until they were right in the middle of the semicircle, then whistled a good imitation of a whippoorwill. But the cry was a strange one to the beastmen, and something rang fowl. One Neanderthal looked up, startled, his mouth opening to cry the alarm—when a dozen Gramarye commandos hit him and his mates.

The rangers surrounded the beastmen completely, so Rod

didn't see what happened; all he knew was that it lasted about thirty seconds, then his men faded back into the trees, leaving three corpses in the center of the glade, pumping their blood into the pale sand.

Rod stared, shaken and unnerved. Beside him, his sergeant grinned. " 'Twas well done, Lord Warlock."

"I'll take your word for it," Rod muttered. "What'd these boys do in peacetime—work in a slaughterhouse?"

The sergeant shrugged. "Any farm lad must know how to slit the throat of a swine, and these ogres are little more."

Rod had to bite back a sudden impulse to explain the conflict as the beastmen saw it. "They're the enemy," he agreed unhappily, "and this is war. They've already pretty well proved that they'll kill us if we don't kill them first." Privately, he wondered how many of them really wanted to.

Later. Right now, it was time to play monster. "Tell the men to spread out along the backtrail, sergeant."

The sergeant turned away to mutter a few words, but that was the only effect Rod saw or heard. He sat his saddle securely anyway, knowing his men had spread out toward the beastmen. He sat securely, and waited.

After about five minutes, the vanguard came up. Their leader saw the corpses in the center of the glade and held out an arm to stop his men. While they stared, shocked, Rod called like a gull, and fifty commandos slid from the brush, swords slashing throats before the beastmen even realized they'd been attacked.

As the first Neanderthals fell, the others turned with a roar, axes whirling down. Rod's men leaped back, but a couple weren't quick enough. He let the anger fuel him as he commanded Fess, "Go!" The great black steel horse leaped out into the battle as Rod shouted, "Havoc!" The beastmen's eyes all riveted on this new threat, so they didn't notice the shadows that slid out of the rushes behind them in answer to Rod's cry. Beastmen began dropping at the rear as Rod and his men began their deadly gavotte, skipping back out of reach of the beastmen's axes as they tried to catch Gramarye glances, but Rod's men held to their hard-learned tactic—staring at the enemy's weapons, not at his pupils. Here and there a soldier accidentally looked at the reddened eyes of the foe, and slowed. It even happened to Rod—being on horseback, he attracted eyes. One Neanderthal managed to catch him squarely, and suddenly he was plowing through molasses, panic touching him as he felt two rival impulses battling in his brain, and realized neither of them was his own.

Then a spreading warmth coursed through his head and down his spine, a familiar touch, and he could almost scent Gwen's perfume as his shield-arm leaped up to give the ax a slight push that deflected it to just barely miss, while his sword stabbed down over the beastman's shield. He felt it sink in, jar against bone, and yanked back on it furiously, turning to the next foeman, trying hard to ignore the falling body.

Then lightning strobe-lit the beach, and thunder broke upon their heads. Rod blocked ax-blows frantically, realizing that almost half his force was frozen. Axes swung and the Gramarye soldiers fell, while their opponents turned to help their fellows gang up on soldiers. Darting frantic glances from one to another, most of the soldiers slipped and chanced to look a Neanderthal in the eye—and froze.

Rod bellowed in anger and fear and chopped down at a beastman. He dodged aside, revealing a grinning face that stared up at Rod, catching his gaze full in the eyes.

It was as though Rod's riposte had slammed into a wall. Frantically, he pushed at the sword, but it wouldn't move, and an ax was swinging up at him. Only a spare tendril lingered in his mind, probing weakly at a dark wall that seemed to have settled there. . . .

Then a blazing shield tore into the dark mass, shredding it to tatters—and Rod's arms answered his summons. He whipped aside as the ax swung past, then bobbed back to stab downward. His men tore into the beastmen like wildcats, outnumbered but determined to bring down ten times their number by sheer ferocity. But more beastmen were welling up behind the vanguard, more and more; and, in a stab of fear, Rod saw a long, slender dragon ship shouldering up out of the drizzle behind the masses of enemy.

But a roaring bellow shook the beach, and the beastmen looked up in sudden terror at five thousand Gramarye soldiers pouring down along the riverbank.

Rod bit back a shout of triumph; all his men kept silence and channeled the surge of energy into a series of quick stabs. Beastmen dropped before them, then came out of their trances enough to turn and defend themselves; but it was frantic and scrambling now, for the soldiers outnumbered them.

Stabbing and blocking fiercely, Rod became dimly aware of a rhythmic rumble coming from the enemy.

"Rod," Fess's voice ground out like a slowing recording, "the strain increases . . . I may fail you. . . ."

"Hold on while you can!" Rod shouted, and mentally prepared himself to leap down and use Fess as a back-shield.

The rumbling grew louder, became coherent; the enemy army chanted, as with one voice, "Kobold! Kobold! Kobold!"

And it almost seemed that their god heard them; the whole riverbank was suddenly transfixed by a shimmering glare, and thunder wrapped them inside a cannon shot.

As the glare dimmed, soldiers slowed. A beastman caught Rod's gaze and he felt himself pushing his arms with agonizing slowness again.

Then the white-hot shield burned through the dark mass again, and his arms leaped free. The whole Gramarye army erupted in a shout of joy and fought with new, savage vigor. A bellow of anger answered them, but it was tinged with despair; and the beastmen seemed to shrink together, forming a wall against the Gramarye spears. But the island wolves harried at that wall, chipping and digging, loosing the blood that it held dammed; and the night was a bedlam of screaming and the crashing of steel.

Suddenly, Rod realized that they were gaining ground. But how could they be, when the enemy had their backs to the water? Looking up, he saw beastmen scrambling single-file back aboard the dragon ships.

"They flee!" he cried, exultant. "The enemy runs! Harrow them!"

His men responded with a crazed scream, and fought like madmen. They couldn't really do much more than scratch and chip; the beastmen's wall was solid, and became all the more so as it shrank in on itself as one boat glided away and another replaced it. But finally, the last few turned and ran to scramble up the sides of the boat. Soldiers leaped to chase them, but Rod, Tuan, and Sir Maris checked them with whiplash commands that echoed through every knight to every sergeant; and, looking up, the soldiers saw the beastmen already aboard poised to throw down everything from axes to rocks upon them. Seeing the soldiers checked, they did throw them, with crazed howls; and shields came up, bouncing the missles away harmlessly. But as they did, the dragon ship slid out into the current, swooped around in a slow, graceful curve, and drifted away downstream.

Tuan stabbed a bloody sword up at the sky with a victorious scream. Looking up, the astonished army realized they had won. Then a forest of lances and swords speared up with a screaming howl of triumph.

Before the echoes had faded, Rod had turned Fess's head downstream again. "You made it through, Old Iron!"

"I did, Rod." The electronic voice was still a little slowed. "They could only come at me from the front in this battle."

Rod nodded. "A huge advantage. Now head for the witches' tent, full speed!"

The sentries outside the tent recognized him and struck their breastplates in salute. Rod leaped off his horse and darted in.

Guttering candles showed young witches and warlocks sprawled crazily all over the floor, unconscious. In the center, Agatha slumped against one tent-post, her head in her hands, and Gwen huddled against the other, moaning and rubbing the front and sides of her head.

Fear stabbed. Rod leaped to her, gathered her into his arms. "Darling! Are you . . ."

She blinked up at him, managed a smile. "I live, my lord, and will be well again—though presently mine head doth split. . . ."

"Praise all saints!" Rod clasped her head to his breast, then finally let the shambles about him sink in. He turned back to Gwen, more slowly this time. "He showed up, huh?"

"Aye, my lord." She squinted against the pain. "When the second bolt of lightning struck, all the younglings were knocked senseless. Agatha and I strove to bear up under the brunt of that fell power, and I could feel Harold's force aiding her. But we all feared a third bolt, knowing we could not withstand it. . . ."

"And Galen was mentally eavesdropping, and knew you probably couldn't hold out against it." Rod nodded. "But he didn't dare take the chance that his 'son' might be burned out in the process, even though that son wasn't born of his body."

"Do not depend on his aid again," came a croak from across the tent, and the pile of cloth and bones that was Agatha stirred. "Beware, Warlock. he doth know that thou wilt now seek to use him by placing Harold at risk."

"Of course." Glints danced in Rod's eyes. "But he'll come, anyway."

*   *   *

Tuan had left squadrons on both banks, chafing with anger at not being able to take part in the battle; but now, as they saw the dragon ships sailing down toward them, they yelled with joy and whipped out their swords.

The beastmen took one look and kept on sailing.

Frustrated, the young knights in charge gave certain orders; and a few minutes later, flaming arrows leaped up to arc over and thud into decks and sails. The archers amused themselves for a few minutes by watching beastmen scurry about the decks in a panic, dousing flames. But as soon as they were all out, the next squad down the river filled the air with fire-arrows, and the fun began all over again. So, even though Tuan sent a squad of revived witchfolk to fly alongside the fleet, keeping carefully out of arrow-range, they weren't needed. Still, they stood by, watchful and ready, as the dragon ships sailed down the Fleuve and out to sea.

On the horizon, the dragon ships paused, as though considering another try. But a line of archers assembled on the sea-cliffs with telekinetic witches behind them, and the resulting fire-arrows managed to speed all the way out to the horizon before they fell to rekindle charred ships.

The dragon ships gave up, turned their noses homeward, and disappeared.

In the midst of the cheering and drinking, Rod shouldered through to Tuan. He grabbed the King by his royal neck and shouted in his ear to make himself heard. "You know it's not really over yet, don't you?"

"I know," the young King replied with dignity, "but I know further that this night is for celebration. Fill a glass and rejoice with us, Lord Warlock. Tomorrow we shall again study war."

He was up and functioning the next morning, though not happily. He sat in a chair in his tent, gray daylight filtering through the fabric all around him. The sky was still overcast, and so was Tuan. He pressed a cold towel against his forehead, squinting. "Now, Lord Warlock. I will hear the talk that I know I must heed: that our war is not done."

Brom O'Berin stepped close to the King's chair, peering up into his face. "I misdoubt me an thou shouldst speak of war when thine head is yet so filled with wine its skin is stretched as taut as a drumhead."

Tuan answered with a weak and rueful smile. " 'Twill do no

harm, Lord Councillor; for I misdoubt me an we shall speak of aught which I know not already.''

"Which is," Rod said carefully, "that if we don't follow them, they'll be back."

Tuan nodded, then winced, closing his eyes. "Aye, Lord Warlock. Next spring, as soon as thunderstorms may start, we shall see them here upon our shores again—aye, I know it.''

Brom frowned. "Yet hast thou thought that they'll have reasoned out a way to conquer all the power our witches can brew up?''

Tuan grimaced. "Nay, I had not. It strengthens my resolve. We must needs bring the war home to them; we must follow them across the sea, and strike.''

"And the time to strike is now," Brom rumbled.

Tuan nodded and looked up at Rod. "Yet how shall we bring our army there, Lord Warlock? Canst thou transport so many men and horses with a spell?''

Rod smiled, amused. "I don't think even Galen could send that many, my liege. But we have discovered that Gramarye has a thriving merchant fleet who would no doubt be delighted to lend their services to helping wiping out a potential pirates' nest.''

Tuan nodded slowly. "I do believe 'twould gain their heart-felt cooperation, an thou wert to word it so.''

"It's just a matter of figuring out their area of self-interest. We've also got an amazing number of fishing boats, and their owners will probably be very quick to agree we should forestall any poaching on their fishing-grounds, before it starts.''

The King nodded—again very slowly. "Then thou dost think we may have transport enow.''

"Probably. And what we lack, I think shipwrights can turn out with around-the-clock shifts by the time we've gathered all the provisions we'll need. No, transportation's not the problem.''

"Indeed?" The King smiled weakly. "What is, then?''

"Fighting the beastmen on their home ground when they're battling for their lives—and for their wives' and children's lives, too.''

Tuan stared at him for a moment. When he spoke his voice was a ghostly whisper. "Aye, 'twill be a bloody business. And few of those who sail shall be wafted home.''

"If we make it a fight to the death," Rod agreed.

"What else can it be?" Brom demanded, scowling.

"A coup d'état." Rod grinned. "According to Yorick and our other beastman-guests, this invasion is the result of a junta managing to seize power in Beastland."

Tuan shrugged, irritated. "What aid is that, if these people have adhered to their new leader?" But as soon as he'd said it, his gaze turned thoughtful.

Rod nodded. "After a defeat like this, they're not going to be very happy with the leadership of that shaman, Mughorck, and his Kobold-god. And from what Yorick said, I kinda got the feeling that they never really were screamingly enthusiastic about him anyway—they were just bamboozled into putting him into power in the panic of the moment. If we can make it clear right from the beginning that we're fighting Mughorck, and not the beastmen as a whole—then maybe they'll be willing to surrender."

Tuan nodded slowly. "Thou dost speak eminent good sense, Lord Warlock. But how wilt thou convey to them this intention?"

"That," Rod said, "is for Yorick to figure out."

"Nothing to it, m'lord." Yorick waved the problem away with one outsized ham-hand. "Oldest thing in the book—a nice little whispering-campaign."

"Whispering-campaigns are *that* old?" Rod had a dizzying vision of 50,000 years of slander. "But how'll you get it started?"

Yorick glanced at his fellows, then shrugged as he turned back to Rod. "No help for it—we'll have to go in ahead of you and do it ourselves." When Rod stared, appalled, Yorick grinned. "What were you thinking of—leaflets?"

"I was really thinking we might be able to do something with telepathy," Rod sighed, "but none of our projectives know the language. Yorick's right—he and his men have got to get the word started somehow. The question is—can we trust them?"

"Trust a man of the foe?" Catharine cried. "Nay, Lord Warlock, I would hope you would not!"

"But he's really on our side," Rod argued, "because he's fighting the same enemy—the shaman, Mughorck."

They sat in a small chamber—only forty feet square—of the royal castle in Runnymede. The Oriental carpet, tapestries on the walls, gleaming walnut furniture, graceful hourglass-shaped chairs, and silver wine goblets belied any urgency. But even though the fireplace was cold, the talk was heated.

"He doth say Mughorck is his enemy," Catharine said scornfully. "Yet, might he not be an agent of just that fell monster?"

Rod spread his hands. "Why? For what purpose could Mughorck send an agent who couldn't possibly be mistaken for a Gramarye native? Not to mention his handful of cronies who don't even speak our language."

"Why, for this very purpose, lad," Brom O'Berin grunted, "that we might send them in to strengthen our attack, whereupon they could turn their coats, warn their fellows, and have a hedge of spears for our soldiers to confront when they land."

"Okay," Rod snorted, disgusted. "Farfetched, but possible, I'll grant you. Still, it just doesn't *feel* right."

Catharine smiled wickedly. "I had thought 'twas only ladies who would decide great matters by such feelings."

"All right, so you've got a point now and then," Rod growled. "But you know what I mean, Your Majesty—there's some element of this whole situation that just doesn't fit with the hypothesis that Yorick's an enemy."

Catharine opened her mouth to refute him, but Brom spoke first. "I take thy meaning—and I'll tell thee the element."

Catharine turned to him in amazement, and Tuan looked up, suddenly interested again.

" 'Tis this," Brom explained, "that he doth speak our language. Could he have learned it from Mughorck?"

"Possibly, if Mughorck's an agent of the Eagle's enemies," Rod said slowly. "If the Eagle taught Yorick English, there's no reason why Mughorck couldn't have, too."

"Still, I take thy meaning." Tuan sat up straighter. "We know that Yorick doth hold the Eagle to be some manner of wizard; if we say that Mughorck is too, then we have pitted wizard 'gainst wizard. Would not then their combat be with one another? Why should we think they care so greatly about us that they would combine against us?"

"Or that Mughorck would oust Eagle only to be able to use the beastmen 'gainst us," Brom rumbled. "Why could we be of such great moment to Mughorck?"

"Because," Fess's voice said behind Rod's ear, "Gramarye has more functioning telepaths than all the rest of the Terran

Sphere together; and the interstellar communication they can provide will in all probability be the single greatest factor in determining who shall rule the Terran peoples.''

And because the Eagle and Mughorck were probably both time-traveling agents from future power-blocs who knew how the current struggle was going to come out and were trying to change it here, Rod added mentally. Aloud, he just said sourly, ''It's nice to know this chamber has such thick walls that we don't have to worry about eavesdroppers.''

''Wherefore?'' Tuan frowned. ''Is there reason to question the loyalty of any of our folk?''

''Uhhhhhh . . . no.'' Rod had to improvise quickly, and surprisingly hit upon truth. ''It's just that I brought Yorick along, in case we decided we wanted to talk to him. He's in the antechamber.''

Catharine looked up, horrified, and stepped quickly behind Tuan's chair. The King, however, looked interested. ''Then, by all means, let's bring him in! Can we think of no questions to ask that might determine the truth or falsehood of this beastman's words?''

Brom stomped over to the door, yanked it open, and rumbled a command. As he swaggered back Rod offered, ''Just this. From Toby's report, the beastmen's village is very thoroughly settled and the fields around it are loaded with corn, very neatly cultivated. That settlement's not brand-new, Tuan. If the Eagle had come here with conquest in mind, would he have taken a couple of years out to build up a colony?''

The young King nodded. ''A point well-taken.'' He turned as the beastman ambled in, and Catharine took a step back. ''Welcome, captain of exiles!''

''The same to you, I'm sure.'' Yorick grinned and touched his forelock.

Brom scowled ferociously, so Rod figured he'd better butt in. ''Uh, we've just been talking, Yorick, about why Mughorck tried to assassinate the Eagle.''

''Oh, because Mughorck wanted to conquer you guys,'' Yorick said, surprised. ''He couldn't even get it started with the Eagle in the way, preaching understanding and tolerance.''

The room was awfully quiet while Tuan, Brom, Catharine, and Rod exchanged frantic glances.

''I said something?'' Yorick inquired.

''Only what we'd all just been saying.'' Rod scratched

behind his ear. "Always unnerving, finding out you guessed right." He looked up at Yorick. "Why'd Mughorck want to conquer us?"

"Power-base," Yorick explained. "Your planet's going to be the hottest item in the coming power-struggle. Your descendants will come out on the side of democracy, so the Decentralized Democratic Tribunal will win. The only chance the losers will have is to come back in time and try to take over Gramarye. When Mughorck took over we realized he must've been working for one of the future losers. . . . What's the matter, milord?"

Rod had been making frantic shushing motions. Tuan turned a gimlet eye on him. "Indeed, Lord Warlock." His voice was smooth as velvet. "Why wouldst thou not wish him to speak of such things?"

"For that they are highly confusing, for one." Catharine knit her brows, but the look she bent on Rod was baleful. "Still, mine husband's point's well taken. For whom dost *thou* labor, Lord Warlock?"

"For my wife and child, before anyone else," Rod sighed, "but since I want freedom and justice for them, and you two are their best chance for that condition—why, I work for you."

"Or in accord with us," Tuan amended. "But hast thou other affiliations, Lord Warlock?"

"Well, there is a certain collaborative effort that . . ."

". . . that doth give him information vital to the continuance of Your Majesties' reign." Brom glanced up at them guiltily. "I ha' known of it almost since he came among us."

Some of the tension began to ease out of Tuan, but Catharine looked more indignant than ever. "Even thou, my trusted Brom! Wherefore didst thou not tell this to me?"

"For reason that thou hadst no need to know it," Brom said simply, "and because I felt it to be Lord Gallowglass's secret. If he thought thou shouldst know it, he would tell thee—for, mistake not, his first loyalty is here."

Catharine seemed a bit mollified, and Tuan was actually smiling—but with a glittering eye. "We must speak more of this anon, Lord Warlock."

But not just now. Rod breathed a shuddering sigh and cast a quick look of gratitude toward Brom. The dwarf nodded imperceptibly.

"Our cause of worry is before us." Tuan turned back to

Yorick. "It would seem, Master Yorick, that thou dost know more than thou shouldst."

Yorick stared. "You mean some of this was classified?"

Rod gave him a laser glare, but Tuan just said, "Where didst thou learn of events yet to come?"

"Oh, from the Eagle." Yorick smiled, relieved. "He's been there."

The room was very still for a moment.

Then Tuan said carefully, "Dost thou say this Eagle hath gone bodily to the future?"

Yorick nodded.

"Who's he work for?" Rod rapped out.

"Himself." Yorick spread his hands. "Makes a nice profit out of it, too."

Rod relaxed. Political fanatics would fight to the death, but businessmen would always see reason—provided you showed them that they could make a better profit doing things your way.

But Tuan shook his head. "Thou wouldst have us believe the Eagle brought all thy people here and taught them to farm enough to support themselves. Where's the profit in that?"

"Well," Yorick hedged, "he does undertake the occasional humanitarian project. . . ."

"Also, for certain assignments you boys probably make unbeatable agents," Rod said drily.

Yorick had the grace to blush.

"Or is it," rumbled Brom, "that he doth fight the future-folk who backed Mughorck? Would thy people not be a part of that fight?"

Yorick became very still. Then he eyed Rod and jerked his head toward Brom. "Where'd you get him?"

"You don't want to know," Rod said quickly. "But we do. How were you Neanderthals a weapon in the big fight?"

Yorick sighed and gave in. "Okay. It's a little more complicated than what I said before. The bad guys gathered us together to use us as a tool to establish a very early dictatorship that wouldn't quit. You'll understand, milord, that we're a bit of a paranoid culture."

"Can't imagine why," Rod said drily.

"What is this 'paranoid'?" Tuan frowned. "And what matters it to government?"

"It means you feel as though everyone's picking on you,"

Yorick explained, "so you tend to pick on them first, to make sure they can't get you. Governments like that are very good at repression."

Catharine blanched, and Tuan turned to Rod. "Is there truth in what he doth say?"

"Too much," Rod said with a woeful smile, "and anyone with witch-power tends to be repressed. Now you know why I'm on your side, my liege."

"Indeed I do." Tuan turned back to face Yorick. "And I find myself much less concerned about thine other associations."

But Rod was watching Catharine closely out of the corner of his eye. Was she realizing that she'd been on the road to becoming a tyrant when she'd reigned alone? Mostly over-compensating for insecurity, of course—but by the time she'd gained enough experience to be sure of herself, she'd have had too many people who hated her; she'd have had to stay a tyrant.

But Tuan was talking to Yorick again. "Why doth thine Eagle fight these autocrats?"

"Bad for trade," Yorick said promptly. "Dictatorships tend to establish very arbitrary rules about who can do business with whom, and their rules result in either very high tariffs or exorbitant graft. But a government that emphasizes freedom pretty much has to let business be free, too."

"Pretty much." Rod underscored the qualifier.

Yorick shrugged. "Freedom's an unstable condition, my lord. There'll always be men trying to destroy it by establishing their own dictatorships. Businessmen are human too."

Rod felt that the issue deserved a bit more debate, but the little matter of the invasion was getting lost in the shuffle. "We were kind of thinking about that whispering campaign you mentioned. Mind explaining how you could work it without getting caught? And don't try to tell me you guys all look alike to each other."

"Wouldn't think of it." Yorick waved away the suggestion. "By this time, see, I'm pretty sure there'll be a lot of people who're fed up with Mughorck. In fact, I even expect a few refugees from his version of justice. If you can smuggle me back to the mainland, into the jungle south of the village, I think I can make contact with quite a few of 'em. Some of them will have friends who'll be glad to forget any chance meetings they might have out in the forest gathering fruit, and the rumor you want circulated can get passed into the village when the friend comes back.''

Tuan nodded. ''It should march. But couldst thou not have done this better an thou hadst remained in thine own country?''

Yorick shook his head. ''Mughorck's gorillas were hot on my trail. By now, he should have other problems on his hands; he won't have forgotten about me and my men, but we won't be high-priority any more. Besides, there might even be enough refugees in the forest so that he's not willing to risk any of his few really loyal squads on a clean-out mission; the odds might be too great that they wouldn't come back.''

The King nodded slowly. ''I hope, for thy sake, that thou hast it aright.''

''Then, too,'' Yorick said, ''there's the little matter that, if I'd stayed, there'd have been no message to pass. Frankly, I needed allies.''

''Thou hast them, an thou'rt a true man,'' Tuan said firmly. Catharine, however, looked much less certain.

Yorick noted it. ''Of course I'm true. After all, if I betrayed you and you caught me, I expect you'd think of a gallows that I'd be the perfect decoration for.''

''Nay, i' truth,'' Tuan protested, ''I'd have to build one anew especially for thee, to maintain harmony of style.''

''I'm flattered.'' Yorick grinned. ''I'll tell you straight-away, though, I don't deserve to be hanged in a golden chain. Silver, maybe . . .''

''Wherefore? Dost thou fear leprechauns?''

Tuan and Yorick, Rod decided, were getting along entirely too well. ''There's the little matter of the rumor he's supposed to circulate,'' he reminded Tuan.

Yorick shrugged. ''That you and your army have really come just to oust Mughorck, isn't it? Not to wipe out the local citizenry?''

''Thou hast it aright.''

''But you do understand,'' Yorick pointed out, ''that they'll have to fight until they know Mughorck's been taken, don't you? I mean, if they switched to your side and he won, it could be very embarrassing for them—not to mention their wives and children.''

''Assuredly,'' Tuan agreed. ''Nay, I hope only that, when

they know Mughorck is ta'en, they'll not hesitate to lay down their arms.''

"I have a notion that most of them will be too busy cheering to think about objecting."

" 'Tis well. Now . . .'' Tuan leaned forward, eyes glittering. "How can we be sure of taking Mughorck?''

"An we wish a quick ending to this battle," Brom explained, "we cannot fight through the whole mass of beastmen to reach him."

"Ah—now we come back to my original plan." Yorick grinned. "I was waiting for you guys to get around to talking invasion. Because if you do, you see, and if you sneak me into the jungles a week or two ahead, I'm sure my boys and I can find enough dissenters to weld into an attack force. Then, when your army attacks from the front, I can bring my gorillas . . .''

"You mean guerrillas."

"That, too. Anyway, I can bring 'em over the cliffs and down to the High Cave."

" 'The High Cave'?'' Tuan frowned. "What is that?''

"Just the highest cave in the cliff-wall. When we first arrived we all camped out in caves, and Eagle took the highest one so he could see the whole picture of what was going on. When the rank and file moved out into huts, he stayed there—so Mughorck will have to have moved in there, to use the symbol of possession to reinforce his power."

"Well reasoned," Brom rumbled, "but how if thou'rt mistaken?''

Yorick shrugged. "Then we keep looking till we find him. We shouldn't have too much trouble; I very much doubt that he'd be at the front line."

Tuan's smile soured with contempt.

"He's the actual power," Yorick went on, "but the clincher'll be the Kobold. When we take the idol, that should really tell the troops that the war's lost.''

"And you expect it'll be in the High Cave too," Rod amplified.

"Not a doubt of it," Yorick confirmed. "You haven't seen this thing, milord. You sure as hell wouldn't want it in your living room."

"Somehow I don't doubt that one bit."

"Nor I," Tuan agreed. He glanced at his wife and his two

ministers. "Are we agreed, then?"

Reluctantly, they nodded.

"Then, 'tis done." Tuan clapped his hands. "I will give orders straightaway, Master Yorick, for a merchantman to bear thee and thy fellows to the jungles south of thy village. Then, when all's in readiness, a warlock will come to tell thee the day and hour of our invasion."

"Great!" Yorick grinned with relief: then, suddenly, he frowned. "But wait a minute. How'll your warlock find us?"

"Just stare at a fire and try to blank your mind every evening for a few hours," Rod explained, "and think something abstract—the sound of one hand clapping, or some such, over and over again. The warlock'll home in on your mind."

Yorick looked up, startled. "You mean your telepaths can read *our* minds?"

"Sort of," Rod admitted. "At least, they can tell you're there, and where you are."

Yorick smiled, relieved. "Well. No wonder you knew where the raiders were going to land next."

"After the first strike, yes." Rod smiled. "Of course, we can't understand your language."

"Thanks for the tip." Yorick raised a forefinger. "I'll make sure I don't think in English."

Rod wasn't sure he could, but he didn't say so.

Yorick turned back to the King and Queen. "If you don't mind, I'll toddle along now, Your Majesties." He bowed. "I'd like to go tell my men it's time to move out."

"Do, then," Tuan said regally, "and inform thy men that they may trust in us as deeply as we may trust in them."

Yorick paused at the door and looked back, raising one eyebrow. "You sure about that?"

Tuan nodded firmly.

Yorick grinned again. "I think you just said more than you knew. Godspeed, Majesties." He bowed again and opened the door; the sentry ushered him out.

Catharine was the first to heave a huge sigh of relief. "Well! 'Tis done." She eyed her husband. "How shall we know if the greatest part of his bargain's fulfilled, ere thy battle?"

"Well, I wasn't quite candid with him," Rod admitted. He stepped over to the wall and lifted the edge of a tapestry. "What do you think, dear? Can we trust him?"

Gwen nodded as she stepped out into the room. "Aye, my

lord. There was not even the smallest hint of duplicity in his thoughts.''

"He was thinking in English," Rod explained to the startled King and Queen. "He had to; he was talking to us."

Tuan's face broke into a broad grin. "So that was thy meaning when thou didst speak of 'eavesdroppers'!"

"Well, not entirely. But I did kind of have Gwen in mind."

"Yet may he not have been thinking in his own tongue, beneath the thoughts he spoke to us?" Catharine demanded.

Gwen cast an approving glance at her. Rod read it and agreed; though Catharine tended to flare into anger if you mentioned her own psi powers to her, she was obviously progressing well in their use, to have come across the idea of submerged thoughts.

"Mayhap, Majesty," Gwen agreed. "Yet, beneath those thoughts in his own tongue there are the root-thoughts that give rise to words, but which themselves are without words. They are naked flashes of idea, as yet unclothed. Even there, as deeply as I could read him, there was no hint of treachery."

"But just to be sure, we'll have Toby check out his camp right before the invasion," Rod explained. "He's learned enough to be able to dig beneath the camouflage of surface thoughts, if there is any."

The door opened, and the sentry stepped in to announce, "Sir Maris doth request audience, Majesties."

"Aye, indeed!" Tuan turned to face the door, delighted. "Mayhap he doth bring word from our sentries who have kept watch to be certain the beastmen do not turn back, to attempt one last surprise. Assuredly, present him!"

The sentry stepped aside, and the seneschal limped into the chamber, leaning heavily on his staff, but with a grin that stretched from ear to ear.

"Welcome, good Sir Maris!" Tuan cried. "What news?"

" 'Twas even as thou hadst thought, Majesty." Sir Maris paused in front of Tuan for a sketchy bow, then straightened up, and his grin turned wolfish. "Three ships did curve and seek to sail into the mouth of a smaller river that runs athwart the Fleuve."

"They were repulsed?" Glints danced in Tuan's eyes.

"Aye, my liege! Our archers filled their ships with fire, the whiles our soldiers slung a weighty chain across the river. When they ground against it and found they could sail no further, they sought to come ashore; but our men-at-arms presented them a hedge of pikes. Nay, they turned and fled." He turned to Rod. "Our thanks, Lord Warlock, for thy good aid in this endeavor!"

Rod started, staring, and Gwen caught his arm and her breath; but Sir Maris whirled back to the King, fairly crowing, "He did seem to be everywhere, first on this bank, then on that, amongst the archers, then amongst the pikemen, everywhere urging them on to feats of greater valor. Nay, they'll not believe that they can lose now."

Gwen looked up, but Rod stood frozen.

"Yet, withal," said the old knight, frowning, "why hadst thou assigned command to me? If the High Warlock were there to lead, he should have had command as well!"

"But," said Tuan, turning to Rod, "thou wast ever here in Runnymede, with ourselves, the whiles this raid was foiled!"

"I noticed," Rod croaked.

"My lord, not all things that hap here are impossible," Gwen sighed.

"Oh, yes, they are. Take you, for example—that someone as wonderful as you could even exist is highly improbable. But that you could not only exist but also fall in love with someone like me—well, that's flatly impossible."

Gwen gave him a radiant smile. "Thou wilt ever undervalue thyself, Rod Gallowglass, and overvalue me—and thus hath made a cold world turn warm for me."

That look in her eyes he couldn't resist; it pulled him down, and down, into a long, deep kiss that tried to pull him deeper. But eventually Rod remembered that he was on the deck of a ship, and that the crew were no doubt watching. He was tempted to consign them all to the Inferno, but he remembered his responsibilities and pulled out of the kiss with a regretful sigh. "We haven't been doing enough of that lately."

"I am well aware of that, my lord." Gwen fixed him with a glittering eye.

"And I thought the Neanderthals had an 'Evil Eye'!" Rod breathed, and turned to hook her hand firmly around his elbow as he strolled down the deck. "For now, however, let's enjoy the seabreeze and the salt air. After all, this is the closest thing to a pleasure cruise we're ever apt to get."

"As thou dost say, my lord," she said demurely.

"Just so you don't mistake my doppelgänger for me," Rod amended.

Gwen shook her head firmly. "That could not hap at any distance less than an hundred feet."

"Well, I hope not—but quite a few people seem to have been making the error."

"Ah, but how well do they know thee?" Gwen crooned. "If they've seen thee at all before, it has been only briefly and from a distance."

"Yeah, but there're some who . . . well, there's one!" Rod stopped next to a brown-robed form that sat cross-legged on the deck, leaning against the rail with a half-filled inkhorn in his left hand, writing in a careful round hand in a book of huge vellum sheets. "Hail, Brother Chillde!"

The monk looked up, startled. Then a smile of delight spread over his face. "Well met, Lord Warlock! I had hoped to espy thee here!"

Rod shrugged. "Where else would I be? It's the King's flagship. But how do you come to be here, Brother Chillde?"

"I am chaplain," the monk said simply. "And I wish to be near to the King and his councillors as may be, an I am able; for I strive to record what doth occur during this war as well as I may."

"So your chronicle's coming well? How far back have you managed to dig?"

"Why, I began four years agone, when the old King died, and have writ down all I've seen or heard that has occurred during, first, the reign of Catharine, then during the reign of both our goodly King and Queen." He beamed up at them. "Yet, in this present crisis I have been fortunate to be in the thick of it, almost from the first. My journal shall be precise, so that folk yet unborn, and many hundreds of years hence, may know how nobly our folk of this present age did acquit themselves."

"A noble goal." Rod smiled, though without, perhaps, as much respect as the project deserved. "Be sure what you write is accurate, though, won't you?"

"Never fear. I've asked several folk for their accounts of each event, and thus believe I've found somewhat of the truth. Yet, for the greater part, I've writ only what I've seen myself."

Rod nodded with approval. "Can't do better than primary source material. May your endeavor prosper, Brother Chillde."

"I thank thee, lord."

And Rod and Gwen strolled on down the deck as the monk bent over his journal again. When they were safely out of earshot, Rod murmured to Gwen, "Of course, eyewitness accounts aren't necessarily what really happened. People's memories are always colored by what they want to believe."

"I can well credit it." Gwen glanced back at the monk. "And he's so young and filled with the ideals of youth! I doubt me not an Catharine and Tuan seem to him impossibly regal and imposing—and the beastmen immensely vile, and . . ."

"Mama!"

Gwen recoiled in surprise, then blossomed into a radiant smile as she realized she was suddenly holding an armful of baby. "Magnus, my bonny boy! Hast thou, then, come to wish thy parents well on this their venture?"

Her eyes darkened as the baby nodded, and Rod guessed she was thinking that Mama and Papa might not come home to Baby. She needed a distraction. "What's he got there—a ball?"

The spheroid was dull and gray, about four inches in diameter—and its surface suddenly rippled. Rod stared.

Gwen saw his look of disgust and said quickly, "Be not concerned, my lord. 'Tis naught but witch moss with which, I doubt me not, he hath been toying."

"Oh." Rod knew the substance well; it was a variety of fungus that had the peculiar property of responding to the thoughts of projective telepaths. Rod had a strong suspicion that it had contributed to the development of elves, werewolves, and other supernatural creatures around the Gramarye landscape. "When did he begin to play with . . ."

He broke off, because the ball was changing in the child's hand—and Magnus was staring at it in surprise. It stretched itself up, flattening and dwindling toward the bottom, where it divided in half lengthwise for half its height, and two pieces broke loose at the sides. The top formed itself into a smaller ball, and dents and lines began to define the form.

"What doth he make?" Gwen whispered.

"I'm afraid to guess." But Rod knew, with a sickening certainty, what he was going to see.

And he was right—for the lump finished its transformation and swung up a wicked-looking war ax, opening a gash of a mouth to reveal canines that would have done credit to a saber-toothed tiger. Its piggy eyes reddened with insane bloodlust, and it began to shamble up Magnus's arm.

The child shrieked and hurled it as far away from him as he could. It landed on the deck, caving in one side; but that side bulged out into its former form as it pulled itself to its feet and shambled off down the deck, looking for something to ravish.

Magnus plowed his head into Gwen's bosom, wailing in terror. "There, love—'tis gone," she assured him, "or will be in a moment . . . ." And she glared at the diminutive monster, eyes narrowing. It took one step, and its leg turned into mush.

"It's a beastman," Rod whispered, "a vicious parody of a Neanderthal."

Another step, and the model beastman turned into a ball again.

"But the kid didn't see any of the battles!" Rod protested. "How could he . . ."

"My lord," Gwen grated, "it will not hold its shape unless I force it. Another mind fights me for the forming of it."

"Then, get rid of it—fast! You never know, it might find another one like it, and breed true!"

"Done," Gwen snapped.

The witch moss turned into a ball so smooth that it gleamed, then shot off the deck and far, far away, heading for the horizon.

Gwen turned her attention back to Magnus. "There, there, child! 'Twas no fault of thine; 'twas some mean and heartless person who crafted thy ball thus, to afright a babe!" She looked up at Rod with murder in her eyes. "Who would ha' done such a thing?"

"I don't know, but I'll find out." Rod was feeling in a mayhem mood himself. He glanced quickly about the decks, even up into the rigging, trying to find anyone gazing at them—but there were only two sailors in sight, and neither was even looking in their direction.

But Brother Chillde still scribbled in his book.

Rod stared. No. It couldn't be.

But . . .

He stepped over to Brother Chillde again, lightly, almost on

tiptoe, and craned his neck to peer over the monk's shoulder
at the words he was writing.

". . . Huge they were," the manuscript read, "with arms
that hung down to their knees, and fangs that sank below their
chins. Their eyes were maddened bits of red, more suited to a
swine than a man, in a head like unto a ball, but too small for
so great a body. Their sole weapon was a huge and murderous
ax, and with it they quested always, seeking for living things to
slay."

"Thou knowest not what thou dost ask," Puck cried.
"Ever was I made for battle, Rod Gallowglass! Hast thou any
comprehension of the opportunities for mischief that occur
when men do war?"

"Very much," Rod answered grimly. "Look, I know it's a
hardship to stay out of the fighting—but you've got to think
of the good of the whole of Gramarye, not just of your own
excitement."

"Who says I must?" the elf demanded with a truculent
scowl.

"I," answered Brom O'Berin; and Puck took one look at
his sovereign's face and shrank back.

"Well, then, so I must," he sighed. "But wherefore must it
be I? Are there no other elves who can execute so simple a
task?"

"None," Rod said with absolute certainty. "It only seems
simple to you. I can think of a few other elves who *might* be
able to bring it off—but you're the only one I'm sure of."

Puck visibly swelled with self-importance.

"You're the only one," Rod pressed on, "who has the imagination, and the gift of gab, to pull this off."

"Thou wilt do it," Brom commanded sternly, "else thou
wilt answer to me, hobgoblin, when the battle's ended."

"Ah, then, I shall," Puck sighed—but preened himself,
too. "E'en so, Warlock—I ken not why the monk will need
one to detail to him what doth occur when he hath two eyes to
see with."

"Yes, well, that's the first thing you'll have to arrange, isn't
it? Some way of making his eyes unusable for the duration of
the battle. Nothing permanent," Rod added hastily, seeing the
gleam in Puck's eye.

"Well-a-day," the elf sighed, "so be it. We shall benight
him only for an hour or two. But what purpose doth that

serve, when I am but to tell to him what doth occur?''

"But you're not," Rod contradicted. "You're supposed to tell him what *isn't* happening."

"What word is this?" Puck stared. "Do I hear aright? I am to say, 'Nay, be of good cheer! It doth not rain, nor doth the moon shine! The soldiers do not shake the beastmen's hands in friendship, nor do they lose a foot of land!' What foolery is this?"

"Not quite what I had in mind, that's for sure." Rod fought a smile. "Don't be so negative, Puck. Think of it like this: 'Our brave, heroic line doth advance, and the murderous mass of craven beastmen stumble toward them with mayhem in their eyes! They catch our soldiers' gazes, and our goodmen freeze, terror-stricken by the Evil Eye! But the witch-folk wrench them free, and the High Warlock doth rise up, a gleaming paragon on a giant steed of jet, to call them onward! Inspired by his valor, our soldier-men take heart; they shout with anger and do charge the foe!' ''

Puck gave him a jaundiced eye. "Thou'rt not slow to trumpet thine own virtues, art thou?"

"Well, not when it's warranted," Rod said, abashed. "And in this case, it's downright vital. Brother Chillde won't believe anything less of me, Puck—and, whatever other effect you achieve, you've got to make him believe what you tell him, totally.''

Air boomed outward, and Toby stood before them. "Lord Warlock, thou'rt wanted on the poop deck."

"From the poop deck?" Rod raised an eyebrow in surprised sarcasm. "All that way? Gee, Toby, I hope you didn't tire yourself out."

The young warlock reddened. "I know thou dost enjoin us, Lord Warlock, to not appear and disappear, or fly, when simple walking will be nearly as fast . . .''

"Darn right I do. Totally aside from what it does to your fitness and your character, there's the little matter of its effects on the non-psi majority."

"I did forget," Toby sighed. "When great events are in train, such matters seem of slight import."

"That's why you need to make normal conduct a habit. But what great event's in train now?"

"*I* am!" the young warlock cried in exasperation. "I have but now returned from bearing word of our arrival to Master Yorick and his band! Wilt thou not come attend to me?"

"Oh!" Rod bolted off his stool, feeling like a pompous idiot. "What an ass I am!"

Puck perked up and opened his mouth.

"Just a figure of speech," Rod said quickly. "But accurate. Here I am, catechizing you about details, when you've just finished a hazardous mission! My deepest apologies, Toby —and I'm glad to see you're back intact. And, of course, you can't report to me here—you've got to say it the first time where the King can hear it."

"No offense, milord," Toby said with a grin. He stepped over to the door and held it open. "And, since *thou* canst not transport thyself from place to place, I'll company thee on foot."

"I, too," Brom growled. "I must hear what progress this grinning ape hath made."

The door slammed behind them, leaving Puck alone to mutter imprecations to himself.

"Welcome, Lord Warlock," Tuan said quietly, as the door closed behind them, "and thou, too, Lord Brom." His eyes glittered. "Now! May we hear this warlock's tale?"

Toby looked around at the glowing eyes, all fixed upon him, and succumbed to sudden embarrassment. "Where . . . what shall I tell?"

"Everything that happened," Rod suggested, "starting from the beginning."

Toby heaved a sigh. "Well, then! I listened for the beastmen's thoughts, and felt a mind belaboring with emptiness. This did resemble the 'sound of one hand clapping' that the High Warlock had told me of, so I drifted toward where it seemed the loudest, and looked down. I was far past the beastmen's village, and the feelings of their thoughts had thinned; but now I felt the thrust of several minds, mayhap threescore. Yet all I saw were treetops."

Rod nodded. "They hid well. What then?"

"I listened close, till the un-clapping mind had begun to think of other matters—yet, even there, no inkling-thought of treachery did come. Therefore did I drift down into a treetop and clambered down into their midst, the less to afright them."

Tuan smiled thinly. "That might somewhat lessen their startlement, I wot—yet not abundantly. What said they when they beheld thee?"

"Oh, the first beastman that laid eyes upon me shrieked and whirled up a war club, and I readied myself to disappear; but I also held up open hands, and he stayed his blow, then nodded toward his left. I went thither, and he followed me, though with ne'er a bit of trust in's eyes. And thus came I unto Master Yorick."

"Where?" Rod pounced on it.

Toby looked up, surprised. "He sat beside a nearly smoke-less fire with several others, only one among many, till he looked up and saw me. Then he stood, and grinned, and came up to me, hand upheld in salute."

Tuan had caught Rod's point. "Ah, then. He sat among his men as an equal, with neither state nor honor."

"None that I could see. I' truth, there were as many women as men around that fire—yet they did defer to him, that much was plain."

"How many were there?" the King demanded.

"A score of men, at least; and he assured me others stood sentry-guard, the whiles a squadron patrolled the jungle's edge, nigh to the village, to aid those who sought to escape. His force, he said, has strength of twoscore and more."

"How many women and children are there?" Catharine sounded anxious.

"A dozen that I could see, of women; each had two babes, or three."

"Thriving little family group." Rod smiled. "If we didn't clean out Mughorck, Yorick'd have his own village going."

"Aye, and betimes the two villages would battle." Tuan smiled with irony. "Mayhap we ought to keep our men at home and let our foemen slay one another."

"Thou canst not mean to say it!" Catharine flared.

"Nor do I," Tuan sighed, "for Yorick and his folk are allies now; and if Mughorck did battle him, Mughorck would surely win, since that he hath thousands. Nay, we must needs strike whiles yet we have a force to aid us. What did he say of the rumor he had hoped he'd seed?"

"He said that in these few weeks time it hath increased amazingly." Toby grinned. "Indeed, saith Master Yorick, ' 'Tis ready to be reaped and sheaved, and gathered into barns.' "

"The seed, then, fell on fertile ground," Brom rumbled.

Toby nodded. "Thus saith Yorick: 'There are some hun-dreds of widows now where there were none two month"

agone—and what hath their blood bought? Why, naught—
save the fear of vengeance.' Aye, milord, these folk were more
than ready to believe that vengeance would be aimed only at
the Kobold and his priest Mughorck.''

"What of the High Cave?" Brom rumbled. "Hath he sign
that the ones we seek do lair therein?"

"They do." Toby nodded. "Those lately come agree with
those who 'scaped two months agone—the Eagle's High Cave
now holds the Kobold and his priests."

"The Eagle—aye. What of him?" Tuan frowned.

"He dwells near them, but not with them," Toby answered,
returning his frown. "Ever and anon doth Yorick go to speak
with him, but he dwells not with his folk."

"Afraid?" Rod demanded.

"Not of Yorick's band. Yet he seems to think Mughorck
might come in search of him, and doth not wish his loyalists to
be caught in a net that might be laid for him."

"I think the Neanderthals aren't the only ones who're
paranoid," Rod noted with a lift of the eyebrow toward Tuan.
"Well, Your Majesty, it sounds as though our partisans are in
good shape, and definitely ready to pitch in on our side."

"I would so conjecture." But Tuan still watched Toby.
"Art thou certain there was no hint of treachery in his manner, nor in his thoughts?"

The young warlock shook his head firmly. "Nay, my liege
—and I did probe. There might be summat hid in the fast-
nesses of his heart . . . but if there is, 'tis beyond my comprehension."

"Mayhap there is," Tuan said frowning, "but when there's
no sign, we would be fools to turn away their aid."

"Still," Rod pointed out, "we could try to be ready for a
last-minute change of heart."

"We must be so, indeed," Tuan agreed. "Let us count the
beastmen loyal only when the battle's won."

"Which will not be easy." Rod stood, frowning down.
"We'll be on the beastmen's home territory this time. They
won't need lightning to bring them their extra power; they'll
have it right there at hand."

"Indeed, 'twill be a most fell battle," Tuan agreed. "Art
thou certain of this ancient wizard's aid?"

Rod started to answer, then hesitated.

"So I feared," Tuan said grimly.

Rod nodded unhappily. "But if he jumped in to save his

'son' once, he's *almost* certain to do it again.''

"Well, one can but pick the strongest ground and do one's best," Tuan sighed. "For, after all, no outcome's certain in battle, commerce, love, or life. Godspeed ye, my commanders —and may we all meet again, when tomorrow's sun hath dawned."

The Neanderthal village breathed uneasily in its slumber, bathed by the moon. The sentries on cliff-top and in small boats were bone-weary but not at all sleepy, for Mughorck had filled them with fear of the wild-eyed, ferocious Flatfaces who were so powerful as to be able to throw off the effects of the Evil Eye. What other powers did they have? How soon would they descend upon the hapless people, filled with vengeful blood-lust?

But, countering these tales, was the rumor that filtered throughout the village now—that the Flatfaces' anger was blunted; that Yorick had pled with them and brought them to see that this madness of raiding and invasion was only Mughorck's doing, and that when the Flatfaces came they would be satisfied with only Mughorck, and his lieutenants. And, of course, the Kobold. . . .

The sentries shuddered. What race of wizards was this, who could dare to strive against a god?

Thus their thoughts ran through the hours while the moon slowly drifted down toward the horizon, then slipped below it—and the land lay shadowed, its darkness lightened only by the stars. The sentries, weary to begin with, began to grow sleepy. The night was almost past; the Flatfaces had not come. For a few more hours, they were safe. . . .

Then they started, staring. What were those dark shapes that scuttled over the water toward the beach, so many as to seem like a field of darkened stars? In disbelief, the sentries squeezed their eyes shut, shook their heads—but when they looked again the squat, dark shapes still drove toward the beach. Surely these could not be the Flatfaces, flooding in so silently. . . .

But the dark shapes plowed up the beach, grinding to a halt, and scores of smaller shadows dropped off their sides. Nightmare though it seemed, this was no dream! The sentries clapped horns and conch shells to their lips, and blew the alarm!

Neanderthals tumbled out of their huts, pulling on helmets,

hefting war axes, groggy but waking fast, calling to one another in alarm.

The Gramarye soldiers formed their line and marched toward the village.

The High Warlock rode back and forth behind the lines, cautioning, "No shouting yet! Remember, silence! The more noise they make, the more eerie we'll seem."

But the beastmen pulled a ragged line together and stumbled toward the Gramarye soldiers with querulous, ragged war cries.

"Now!" Rod bellowed, and the soldiers charged with a hundred-throated ear-splitting shriek.

The lines crashed together, and the long pikes did their murder. Axes chopped through their shafts, but the beastmen died. Then, here and there, a beastman began to catch a soldier's eyes, and the Gramarye line slowed as its members began to freeze.

In the flagship's cabin, the witches and warlocks sat in a circle, hands joined, staring at the ceiling.

The Gramarye line gained speed again as the numbing darkness lifted from the soldiers' minds.

Frantically, the beastmen reached for the power of the Kobold.

A second wave of Gramarye soldiers charged up the beach, and new pikes poked through the line. The first wave retreated, minds dizzy from the Evil Eye.

"We are come, Lord Warlock," Tuan called, as he reined in his steed next to Fess. "Do as thou must; Sir Maris and I will care for our men."

"All thanks, my liege!" Rod called back. He ducked down, lying flat on Fess's back. "Now, Steel Steed! Head for the low scrub!"

The robot-horse leaped into a gallop, heading for the brush and low trees at the edge of the beach. "Rod, this subterfuge is scarcely needed! My thoughts were not even growing fuzzy yet!"

"For once, I'm not worried about you having a seizure in the middle of a battle."

"Then, why this retreat?" Fess slowed and halted behind a screen of brush.

"Just wait. Trust me." Rod parted the bushes and peeked out toward the beach. The battle was raging nicely, he noticed. But that wasn't his prime concern. He scanned the beach—

more especially, the brush. It was very dark, so of course he couldn't be sure. The Gramarye soldiers had lighted torches to see their enemy by, and the light spilled over, dimly illuminating the edges of the beach; he thought he could just barely make out some dim, amorphous mass, bulging very slowly, and growing larger—but he couldn't be sure.

The second wave of soldiers had carried the charge almost into the Neanderthal camp before sheer reflex had made individual beastmen begin seeking out the eyes of single opponents. Power flowed into the beastmen; their eyes burned more brightly. The Gramarye line slowed to a grinding halt.

In the flagship's cabin, Agatha and Gwen squeezed the hands of the witches to each side of them and shut their eyes, bowing their heads.

Pikes, spears, and swords began to move again, slowly, gathering force to block the beastmen's swings.

The beastmen chopped hysterically in the desperation born of superstitious fear—but wildly, too, dropping their guards. The pikes drove in, and blood flowed out.

Coming down the gangplank, Brother Chillde tripped, stumbled, and fell, sprawling on the sand with a howl of dismay.

Puck chuckled, tossed aside the stick he'd jabbed between the monk's feet, and scurried to his side, moving his hands in arcane, symbolic gestures, and chanting under his breath,

> "Chronicler, whose zeal doth blind thee
> To the truth t'which sight should bind thee,
> Be thou bound in falsehood's prison!
> For an hour, lose thy vision!"

"What . . . what doth hap?" Brother Chillde cried, pushing himself up out of the sand. He glanced about him, then squeezed his eyes shut, shook his head, and opened them again. "What! Is the night become so dark? Is there no light at all?" Then his face twisted into a mask of terror as the truth hit him. "I am blinded! Heaven forgive me—my sight is lost!"

"Here, now, fellow," Puck growled in a deep and throaty voice as he strode up to Brother Chillde, "what ails thee? Eh, thou'rt o' the cloth!"

"Oh, kind sir!" Brother Chillde flailed about him, caught

Puck's shoulder, and grasped it. "Have pity on me, for I'm struck blind!"

"What sins are these," Puck rumbled, "that must needs meet such desperate punishment?"

"I cannot say." Brother Chillde bowed his head. "Pride, mayhap—that I should dare to scribble down all that did hap within this war. . . ." His head snapped up, sightless eyes staring. "The battle! Oh, stranger, take pity! I have labored all these months to record in writing each separate event of this war! I cannot miss the knowledge of the final battle! Pray, have mercy! Stay, and speak what thou dost see! Tell me the course of the day!"

"I should be gone," Puck growled, "to aid in tending other wounded."

"Hast thou hurt, then?" Brother Chillde was suddenly all solicitousness, groping about him. "Nay, let me find it! I shall bandage . . ."

"Spare thy trouble," Puck said quickly, "for the flow already hath been stanched. Yet I'll own I have no occupation now. . . ."

"Then, stay," Brother Chillde implored, "and speak to me of all that thou mayst see."

"Well, I will, then," Puck sighed. "Attend thou, then, and hear, for thus it doth occur."

"May Heaven bless thee!" Brother Chillde cried.

Puck took a deep breath, recalling the main thrust of Rod's prompting. "The beastmen and our brave soldiers are drawn up in lines that do oppose. They grapple, they struggle; battle axes flail; pikes hover and descend. The clank of arms doth fill the air, and soldiers' groans and horses' neighs—eh, but that thou canst hear of thine own."

"Aye, but now I ken the meaning of the sounds!" Brother Chillde clutched Puck's shoulder again. "But the High Warlock! What of the High Warlock?"

"Why, there he rides," Puck cried, pointing at empty air. "He doth rise up on's huge black horse, a figure strong and manly, with a face that doth shine like unto the sun!" He grinned, delighted with his own cleverness. "Nay, his arms are corded cables, his shoulders a bulwark! He fairly gleams within the starlight, and his piercing eye doth daunt all who do behold him! Now rides he against the center of the line; now doth it bend and break! Now do his soldiers rush to widen the breach that he hath made!"

* * *

In the scrub brush, Rod eyed the heaving lump of jelly apprehensively. He'd watched smaller lumps of fungus ooze over to merge with it; the whole mass had grown amazingly. Now it was bulging very strangely, stretching upward, higher and higher, coalescing into a giant double lump. It thrust out a pseudopod that began to take on the shape of a horsehead, and the top narrowed from front to back and broadened from side to side. A piece split off on each side to assume the shapes of arms; a lump on top modeled itself into a head.

"I can scarcely believe it," Rod hissed.

"Nor I." Fess's voice wavered. "I know of the fungus locally termed witch moss, and its link to projective telepaths —but I never suspected anything on this scale."

Neither had Rod—for he was staring at himself. Himself the way he'd always wanted to be, too—seven feet tall, powerful as Hercules, handsome as Apollo! It was his face; but with all the crags and roughness gone, it was a face that could have dazzled a thousand Helens.

"Terre et ciel!" the figure roared, hauling out a sword the size of a small girder, and charged off into the battle on a ten-foot war-horse.

"Brother Chillde," Rod sighed, "is one hell of a projective!"

"He is indeed," Fess agreed. "Do you truly believe he does not know it?"

"Thoroughly." Rod nodded. "Can you really see the Abbot letting him out into the world if he knew what Brother Chillde was?" He turned Fess's head away. "Enough of the sideshow. He'll keep the beastmen busy—and anybody who's looking for me will see me."

"Such as Yorick?" Fess murmured.

"Or the Eagle. Or our own soldiers, come to that—'my' presence there will sure lend them courage—especially when I look like that!" He sort of hoped Gwen didn't get a close look at his doppelgänger; she might never be satisfied with reality again. "Now we can get on with the real work of the night— and be completely unsuspected, too. To the cliff-face, Fess— let's go."

The robot-horse trotted through the starlight, probing the brush with infrared to see the path. "Is this truly necessary, Rod? Surely Yorick has an adequate force."

"Maybe," Rod said with a harsh smile, "but I'd like to give

him a little backup, just in case.''

''You do not truly trust him, do you?''

Rod shrugged. ''How can you really trust anybody who's always so cheerful?''

On the beach, Brother Chillde cried, ''Why dost thou pause? Tell me!''

But Puck stared, stupefied, at the giant shining Rod Gallowglass who galloped into the fray.

''The High Warlock!'' Brother Chillde chattered, ''The High Warlock! Tell me, what doth he?''

''Why . . . he doth well,'' Puck said. ''He doth very well indeed.''

''Then he doth lead the soldiers on to victory?''

''Nay . . . now, hold!'' Puck frowned. ''The soldiers do begin to slow!''

'' 'Tis the Evil Eye!'' Brother Chillde groaned, ''and that fell power that doth bolster it!''

It did seem to be. The soldiers ground to a virtual halt. The beastmen stared a moment in disbelief, then shouted (more with relief than with bloodlust) and started chopping.

In the witche' cabin, the young folk grimaced in pain, shoulders hunching under the strain as a huge, black amoeba strove to fold itself over their minds.

Rod and Fess galloped up the series of rock ledges that led to the High Cave, and found Brom waiting.

Rod reined in, frowning up at the dwarf where he stood on a projection of rock a little above Rod's head.

''Didn't expect to find *you* here, Brom. I'm glad of it, though.''

''Someone must see thou dost not play the fool in statecraft in the hot blood of this hour,'' the dwarf growled. ''I fail to see why thou wilt not trust these beastmen allies by themselves; but, if thou must needs fight alongside of them 'gainst the Kobold and, mayhap, against *them*, when the Kobold is beaten, I will fight by thy side.''

''I'm grateful,'' Rod said, frowning. ''But what's this business about beating the Kobold? It's only a wooden idol, isn't it?''

''So I had thought, till I came here,'' Brom growled. ''But great and fell magic doth lurk on this hillside, magic more than mortal. Mughorck is too slight a man for the depths of this foul power, or I mistake him quite. I feel it deep within me, and . . ."

There was a yell up ahead of them within the cave, then the clash of steel and a chaos of howling.

"It's started," Rod snapped. "Let's go."

Fess leaped into a gallop as Brom hurtled through the air to land on the horse's rump. Rod whipped out his sword.

They rode into a mammoth cave more than a hundred feet deep and perhaps seventy wide, coated with glinting limestone, columned with joined stalactites and stalagmites, and filled with a dim eldritch light.

Three Neanderthals lay on the floor, their throats pumping blood.

All about the cave, locked pairs of Neanderthals struggled.

But Rod saw none of this. His eyes, and Brom's, went straight to the dais at the far end of the cave.

There, on a sort of rock throne, sat a huge-headed, pot-bellied thing with an ape's face, concave forehead, and bulging cranium. Its limbs were shriveled; its belly was swollen, as though with famine. It was hairless and naked except for a fringe of whiskers around its jowls. Its eyes were fevered, bright, manic; it drooled.

Two slender cables ran from its bald pate to a black box on the floor beside it.

The spittle dribbled from its chinless mouth into its scanty beard.

Behind it towered three metal panels, keys and switches, flashes of jeweled light, and a black gaping doorway.

At its feet, Yorick and a short skinny Neanderthal strained, locked in combat.

Its eyes flicked to Rod's.

Icicles stabbed into Rod's brain.

The monstrosity's eyes flicked to Brom's, then back to Rod's.

Brom moved slowly, like a rusted machine, and the Kobold's eyes flicked back to him. Brom moved again, even more slowly.

The Kobold's jaw tightened; a wrinkle appeared between its eyes.

Brom froze.

In the witches' cabin, the air seemed to thicken next to Agatha, like a heat haze. It began to glow.

A young witch slumped unconscious to the ground. A fourteen-year-old warlock followed her into a blackout, then a fifteen-year-old. A few moments later, a seventeen-year-old witch joined them, then a young warlock in his twenties.

One by one, the young psis dropped, to sprawl unconscious.

Agatha and Gwen caught each other's free hands, bowing their heads, every muscle in their bodies rigid, hands clasped so tightly that the knuckles whitened.

Then Gwen began to sway, only a centimeter or so at first, then wider and wider till suddenly her whole body went limp and she fell.

Agatha dropped Gwen's hands, clenched her fists; her face tightened into a granite mask and a trickle of blood ran down from the corner of her mouth.

Above her, the heat haze brightened from red to yellow. Then the yellow grew brighter and brighter.

A blast shook the tent, a hollow booming, and Galen knelt there before Agatha. He clutched her fists, and his shoulders heaved up, hunching under some huge, unseen weight. He bowed his head, eyes squeezing shut, his whole face screwing up in agony.

The heat haze's yellow dimmed, became orange.

On the beach, the soldiers began to move again, slowly at first, then faster and faster, stepping aside from ax-blows, returning pike-stabs.

The beastmen howled in fear and fought in panic.

But the High Cave lay silent, like some fantastic Hall of Horrors in a wax museum. An occasional whine or grunt escaped the Neanderthals frozen body-to-body in combat, straining each against the other—Kobold's men to Eagle's partisans, Mughorck locked with Yorick.

Rod and Brom stood frozen, the Kobold's glittering, malevolent eyes fixed on them, holding its frozen prey in a living death.

There was agony in Rod's eyes. A drop of sweat ran down from his hairline.

Silence stretched out in the glimmering, ghostly elf-light.

On the beach, the soldiers slowly ground to stasis again, their muscles locking to stone.

The Neanderthals roared and swung their axes like scythes,

mowing through the Gramarye ranks, their victory song soaring high.

In the cabin, Galen bent low, the black weight pressing down, squeezing, kneading at his brain. The other soul was still there with him, fighting valiantly, heaving with him against the dark cloud.

And the High Cave lay silent.

A crowing laugh split the air, and a wriggling infant appeared on Rod's shoulders, straddling his neck, chubby hands clenched in his hair, drumming his collarbone with small heels. "Horsey! Gi'y'up! Da'y, gi'y'up!"

The Kobold's gaze focused on the baby boy.

Magnus looked up, startled, and stared at the creature for a moment, then darted a glance at his frozen father. Terror started to show around the edges of the boy's expression; but hot, indignant anger darkened his face faster. He clutched his father's temples and glared back at the monster.

Rod shuddered, his neck whiplashing as the dark mantle wrenched free of his mind.

He tore his eyes from the Kobold's, saw Mughorck and Yorick locked straining in the embrace of hatred.

Rod leaped forward, ducking and dodging through the paired immobile Neanderthals, and sprang. His stiffened hand lashed out in a chop at the back of Mughorck's neck. The skinny tyrant stiffened, mouth gaping open, and slumped in Yorick's arms.

Yorick dropped the contorted body and lunged at the black box, slapping a switch.

Slowly, the Kobold's eyes dulled.

Galen's body snapped upward and back.

His hands still held Agatha's.

For a moment, minds blended completely, point for point, id, ego, and conscience, both souls thrown wide open as the burden they had strained against disappeared—open and vulnerable to the core. For one lasting, soul-searing moment, they knelt, staring deeply into each other's eyes.

Then the moment passed. Galen scrambled to his feet, still staring at Agatha, but his eyes mirrored panic.

She gazed up at him, lips slowly curving, gently parting, eyelids drooping.

He stared, appalled. Then thunder cracked, and he was gone.

She gazed at the space he'd filled with a lazy, confident smile.

Then a shout of joy and triumph exploded through her mind. Her gaze darted upward to behold the heat haze one last time before it vanished.

On the beach, the Gramarye soldiers jerked convulsively and came completely to life, saw the carnage around them, the mangled remains of friends, brothers, and leaders, and screamed bloody slaughter.

But a howl pierced the air, freezing even the soldiers. They stared as a beastman in the front line threw down his ax and shield and sank to his knees, wailing and gibbering to his mates. They began to moan, rocking from side to side. Then, with a crash like an armory falling, axes and shields cascaded down, piling up in waist-high windrows.

Then the beastmen sank to their knees, hands upraised, open, and empty.

Some of the soldiers snarled and hefted their pikes; but Tuan barked an order, and knights echoed it; then sergeants roared it. Reluctantly, the soldiers lowered their weapons.

"What hath happed?" Sir Maris demanded.

"I can only think 'tis some event within their minds," Tuan answered in a low voice, "mayhap to do with that fell weight being lifted from ours."

"But why have they not fought to the death?"

"For that, haply we may thank Master Yorick's rumor-mongering." Tuan squared his shoulders. "Yet, when we bade him spread that word, we did effectively make compact with him, and with all his nation. Bid the men gather up the weapons, Sir Maris—but be certain they do not touch a hair of any beastman's head!" He turned his horse away.

"Why, so I shall," the old knight growled reluctantly. "But whither goest thou, my liege?"

"To the High Cave," Tuan said grimly, "for I misdoubt me as to what occurreth there."

Fess's hooves lifted, slamming down at the back of a Neanderthal's head. The beastman slumped.

Rod caught two beastmen by the neck, yanked them apart, and smashed their heads back together. He turned away, let-

ting them drop, and saw a pair of rocks flying through the air
to brain two beastmen. "Tag!" cried Magnus; and, as the
Neanderthals fell, he gurgled, "Fun game!"

Rod repressed a shudder, and turned just in time to see
Brom heave at a beastman's ankles. The Neanderthal fell like
a poleaxed steer, and Brom sapped him with the hilt of his
knife.

But beastmen came in mismatched pairs here, and Brom
had guessed wrongly. The other half roared and lunged at
him.

The dwarf grabbed an arm and pulled sharply. The beastman doubled over, his head slamming against the rock floor.

"Nice work," Rod called approvingly. "That's why I've
been knocking out both halves of each couple. We can win-
now out the friends from the foes later."

Yorick finished trussing up Mughorck like a pot roast, and
turned to join the battle; but just as he did, Fess nailed the last
beastman. "Aw-w-w! I always miss the fun!"

Rod looked around the huge cave and saw that there was
nothing left standing except himself, Brom, Fess, Yorick,
and Magnus. Though Magnus wasn't really standing, actually; he was floating over an unconscious beastman, lisping,
"S'eepy?"

"Hey, we did it!" Yorick strode around Mughorck's inert
form with his hand outstretched—but he kept on rounding,
circling further and further toward the mouth of the cave as he
came toward Rod. Rod suddenly realized Yorick was pulling
Rod's gaze away from the back of the cave. He spun around
just in time to see the black doorway behind the monster glow
to life, a seven-by-three-foot rectangle. Its light showed him a
short twisted man. From the neck down, he looked like a
caricature of Richard III—an amazingly scrawny body with
a hunched back, shriveled arm, shortened leg—and so slender
as to seem almost frail.

But the head!

He was arresting, commanding. Ice-blue eyes glared back at
Rod from beneath bushy white eyebrows. Above them lifted a
high, broad forehead, surmounted by a mane of white hair.
The face was crags and angles, with a blade of a nose. It was a
hatchet face, a hawk face . . .

An eagle's face.

Rod stared, electrified, as the figure began to dim, to fade
Just as it became transparent, the mouth hooked upward in

sardonic smile, and the figure raised one hand in salute.

Then it was gone, and the "doorway" darkened.

"Impressive, isn't he?" Yorick murmured behind him.

Rod turned slowly, blinking. "Yes, really. Quite." He stared at Yorick for a moment longer, then turned back to the "doorway."

"Time machine?"

"Of course."

Rod turned back. "Who is he? And don't just tell me the Eagle. That's pretty obvious."

"We call him 'Doc Angus,' back at the time lab," Yorick offered. "You wouldn't have heard of him, though. We're very careful about that. Publicly, he's got a bunch of minor patents to his credit; but the big things he kept secret. They just had too much potential for harm."

"Such as—a time machine?"

Yorick nodded. "He's the inventor."

"Then"—Rod groped for words—"the anarchists . . . the totalitarians . . ."

"They stole the design." Yorick shook his head ruefully. "And we thought we had such a good security setup, too! Rather ingenious how they did it, really. . . ." Then he saw the look on Rod's face, and stopped. "Well, another time, maybe. But it is worth saying that Doc Angus got mad at them—real mad."

"So he decided to fight them anywhere he could?"

Yorick nodded. "A hundred thousand B.C., a million B.C., one million A.D.—you name it."

"That would take a sizable organization, of course."

"Sure—so he built one up and found ways to make it finance itself."

"And if he's fighting the futurian anarchists *and* the futurian totalitarians," Rod said slowly, "that puts him on *our* side."

Yorick nodded.

Rod shook his head, amazed. "Now, *that's* what I call carrying a grudge!"

"A gripe," Yorick chuckled. "That's the name of the organization, actually—G.R.I.P.E., and it stands for 'Guardians of the Rights of Individuals, Patentholders Especially.' "

Rod frowned. Then understanding came, and the frown

turned to a sour smile. "I thought you said he didn't patent the time machine."

"That just made him madder. It was his design, and they should have respected his rights. But the bums don't even pay him royalties! So he gathered us together to protect patent rights up and down the time line, especially his—and democracy guards individual rights better than any other form of government, including patent rights; so . . ."

"So he backs us. But how does that tie in with several thousand psionic Neanderthals cavorting around our planet?"

Yorick tugged at an earlobe, embarrassed. "Well, it wasn't supposed to work out quite this way. . . ."

"How about telling me how it *was* supposed to work?" Rod's voice was dangerously soft.

"Well, it all began with the totalitarians . . ."

Rod frowned. "How?"

"By tectogenetics." Yorick hooked a thumb over his shoulder at the Kobold. "You may have noticed they're pretty good at it. The future has worked up some dandy genetic engineering gadgets."

Rod nodded, still frowning. "All right, I'll buy it. So, what did they engineer?"

"Evil-Eye Neanderthals." Yorick grinned. "They cooked up a strain of mutant projective telepaths and planted 'em all over Terra. Figured they'd breed true and become dominant in whatever society they were in—take over completely, in fact. It would've made things a lot easier for the futurians if they'd been able to prevent democracy's ever getting started at all."

Rod shuddered. "It sure would have." He had a quick mental vision of humanity evolving and progressing down through the long road of history, always shackled to the will of one group of tyrants after another. "I take it they're genetically a different race from the other Neanderthals."

Yorick nodded. "Can't interbreed to produce fertile offspring. So they'd stay a minority and they wouldn't dare loosen the reins, for fear of being wiped out by the non-psis."

Rod began to realize that humanity had had a close call. "But you caught them at it."

Yorick nodded. "Caught 'em, and managed to persuade all the little groups of projectives to band together. The totalitarians made the mistake of just letting nature take its course: they left 'em unsupervised."

"Which you didn't, of course."

"Well, we thought we were keeping a close watch." Yorick seemed embarrassed. "But the totalitarians dropped some storm troopers on us one night, killed most of the GRIPE force and chased away the rest, then set up a time machine and herded all the Neanderthals to Gramarye."

Rod's eyes widened. "Now it begins to make sense. What'd they expect the beastmen to do, take over right away?"

"I'm sure they did. Leastways, by the time we managed to find 'em again they were running around in horned helmets and talking about going a-viking—and I don't think they dreamed that up on their own."

"So you hit the totalitarian force with everything you had and stole your Neanderthals back. But why couldn't you have taken them someplace else?"

"Have pity on the poor people, milord! Would you want them to spend their whole existences being balls in a cosmic game of Ping-Pong? No, we figured it was better to let them stay and try to keep them under protection. We mounted a strong guard—but we forgot about infiltration."

"Mughorck." Rod's mouth twisted. "Then he isn't really a Neanderthal?"

"Oh, he's the genuine article, all right—just as much as I am!"

Rod stared at Yorick. Then, slowly, he nodded. "I see. They 'adopted' him in infancy and raised him to be an agent."

Yorick nodded. "A farsighted plan, but it paid off. When the fat hit the fire we couldn't do anything about it. It was either kill the people we'd been trying to civilize, or run—so we ran." For a moment, he looked miserable. "Sorry we slipped up."

Rod sighed. "Not much we can do about it now, I suppose."

"No, not really," Yorick answered. " 'Fraid you're stuck with 'em."

It was the perfect moment for Tuan to come charging into the cave.

He took one look at the Kobold and sawed back on the reins, freezing—just for a moment, of course; the monster was shut down. But it was a sight to give anyone pause.

Behind him, sandals and hooves clattered and Brother Childe jerked to a halt to stare, paralyzed, at the monster. "My liege . . . what . . .''

Tuan turned to him, frowning, then caught a glimpse of what was behind the monk. He looked again, and stared. "Lord Warlock!"

Rod turned, frowning. "Yes?"

"But how didst thou . . ." Tuan turned back to him, and whites showed all around his eyes. "But thou wert even now . . ." He jerked around to stare past Brother Chillde again.

Rod followed his gaze, and saw . . .

Himself.

A giant self, astride a behemoth of a horse; a handsome self, with the form of a Greek statue.

Brother Chillde stared at the double, then whipped around to stare at Rod, then back to the double, back to Rod—and the double began to shrink, the horse began to dwindle; the doppelgänger's face became more homely, its features more irregular, its muscles less fantastic—and Rod found himself staring at an exact duplicate of himself.

Brother Chillde's gaze still swiveled back and forth from one to the other like a metronome. "But what . . . how . . ."

"By thyself," Brom rumbled behind him. "It is thou who hath made this co-walker, friar, though thou didst not know it."

Brother Chillde sighed as his eyes rolled up and his knees buckled. He collapsed in a dead faint.

"He'll get over it," Rod assured the company.

"Thy double will not," Brom snorted as he watched the co-walker blur, sag, and melt into a huge heap of fungus.

A sponge rubber club hit Rod in the back of the neck, and a little voice demanded fretfully, "Gi'y'up!"

Rod grinned, reached up, and plucked his son off his shoulders.

Magnus's eyes went round and wide; foreboding entered his face. "Naw'y baby?"

"Not this time." Rod tried hard to look severe, and failed. "No, good baby. By accident, maybe, but good baby, anyway." He tickled Magnus's tummy, and the baby chuckled and squirmed. "But Daddy's busy just now, and I've got a job for you."

Magnus bobbed his head. "Baby help!"

"Right." Rod pointed to the heap of witch moss. "Ge of that for me, will you?"

The baby frowned at the pile, then screwed his face up

tense concentration. The fungus began to twitch, to heave; it separated into fifty or sixty fragments, each of which stretched up, developed arms and legs, helmets, shields, and armor—and an army of toy knights stood waiting at attention.

"Pretty!" Magnus chirped, and drifted up out of Rod's arms. "March!"

He drifted toward the doorway, calling commands that were frequently incomprehensible as his new model army marched before him out the cave-mouth and down the ramp.

A broomstick swooped in the entrance just before Magnus left it, and an arm reached out and pulled him firmly against a hip. "And where wouldst thou go, my bonny babe?"

"Mommy!" Magnus cried in delight and threw his arms around her neck.

Another broomstick wobbled in beside Gwen's. Agatha cast a brief smiling glance at the pair, then came in for a landing.

"Hail, reverend dame!" Tuan called. "Are all thy witches well?"

"All," Agatha agreed, hobbling forward. "But then, I'm certain the High Warlock could ha' told ye as much."

Tuan cast a questioning glance at Rod, who nodded. "I didn't really *know*, you understand—but when the mental fog lifted for the third time, I was pretty sure." He turned to Agatha. "And how's your son?"

"Vanished," Agatha retorted, "and with joy; for when that unholy weight lifted from our minds, Galen's thoughts blended fully with mine and, from their combination, Harold was able to lift what he required. He's homeward sped, to wake his body."

Rod eyed her narrowly. "You don't exactly seem heart-broken."

"I am not." Her eye glinted. "I've knowledge of the old stiff stick now; I've seen deeply into him, and know what he holds hid."

Rod frowned, puzzled. "And that's enough to make you happy?"

"Aye; for now I'll invade his Tower truly."

"But he'll throw you out again!"

"I think not." Agatha's smile widened into a grin. "I think t he will not."

od stared at her for a long moment; then he shrugged. must know something I don't know."

"Aye." Gwen met Agatha's eyes with a smile that held back laughter. "I think she doth."

"Godspeed ye, then." Tuan inclined his head towards Agatha. "And the thanks of a kingdom go with thee. If thou wilt come to Runnymede in some weeks time, we'll honor thee as thou shouldst be."

"I thank thee, Majesty," Agatha rejoined, "but I hope to be too deeply occupied for such a jaunt."

Tuan's eyebrows shot up in surprise, but Agatha only dropped a curtsy, albeit a stiff one, and snapped her fingers. Her broomstick shot up beside her; she leaped astride it and floated up into the air.

"Milords, uncover!" Tuan snapped—entirely unnecessary, since no male present was wearing a hat. But they all dutifully pressed their hands over their hearts in respect as they watched the veteran witch sail out the cave-mouth and up into the night.

Rod turned to Gwen with concern. "That's a long way to go, all the way back to the mainland—and after all the drain of the battle, too! Is she going to be all right?"

"Fear not, my lord," Gwen said, with a secretive smile. "I believe she shall fare excellently."

Rod frowned at her, wondering if he was missing something.

Then he sighed and turned away. "Oh, well, back to the aftermath. What do you think we should do with Brother Chillde, my liege?"

Tuan shrugged. "Tend him when he doth wake; what else is there to do? But why was he so taken at the sight of thy double?" He shuddered, "And, come to that, who did craft it?"

"He did," Rod answered. "He's a very powerful projective telepath, but he doesn't know it—and he watched the battles very intensely, trying to remember everything that happened. But he wasn't trained as an observer, so he kept getting what he really *did* see confused with what he *wanted* to see—and what he wanted to see most was the High Warlock performing feats of valor." Rod had the grace to blush. "I'm afraid he's come down with a bad case of hero-worship."

"I comprehend," Tuan said drily.

"Well, not completely. For this final battle, I'm afraid we used the poor young fellow. I persuaded Puck to make Brother Chillde temporarily blind and to describe the High

Warlock the way Brother Chillde wanted to see him—bigger than life, impossibly perfect. The poor friar was sucked in totally, and unknowingly created a witch-moss High Warlock who helped the troops keep up their courage, and had everybody thinking I was down here so my visit to the High Cave could be a complete surprise. Not that it did much good," he answered, with a glance at the Kobold.

"Aye—the monster." Tuan followed his gaze. "We must make disposition of it, must we not?"

The whole company turned to stare at the false god.

"What is this fell creature?" Tuan breathed.

"A Kobold," Rod growled, face twisting with disgust and nausea. "Does it need any other name?"

"For you and me, yes," Yorick growled. "What do you think it was, Lord Warlock? A chimpanzee?"

"Its parents were." Rod turned away. "I can't see much in the way of surgical scars, so I'm pretty sure they were; but the normal strain might be quite a few generations back. It's obviously been genetically restructured; that's the only way you could get a monster like that." He turned back to the Kobold. "Of course, I suppose you could say it's a tectogenetic masterpiece. They doctored the chromosomes to make the poor beast into a converter—feed current into it, DC, I suppose, and out comes psionic energy." He dropped his gaze to the black box, then looked a question at Yorick.

The Neanderthal nodded, nudging the black box with his foot. "Atomic-power pack. Wish I could figure out how to shut this thing off permanently."

"You mean it's liable to go on again?"

"Not unless somebody flips the switch." Yorick eyed the monster warily. "Still, it would be an almighty comfort if that were impossible." He cocked his head on one side and closed one eye, squinting, looking the Kobold up and down. "I suppose it *is* a triumph of genetic engineering, if you look at it the right way. That bulging cerebrum can handle one hell of a lot of power. And no forebrain, did you notice that? Lobotomy in the womb. It can't do anything on its own. No initiative."

"Just a living gadget," said Rod grimly.

"Which may be just as well," Yorick pointed out. "We might conjecture about what it would do if it had a mind of its own. . . ."

Rod shuddered, but growled, "It couldn't do much. Not ~~wi~~th those atrophied limbs. All it can do is just sit there." He swallowed hard and turned away, looking slightly green. "That forehead . . . how can you just sit there and look at it?"

"Oh, it's a fascinating study, from a scientific viewpoint," Yorick answered, "a real triumph, a great philosophic statement of mind over matter, an enduring monument to man's ingenuity." He turned back to Rod. "Put the poor thing out of its misery!"

"Yes," Rod agreed, turning away, slightly bent over. "Somebody stick a knife in the poor bastardization!"

Nobody moved. Nobody spoke.

Rod frowned, lifted his head. "Didn't anybody hear me? I said, kill it!"

He sought out Tuan's eyes. The young King looked away.

Rod bowed his head, biting his lip.

He spun, looking at Yorick.

The Neanderthal looked up at the ceiling, whistling softly.

Rod snarled and bounded up to the dais, dagger in his hand, swinging up fast in an underhand stab.

His arm froze as he looked into the dulled eyes, looked slowly up and down the naked, hairless thing, so obscene, yet so . . .

He turned away, throwing down his knife, growling low in his throat.

Yorick met his eyes, nodding sympathetically. "It's such a poor, pitiful thing when the power's turned off, milord—so weak and defenseless. And men have done it so much dirt already. . . ."

"Dogs!" roared Brom, glaring about at them. "Stoats and weasels! Art thou all so unmanned as to let this thing live?"

He whirled about where he stood on the dais, glowering at the silent throng before him. He snorted, turned about, glaring at them all.

"Aye," he rumbled, "I see it is even as I have said. There is too much of pity within thee; thou canst not steel thyselves to the doing of it; for there is not *enough* pity in thee to force thee to this cruel kindness."

He turned, measuring the Kobold up and down. "Yet must it be done; for this is a fell thing, a foul thing out of nightmare, and therefore must it die. *And will no man do it this courtesy?*"

No one moved.

Brom looked long and carefully, but found only shame in each glance.

He smiled sourly and shrugged his massive shoulders. "This is my portion, then."

And, before anyone quite realized what he was doing, the dwarf drew his sword and leaped, plunging his blade up to the hilt in the Kobold's chest, into its heart.

The monster stiffened, its mouth wrenching open, face contorting in one silent, simian scream; then it slumped where it sat, dead.

The others stared, horrified.

Brom sheathed his sword, touched his forelock in respect where he stood on the arm of the Kobold's stone chair. "Good lasting sleep, Sir Kobold."

" 'Twas an ill deed," said Tuan. "It could not defend itself." But he seemed uncertain.

"Aye, but soulless it was, also," Brom reminded. "Forget that not, Majesty. Is it dishonor to slaughter a hog? Or to stick a wild boar? Nay, surely not! But this thing ha' wrought death and was now defenseless; and therefore no man would touch it."

The cavern was still; the company stood awed by the event.

Yorick broke the silence. "Well, then, my people's god is dead. Who shall rule them in his stead?"

Tuan looked up, startled. "Why, the Eagle! Say to him that I would fain parley with him that we may draw a treaty."

But Yorick shook his head. "The Eagle's gone."

"Gone?" Tuan said blankly.

"Thoroughly," Rod confirmed. "I saw him disappear myself."

"But . . . why," Tuan cried, "when his people were his again?"

"Because they don't need him any more," Yorick said practically.

"But . . . then . . . wherefore did he remain when he'd been overthrown?"

"To make sure they were freed from Mughorck," Yorick explained. "After all, he's the one who really masterminded my end of the invasion, you know."

"Nay, I did not. Who now shall rule thee?"

Yorick spread his hands. "To the victor go the spoils." He dropped to one knee. "Hail, my liege and sovereign!"

Tuan stared down at him, horrified.

"Thou canst not well deny him," Brom said, *sotto voce*.

"Thus hath it ever been—that the victor governed the vanquished."

And that, of course, settled it. In a medieval culture, tradition ruled.

"Well, then, I must," Tuan said, with ill grace—but Rod noticed he stood a little straighter. "Yet how is this to be? I've a kingdom already, across the wide sea!"

"Oh, I could run the place for you, I suppose," Yorick said, carefully casual, "as long as you're willing to take the final responsibility."

"That I can accept," Tuan said slowly, "an 'tis understood that thou wilt govern in my stead."

"Glad to, I assure you! For the first year or so, anyway. But don't worry about what happens after that; I've got a very likely-looking lieutenant who should fit the bill perfectly. He's even learning English. . . ."

The prisoners were assembled beneath the High Cave, all four thousand of them. Four soldiers stood on the ledge, two to either side of the cave-mouth. At some unseen signal, they flourished trumpets and blew a fanfare.

Inside the cave, Rod winced. They were beginning to get the idea that pitch wasn't just a matter of personal taste, but they had a long way to go.

Four knights rode out of the cave in full armor, raising their lances with pennons at their tips. They sidestepped, leaving the center clear. After them came Yorick—and then, just as the sun rose, Tuan stepped out onto the ledge, gilded by the dawn.

An awed murmur ran through the crowd below.

Yorick stepped up a little in advance of Tuan and to his side, and began to bellow in the Neanderthal language.

"I'll bet he's telling them the sad news," Rod muttered, "that the Eagle's gone."

A groan swept the crowd.

Brom nodded. "Thou hast the right of it."

Yorick started bellowing again.

"Now he's telling them they've got a new king," Rod muttered.

"Emperor!" Yorick shouted.

Tuan looked up, startled.

Inside the cave, Gwen shrugged. "He is, in all truth—and Catharine's an empress."

"Sure," Rod agreed. "It just hadn't hit him before."

A thunderous cheer split the air.

"I'd wager Yorick hath but now told them that he will rule as viceroy," Brom said drily.

Rod nodded. "Logical guess."

There was a pause, and they could hear Yorick's stage whisper: "A speech might be appropriate, my liege."

The pause lengthened; then Tuan cried out, "I am thy new ruler!" and Yorick bellowed the translation.

The crowd cheered again.

"Now they know it won't be a real conquest," Rod murmured.

Tuan went on, with frequent pauses for translation. "I am thy new ruler and will never forsake thee. Yet, since I cannot abide here with thee, I give to you a viceroy to rule in my stead. Thou hast called thyselves the People of the Kobold . . . and did worship a goblin . . . calling it thy god. This god was false . . . and the mark of it was . . . that it demanded thy worship, which should go to the One True Unseen God only. I shall not demand such worship . . . only fealty and loyalty. An thou wilt be loyal to me and my viceroy, I shall be true to thee."

"He does it well, don't you think?" Rod said softly.

Brom and Gwen nodded. "He ever hath," said the dwarf. "Yet wilt thou, I wonder?"

Rod frowned. "What do you mean? I don't have to do any speechifying!"

"Nay," Brom agreed, "but thou'lt now have to be the mainstay of two nations, the power behind two thrones."

"Oh." Rod's mouth tightened. "Yeah, I know what you mean. But honestly, Brom, I don't know if I can handle all that."

"Aye," Gwen sympathized. "The two lands are more than thirty leagues apart!"

"I know," Rod said heavily. "And I can't be in two places at the same time, can I?"

MORE SCIENCE FICTION!
ADVENTURE